Peggy —

Now faith is being sure of what we hope for and certain of...

What We Don't See

Hebrews 11:1

LeighAnne Clifton

LeighAnne Clifton

What We Don't See: Book 3 in the Together for Good Series by LeighAnne Clifton

Copyright © 2022. All rights reserved.

ALL RIGHTS RESERVED: No part of this book may be reproduced, stored, or transmitted, in any form, without the express and prior permission in writing of Pen It Publications. This book may not be circulated in any form of binding or cover other than that in which it is currently published.

This book is licensed for your personal enjoyment only. All rights are reserved. Pen It Publications does not grant you rights to resell or distribute this book without prior written consent of both Pen It Publications and the copyright owner of this book. This book must not be copied, transferred, sold or distributed in any way.

Disclaimer: Neither Pen It Publications, or our authors will be responsible for repercussions to anyone who utilizes the subject of this book for illegal, immoral or unethical use.

This is a work of fiction. The views expressed herein do not necessarily reflect that of the publisher.

This book or part thereof may not be reproduced in any form, stored in a retrieval system, or transmitted in any form by any means-electronic, mechanical, photocopy, recording or otherwise-without prior written consent of the publisher, except as provided by United States of America copyright law.

Published by Pen It Publications in the U.S.A.

713-526-3989 www.penitpublications.com

ISBN: 978-1-63984-283-4

Edited by Kristin Campbell

Cover Design by Donna Cook

Acknowledgments

Publishing is a long journey no writer takes alone. Without the help, support, brain-power, talent, and dedication of a few people, this book would have never come to life. My gratitude runs deep for the folks involved in making What We Don't See a reality.

Dear sisters in the Lord - Jane, Beth, and Mary (also my niece!) –willingly read this book in its infancy and shared their thoughts, knowledge, and wisdom. You are each incredibly gifted and remarkably generous.

Kristin, editor extraordinaire, whose skill at polishing a manuscript until it sparkles... well, it's amazing. My engineer side appreciates your consistency and attention to detail. My creative side revels in your ability to apply tiny tweaks and reveal the stronger story. And my human side thanks you for being willing to enter a discussion, hear me out, and – when needed – change my mind!

Donna's power to distill an entire story into a single, stunning, impactful cover image continues to amaze. This may be my favorite cover yet!

As I was submitting this book, Kenney took on the huge task of leading the folks who call Pen It Publications their other family. It couldn't have been an easy undertaking, but I'm so grateful to be part of it. You've been instrumental in making this book available to all the readers who want to know what happens next in the small Southern town of Burton, South Carolina. And you continue to carry us forward, desiring for us both excellence and success.

Teresa graciously lent her name to a supporting character. Thanks for playing along, my dear friend.

Writing can be lonely work. Thank you, Bill, for understanding when I had to sit at the computer just a few more hours to get a scene just right. Thank you to my kids who spread the word about my books. Family is a gift from the Lord, and I'm greatly blessed!

Dedication

This book is dedicated to the faithful people who invest their time, energy, resources, and – most importantly – unceasing prayers to saving the lives of the unborn. You are heroes.

Your hands made me and formed me;
give me understanding to learn your commands.
Psalm 119:73 (NIV)

Children are a heritage from the Lord,
offspring a reward from Him.
Psalm 127:3 (NIV)

Other Books by LeighAnne Clifton

The Together for Good Series (inspirational romance)
All Your Heart
Ready to Forgive

Children's Book

The Little Vessel

Contents

At the Hospital	1
Change Is Coming	11
Baby News	23
Shadow of a Shattered Dream	33
What Next?	45
Proposed Changes	55
The Decision	65
Move-In Day	75
Big News and Little Kittens	85
A Production and a Proposal	97
Difficult Things	107
Broken Relationship	121
Scattered and Gathered	129
New Life	139
Welcome Aboard	145
Old Friends	155
Going on a Trip	163
Sleepy	169
It's Show Time	175
Intrusion	181
Anniversary Gifts	187
Confessions	193
Back to Reality	199
The Harvest Tea Preparations	207
Announcements	215
Plan in Motion	225
Fissures	231
All Wrong	243
In the Open	253
Around the Hall	263
Tea Talk	271
Epilogue	277

*Now faith is confidence in what we hope for
and assurance about what we do not see.
Hebrews 11:1 (NIV)*

*But if we hope for what we do not see, we wait for it with patience.
Romans 8:25 (ESV)*

At the Hospital

He held her fragile hand in his, the quiet beeps and whirs of the machines attached to her body drowning out all thought. Two days ago, she had been lively and making plans for the Memorial Day party. Now her eyelashes twitched against her face, but her body remained motionless.

Exhausted, he rested his arms on the bedrail and let his head fall onto them. Two days, and he hadn't left her side, despite the doctors and nurses pleading with him to do so.

He heard the door open behind him but didn't bother to sit up. He knew the drill by now. A nurse came in every hour or so, checked her vitals, made notes in a laptop, sometimes administered medication into the tube that snaked its way into her tape-covered left hand. He had no strength left to make small talk. If there was a change in her condition, he hoped they would tell him.

Terry jumped at the touch on his shoulder. *Did I doze off?*

Confused, he looked up to see Alex's chocolate brown eyes filled with unspoken questions, her hand pressed against his back. Chad stood close behind her, concern and sorrow etched into his face.

"We left North Carolina as soon as we could wrap things up," Alex said, although her voice was so quiet that Terry wondered if she had really said anything or if he had imagined it. Again.

He had prayed for them to come, and now here they were. Was this real? Or just a hazy, exhaustion-induced dream?

"Where's Lydia?" he asked, looking from Alex to Chad and back again.

"Charmain offered to watch her, so we dropped her off at Together for Good. She thinks it's a sleepover with Aunt Char at Miss Matilda's place." Alex choked on the words, unable to continue.

Chad touched his wife's shoulder, and she turned toward him, collapsing and resting her tear-stained face against his broad chest.

The depth of their love for each other filled the space around them. The way they spoke to each other, the way they laughed together, and now, in the way they comforted each other. And, although he would never begrudge them the life they'd worked to build, Terry's heart ached as he observed the bond they shared. He'd given up hope of finding what they had.

"How is she?" Chad asked over Alex's head, causing her to pull away slightly and watch Terry's face as he answered.

"Stable. The doctors say she was lucky to have received help as quickly as she did." Terry wiped a hand over his face, two-day-old stubble scratching his palm. "Time is critical when someone has a stroke."

Terry had waited until yesterday morning to call the Whites, not wanting to worry them without also being able to provide them with definitive information. Once the doctors confirmed she'd had a stroke, he'd called to break the shocking news to his friends.

A stroke.

The word still clenched his heart in fear. It sounded so ominous. So final. And yet, here she lay, still alive. Still breathing.

"What's the prognosis?" Alex's face pinched, as if she didn't really *want* to know the answer. Instead, she *needed* to know. The distinction was real.

Terry shook his head, wishing he had better news. Or any news, for that matter.

"They just don't know yet. Considering her age, Aunt Tilley may make a full recovery, or she may have to go to a nursing facility. We won't know until she wakes up." He turned away from their concerned scrutiny to continue his vigil of watching and waiting.

"Why is her right arm wrapped in bandages? It looks like the IV is going to her left hand."

Terry nodded at Chad's observation. He told the couple that Aunt Tilley's right hand was swollen and began bruising soon after she came in. In her unresponsive state, they'd had to do an x-ray and determined she'd broken it, probably when she fell after losing consciousness.

"Terry, why don't you run home and get a shower? Grab a bite to eat. Maybe take a quick nap. We'll sit here and call you if there's any change." Alex's eyes swam in unshed tears as she spoke. "I promise."

"I can't leave her. What if …?" He felt tears sting his own eyes, his voice cracking as the emotions finally surfaced. "I can't lose her, Alex."

"No, none of us can." The forcefulness in Alex's voice startled both men. "But we can't think like that, Terry. We'll wait for God's timing to heal her. In the meantime, sitting here without food or sleep won't do anyone any good. You look terrible." She winced. "Sorry, but it's true."

Terry smiled for the first time in days. He could count on Alex to tell it like it was, as she'd done since she'd found herself stranded in Burton four years ago. Her presence had caused upheaval in Terry's life, but he'd needed it. If he were honest with himself, once he'd made peace with all the changes of the last few years, he'd settled in quite well to his new normal.

"I guess a quick trip home might do me good, now that y'all are here with her."

Alex stepped out of the room and into the hallway with Terry, leaving Chad to take his post in the hard hospital chair that Terry had vacated.

"I mean it, Terry. Get some food and rest. You won't do her any good if you collapse from exhaustion or stress. You don't want to end up in a room down the hall, do you?"

He rubbed his eyes, which felt like they were lined with sand paper, knowing she spoke the truth. Then, remembering where Chad and Alex had been, he sucked in a quick breath and snapped his gaze to Alex. "Oh, my goodness, Alex. I completely forgot to ask. How did it go in Woodvale? Did Karen agree to the terms of the will?"

Alex sighed and avoided looking him in the eye. She shook her head as she spoke. "It went as well as can be expected, I guess. Mother doesn't seem content with J.T.'s wishes, as specified in his revised will. The lawyers are trying to reason with her. She still believes, though, as his widow, she's entitled to everything, no matter what his instructions were." She looked up, and Terry noticed the dark shadows beneath her eyes.

Guilt washed over him for about the hundredth time in the last couple of days.

Alex had volunteered to go to Woodvale to try to reason with her mother. They'd all known it would probably be a losing battle.

Before J.T. had died last year, he'd revised his beneficiaries for many of his significant assets. Although everything had been professionally prepared by J.T.'s attorneys and properly witnessed and filed, Karen continued to grasp at any straw that might somehow reverse J.T.'s decision to leave the bulk of his fortune to Alex and Terry. Karen had received his life insurance and a substantial monthly allowance. However, J.T. had clearly specified how his other assets—financial accounts, real estate, business holdings—were to be divided between Alex and Terry.

"She's still having a hard time believing you're his son. And, we all know what she thinks about Lydia."

When Karen had shown up uninvited to Alex and Chad's wedding with the news of J.T.'s death, she'd made it clear she thought Terry was

Lydia's father. She'd refused to acknowledge the fact that their physical resemblance arose from common parentage. Namely, J.T.

Alex kept the information about the trip vague, which Terry surmised was her way of trying to spare his already frayed nerves from any of the disturbing details of her encounter with Karen.

He nodded, feeling the combined weight of stress, fear, and uncertainty from the past couple of days finally taking their toll, slamming into him like a truck. A Mack truck.

How am I going to make it to the car? And drive home?

"Thanks, Alex. I'm so sorry you had to deal with that. I wish I'd been with you. But if I had, I wouldn't have been here when …" He glanced at the door to Aunt Tilley's room.

"Stop it, Terry. Chad's in there now. I'll be here with him in case we need coffee or snacks. If there's any change, we'll call you immediately. You don't need to think about anything else right now. It'll all work out somehow. God's in complete control." She placed a hand on his back and guided him in the direction of the elevator down the hall.

He knew when he'd been dismissed, even if it was politely by a Southern lady.

"Thanks, Alex," he called over his shoulder while he punched the *down* button.

She didn't hear him. She'd already disappeared back into the room.

§§§

Humming the tune to Miss M.'s favorite hymn, Chad stroked the soft skin on her arm, now speckled by age and leathery from years in the sun.

He knew if anyone could get Terry to take a much-needed break, it was Alex. She excelled at taking care of others. In less than a year, she had him eating healthy food, taking walks at night, and popping a vitamin each morning. He'd never felt so good.

Right now, though, his heart hurt, and it had nothing to do with his newly-improved cardiovascular condition. He bowed his head, begging God to spare this lady, who'd once been his lifeline, who'd saved countless babies, and led many of their mothers to the Lord. Chad knew God's timing was perfect, but his petition today was for more time. He had so much more he needed to tell her. So much more to learn from her.

The sound of the opening door interrupted Chad's prayer. He watched as Alex, concern distorting her beautiful features, came back into the room. When she massaged his tight shoulders, he felt his muscles relax a bit. He tilted his head from side to side, happy to let go of some of the tension that had been building.

"Any change?" she asked, though their friend clearly continued to lie still as a stone.

Chad shook his head as he stood and offered Alex his seat. It might be a time of crisis, but the manners he'd learned as a child, from the woman in the bed beside them, would always prevail. He moved around the bed and pulled another chair close. He caught Alex's eye across the crisp white coverlet and saw the fear there. Reaching across, he took her hand.

"It's going to be okay, babe."

"How do you know that, Chad? What if it isn't?"

He'd wrestled with this question the whole way back from North Carolina. But as he had prayed a few minutes ago, he understood that, regardless of Miss M.'s condition in the foreseeable future, he and Alex would get through it together. He worried about Terry, though. His aunt was all he had left. Chad wasn't sure how he would cope if the Lord called her home.

"If it isn't, then we'll get through it together," Chad said, finally giving voice to the possibility of a less-than-ideal outcome. "This is one of those shadows we mentioned in our vows. You see that, right?"

She nodded but focused her stare on Miss M.'s peaceful, motionless face.

"We couldn't talk much about what you found out from Terry on the drive back from Woodvale." Chad knew Alex wanted to keep the news from Lydia until they knew more definitively what the prognosis was. "So, what happened? Who found her?"

Alex dragged her eyes back to Chad and took a deep breath.

"She was having coffee with the residents when she started slurring her words. Within a few seconds, she dropped her mug. One of the girls told Terry that the right side of her face looked kind of like it was melting." Alex brought a hand to her mouth, pausing a moment before continuing. "That's when they called 911. She collapsed before they arrived."

She went on to describe the call that Terry had received, telling him that his aunt had been admitted with all indications of having suffered a stroke. He'd dropped everything he'd been doing and hadn't left her side since. All they could do now was wait, and pray, and hope she suffered no long-lasting effects.

One huge factor in her favor was that the skilled EMTs, who had responded, had administered the proper medication within minutes. Time was everything in these situations.

"Why did Terry wait so long to call us?" Chad asked.

"He said he knew we were in the midst of our own troubles, which I think he feels partly responsible for." Alex shook her head. "Just think, though. What if he'd gone up there to meet with J.T.'s lawyer instead of us? He wouldn't have been here when Miss Matilda needed him. I think he's aware of that, too."

Chad didn't point out Terry's inability to do anything short of camping out at his aunt's bedside. He understood the importance of being present in times of crises, even if it only served as a balm to one's own conscience.

"Babe, it's late. Why don't you go home and get some sleep, too? These last couple of days have been rough." Chad understood the toll the meetings at the lawyer's office had taken on his wife. "I can sit here and let y'all know if anything changes."

But Alex shook her head and rose from her chair. Within seconds, she'd converted it into something that resembled a bed. Chad knew all too well the comfort level of the apparatus left much to be desired. He'd spent an uncomfortable and sleepless night on a similar contraption the night before Lydia had been born.

Alex flourished a hand wave at her accomplishment. "You lie down and rest," she said. "You drove the whole way back and must be running on fumes. I'll stop by the nurses' station on my way to get coffee and ask a nurse to bring you a pillow and blanket."

While she spoke, he had risen from his chair, his tired and aching limbs protesting against the movement, and crossed the room to stand before her. Leaning down, he gently kissed her forehead, then the tip of her nose,, and then her lips. She smiled as he pulled back, tilting her head back to look up at him.

"What was that for?" she asked, a happy twinkle in her eye for the first time in days.

"That," he said, pausing to kiss her one more time, "was for being the best thing that ever happened to me."

§§§

Alex found herself still smiling as she rode the elevator down to the first floor, in search of a round-the-clock coffee stand. Chad believed she was his blessing, but she knew the truth. She and Lydia were truly the blessed ones. Chad had endured quite a bit, both in his lifetime and in their relationship, but through it all, he remained her friend, her protector, and her hero.

She felt her watch vibrate, indicating an incoming text.

When Chad had first gotten her the device for Christmas, she wondered what was going on—crazy sounds and vibrations issued forth at the most random times—and if she'd ever get accustomed to the constant beeps and buzzes. Eventually, she'd figured out how to check her watch to see who was trying to reach her. Considering her phone stayed buried in the depths of the enormous bag that she called a purse, it really was convenient technology.

Looking at her wrist, she saw Chad's name scrolling across the watch face. *He probably wants to remind me to get the sugar substitute in his coffee.*

Alex had been working hard to change some of Chad's bachelor habits, including his health-care routine. More veggies, less sugar, more exercise. He protested but, in general, he'd been a pretty good sport about having his lifestyle revamped.

She smiled as she searched for her phone among the contents of her purse. She almost dropped it when she read the text.

Moving fingers and mumbling. Come back! Now!

The elevator doors inched open, and Alex squeezed through before they finished. She didn't have time to wait for it to go through its turtle-slow machinations back up to her floor. Instead, she bolted past startled hospital visitors and staff in the lobby, found the stairs, and bolted up them two at a time to the third floor. She sprinted to Miss Matilda's room and burst in the door, out of breath.

"Alex, dear, why are you breathing so hard? You haven't been running around like a chicken with its head cut off, have you? That's not at all ladylike."

Alex had never been so happy to have her adherence to etiquette questioned.

Change Is Coming

The nurses arrived on Alex's heels, checking vital signs and pummeling Miss Matilda with questions.

"What's your name, ma'am? Do you know where you are? What day it is? What year it is? Who is President of the United States?" The questions came faster than a healthy young person could field, much less an older lady waking up from two days of unconsciousness.

Then they turned their attention to Chad. "Sir, when did she first exhibit any indication of awakening? Are you her next-of-kin? Has her doctor been notified of her change in condition?"

Chad, looking like a deer in the headlights, peered from one nurse to the next as they peppered him with questions.

Eventually, a middle-aged, scrub-clad gentleman with a stethoscope draped around his neck ushered Chad and Alex out the door with instructions to stay in the hospital in case the nursing staff needed to contact them.

As the door closed softly behind them, all they could do was stand in the hall, looking at one another and blinking at the whirlwind that they'd been ejected from.

"What do we do now?" Chad asked, running his fingers through his wispy, strawberry blond hair.

"I don't know about you, but I could really use that coffee right about now." Alex turned toward the elevator once again to finally make her coffee run but stopped when Chad put his hand on her shoulder. Annoyed that her quest for caffeine was being delayed further, she turned to him, uncertain why he hesitated.

"Should we call Terry?"

"Oh, he just left. And he was so exhausted. Why don't we go get our coffee and come back up here? Maybe by then, they can tell us more. We'll call Terry once we have some real news."

Chad gave Alex a thumbs-up and took her hand. Together, they called to the person on the elevator to hold the door.

§§§

Terry stepped off the elevator, walking faster than appropriate for a visitor on a hospital floor. When he'd gotten home, he'd wolfed down a sandwich and taken a quick shower before lying down to rest his eyes. Alex's call had pulled him out of a deep sleep, and he'd seen that he'd been out for over an hour. He recalled how his chest had constricted when he'd seen Alex's name on his phone.

He didn't know if it was the fantastic news that Alex had given him, the food, or the much-needed rest that had him feeling better than he had in days. *Probably a combination of all three*, he acknowledged.

Stepping into the floor's waiting room, he felt ... What was that feeling? Lighter. Not physically, but emotionally, mentally. Letting his breath out between pursed lips, he lifted a silent prayer of thanks for the improvement in Aunt Tilley's condition.

"Hey, bud. You look much better," Chad said, shaking Terry's hand and clapping him on the back.

"I feel better. What's going on? All Alex would tell me was Aunt Tilley woke up."

"Yep." Chad nodded. "And she's just as feisty as ever."

Smiling, Terry folded his long frame into a tiny waiting room chair as Chad and Alex plopped onto the squeaky, vinyl-covered sofa across from it.

"Hey, Terry," Alex said. "I'm sorry I was vague on the phone. Let me fill you in on what we know."

Alex told Terry how pleased, and surprised, the doctor was with his aunt Tilley's condition. She had full mobility in her arms and hands, legs and feet, although the break in her right wrist caused her quite a bit of pain. And her speech was completely normal. Dr. Duncan, the neurologist, had actually used the word "miracle" to describe her recovery.

"Well, that's great news!" Terry said. His prayers had been answered in a mighty way. But the look on Alex's face told him that she wasn't finished. "So, what's the catch? When can she go home?"

"Dr. Duncan thinks she needs to be monitored closely for the next several weeks. You know, take it easy, relax." Alex chose her words carefully, an intensity in her stare.

Terry nodded slowly, trying to wrap his mind around her underlying message. Aunt Tilley was going to need help running Together for Good.

"She needs to start a physical therapy routine to help her regain full strength," Alex continued. "Plus, while her right arm is in a cast, she won't be able to do much by herself."

"Sounds like she's going to need a lot of help for a while. It's going to be hard to ask her to step back from what she's done her whole adult life, even if it is temporary." Terry tamped down an apprehensive feeling that threatened his self-control. "Have either of you ever known Aunt Tilley to relax for a minute? Much less for several weeks?"

Chad cleared his throat and looked at Alex, arching one brow at her.

There's something else they're not telling me.

Terry's senses went on high alert, and his gut tightened in anticipation of what other news awaited him.

"Well, Terry, here's the thing. We don't ... That is, the doctors think ... What I'm trying to say is ..." Chad danced around the thing he was trying to say, unable to voice his thoughts and making Terry more anxious by the second.

"What Chad means," Alex interrupted, putting her hand on Chad's, "is it could be quite some time before Miss Matilda is able to run the home again."

Terry felt the blood drain from his face as he shook his head in disbelief, looking at his two friends as if they'd sprouted horns.

"I don't understand. You just told me she'd made a miraculous recovery. She's got the use of her arms and legs. She can speak. What's the problem?" He wanted to understand the whole situation before he went in to talk to her, but something wasn't adding up.

Terry rose and paced the length of the waiting room, needing to busy himself somehow. Walking past the waiting room door, he caught a glimpse of Dr. Duncan leaving Aunt Tilley's room. Terry waved to him and, within seconds, the doctor joined the group.

Alex and Chad stood, shuffling past Terry to get to the waiting room exit and give Terry some privacy with the doctor. However, Terry raised his hand to halt them, needing reinforcement and someone else to hear the doctor's explanation and instructions. Despite his brief rest, Terry wasn't convinced he'd be able to process all the information Dr. Duncan looked prepared to hurl at him.

Chad nodded and took Alex's hand. They stood, quietly attentive, allowing Terry and the doctor to carry on their conversation.

"Mr. Lovell, I'm glad your friends convinced you to take a break. Your aunt is actually doing much better," Dr. Duncan said, taking a seat and motioning for Terry to do the same. "You know, Mr. Lovell, I've admired Miss Gault for a long time for the work she does at the home. A couple of years ago, during one of her regular appointments, she invited me out for a tour. It truly is incredible how hard she works to save those babies and make the mamas feel loved."

"Thanks, Doctor. Aunt Tilley is a force of nature, that's for sure. So, what happens next?" Terry sat, but he didn't have time to waste on small talk, and he knew the doctor didn't either.

"Well, it's like I was telling Mr. and Mrs. White, your aunt may go home soon. Possibly tomorrow. But she needs to rest and be observed for several weeks. Maybe a few months. After that, I'd really like to see her slow down her pace a bit. In the years that your aunt has been my patient, I've learned how demanding it is to run the home. She tends the garden, does the grocery shopping, and supervises most of the cooking. She's also up at all hours of the night when a girl goes into labor. She won't be able to do these things while she's in the cast, and I can't be certain of her overall strength until we do some more tests. Also, she'll need to start a mandatory physical therapy regimen. It'll take a fair amount of time each day and could leave her exhausted afterward, especially in the beginning." The doctor placed a hand on Terry's shoulder. "It's time for your aunt to step back a bit and take care of herself for a change."

Terry appreciated the fact that Dr. Duncan knew how hard Aunt Tilley worked. The thing that concerned him, though, was that the man had no idea how integral her work was to her existence. What would she do if she didn't run Together for Good? It was all she'd ever done. It was her life's purpose.

Terry tipped his head backward, staring at the ceiling as if the answers were written up there. "Has anyone told her?"

"No. I wanted to discuss it with you first, to see if you had any viable options we could present to her."

A smile played at Terry's mouth. Dr. Duncan obviously knew Aunt Tilley. She wouldn't be told to give up Together for Good without a fight. And, even if she lost that fight, she'd most likely leave a bloody trail in her wake.

As chairman of the board and one of the home's major benefactors, Terry kept tabs on what it cost to run the place. The prices for maintenance, utilities, food, medical care, and a whole host of other things just kept increasing. Aunt Tilley lived simply and didn't require much in the way of a salary. Knowing all this, Terry questioned the economic feasibility of hiring an employee to run the place.

He knew if he let the place go under, however, he'd never be able to live with himself. He owed it to the woman who'd been his anchor in the storm, as she'd been to countless girls and their babies, to ensure the continued operation of the home.

And it wasn't just Aunt Tilley's life's work at stake here. Terry's parents, Sarah and Charles Lovell, had founded the home decades ago. And his own birth mother had lived there briefly. Simply put, Together for Good was as much a part of him as his right hand. He couldn't, in good conscience, do anything to jeopardize it, or allow it to fail.

Standing in the cramped waiting room, Terry looked at his friends while they stared back at him with questions in their eyes. The pressure to make the right decisions, whatever they were, weighed on him like a huge stone. Add the exhaustion creeping back into his bones, and Terry wanted nothing more than to run out the door, get in his car, and drive until he ran out of gas. But Terry was done with running away from his problems.

"Can we just talk to her about the immediate future, Doctor? Not get into any discussion of long-term options for now?" Terry asked. "Let's take this one step at a time. We're going to need to put our heads together and figure out some arrangements for further down the road. There's no need to worry her unnecessarily right now."

"Of course. I understand." Dr. Duncan nodded.

"May we see her now?" Alex asked.

"You may go in, but don't stay long. She needs her rest if she's going to leave tomorrow." The doctor then said goodbye and departed, disappearing into the room across the hall.

Terry, Alex, and Chad stared at one another, each of them wondering how God would orchestrate the massive changes necessary in Matilda's life. Who would He choose to take over the operation of Together for Good?

"So ... who's going to tell her?" Alex was the first to speak up.

As the trio filed out of the waiting room and into the hallway, a cloud of noxious perfume assailed them, followed quickly by an elderly lady who was trying to look twenty years younger, unsuccessfully. Her straw-like, platinum hair sat piled on her head in an odd style that was something between a messy bun and a bouffant. Her clothes, from her flowing jungle-print caftan down to her leather sandals, made her look as if she could have either stepped out of the sixties or off the set of an island-themed movie. She ran to Terry and took his face in her hands, making him wince as her needle-sharp nails dug into his cheeks. Up close, Terry saw the bright rouge and neon blue eyeshadow had settled into the deep creases on her face.

"Oh, Terry, look how tall and handsome you've gotten. I came as soon as I heard." The lady wrapped Terry in a stifling hug, pinning his arms to his side.

He shot his friends a wide-eyed look, pleading for help.

"Um ... I'm Alex White. And you are ...?" Alex's etiquette training kicked in, and she attempted to defuse the situation while also trying to determine who the crazy lady was.

"Oh, my goodness," the lady breathed. "How rude of me. Allow me to introduce myself. I'm Dorothy, one of Matilda's oldest and dearest friends." She shook each of their hands as she spoke, so she missed the look of mingled disbelief, horror, and confusion that passed among them.

By the time the introductions were complete, Terry had regained his composure ... and the feeling in his arms.

"I'm sorry, Miss …? I missed your last name," he said, wrangling information out of her without stooping to her level of rudeness.

"Honey, I'm no *miss*. I'm divorced. Three times actually."

"Not surprising," Chad whispered in Alex's ear.

She shoved an elbow into Chad's ribs and bit the inside of her cheek hard to keep from giggling.

"I'm Dorothy Comstock now." Dorothy's rambling didn't miss a beat. "Matilda knew me as Dot Smith years ago. When can I see her? The ladies at the church said she was on this floor."

When Alex explained only family and close friends were briefly allowed into the hospital room, Dorothy's eyebrows—or, rather, the dark pencil lines that served as her brows—pulled together. Alex couldn't decide if it was a show of anger or frustration. She looked to Chad and Terry for some assistance. Chad simply stood and stared at the whole scene, mouth hanging open in disbelief. Luckily for Alex, Terry shook off the woman's invasion of his personal space and stepped forward.

"Mrs. Comstock, we'll be sure to pass along your concern to Aunt Tilley. If you'll leave your name and number at the nurse's station, I'll have my aunt contact you when she's feeling strong enough for visitors. I'm sure she'll be touched that you stopped by."

"*Hmph*. I drove all this way to the hospital, and this is the reception I get? I'm appalled at how you young folks have done away with good old-fashioned Southern hospitality." With one final dagger-throwing glare at each of them, she turned and stormed out of the room, her flip flops clapping with each angry step.

"Did that really just happen?" Chad asked, his trance finally broken.

Alex and Terry chuckled at the shell-shocked look on his face.

Despite her brashness, Mrs. Dorothy Comstock's unexpected appearance had accomplished one important goal—defusing the tension the three felt over breaking the news about how Matilda's recovery was about to change her life.

§§§

"That's the plan, Miss Matilda."

Alex had drawn the short straw, so here she stood, explaining to Miss Matilda how her life would change for the foreseeable future while the men stood on the far side of the room, not daring to meet the old lady's eyes.

Big scaredy cats.

After making a few quick phone calls, the three of them had pieced together a temporary plan that would allow someone to keep an eye on Miss Matilda at all times and still ensure Together for Good had a competent caregiver present.

"But, what about Charmain's job, dear?"

She might have suffered a stroke, but it hadn't affected her reasoning capabilities in the slightest. Alex had hoped she'd simply accept their plan to have Charmain trade places with Miss Matilda, putting the older lady in close proximity to Chad and Alex where they could watch her without seeming intrusive.

Charmain lived in the little guest cottage behind Alex and Chad's home. It was the same place Alex had remodeled when she had moved in right after Lydia's birth. Once Chad and Alex were married, Alex and Lydia had moved into the big farmhouse that Chad and his sister had inherited from their dad, essentially trading places with Charmain. Alex continued to use the garage-turned-workshop attached to the little cottage as the headquarters for her growing upcycled home décor business.

"Charmain's got some vacation time she needs to use," Alex said, praying her guilty conscience over the white lie wasn't written all over her face. She then shot a warning look at Chad, indicating he shouldn't contradict her.

Actually, Charmain had pulled strings, bargained with co-workers, and promised to work the next two holiday shifts to be able to take the upcoming week off. She'd only been working at the trendy downtown boutique for a few months, but management had been willing to give her the time off, due to the nature of the emergency. The fact that everyone in Burton loved Miss Matilda had helped, too.

The young people described the details of their plan, knowing they needed a rock-solid proposal in order for Miss Matilda to go along with it. Chad, Lydia, and Charmain would take Char's car home, leaving Alex to spend tonight at Together for Good. Charmain had promised Alex that she'd be packed and ready to move into Miss Matilda's cottage by tomorrow afternoon. Alex hoped Char would have enough time, and the inclination, to clean up a bit before Miss Matilda came to stay. Tidiness wasn't Charmain's strongest trait. Regardless of the housekeeping situation, they all had to trust the plan that they'd made for Miss Matilda's care.

"Well, if you ask me, y'all are going to a lot of trouble. Unnecessarily, I might add." Miss Matilda wasn't taking it well, but she also wasn't causing much of a ruckus.

Alex accepted their small victory.

"Maybe so, but Dr. Duncan said he'd feel better knowing you're being pampered for a while." Alex remained deliberately vague about the exact timeframe, knowing her words could be used against her, especially if Miss Matilda discovered the slightest chink in what they hoped was an iron-clad plan.

She watched Miss Matilda, her complexion still a bit chalky, mull the information over in her head. Finally, the older lady sank back against the pillows and closed her eyes. "If y'all think it's for the best, I'll agree to it. But, remember this"—she snapped her eyes open and bore her gaze into Alex's—"I don't have to like it," she finished, turning her fierce stare to the two cowards in the corner.

Alex tried with all she had to suppress a grin … and failed.

"It's not funny, Alex. Even with this ridiculous thing on"—she tilted her head in the direction of her broken arm—"I'm not an invalid, and I won't be treated like one." Miss Matilda's tone was indignant as she defended her independence.

"Nobody said you're an invalid, Aunt Tilley," Terry finally spoke up. "We just want to make sure you have the best chance possible for making a complete recovery. We love you."

The last thing Alex wanted was to patronize the strong, capable woman who'd rescued her and Lydia from Alex's potentially disastrous decision. It had been Miss Matilda who'd shown Alex the tiny life within her at a time when Alex had been considering an abortion. Now she couldn't imagine life without Lydia, and she had Miss Matilda to thank.

Alex owed her daughter's life to this woman's dedication to saving babies. She'd do whatever she needed to do to get their old friend back on her feet.

§§§

"I think that went well, considering how badly it could have gone." Chad reached for her hand as they walked to the parking garage.

"Yeah, I really appreciate you and Terry jumping in to help me explain." Alex playfully nudged Chad's ribs with her elbow. When he grinned but didn't reply, Alex sobered. "Do you think we're doing the right thing, honey?" She'd started second-guessing their plan and needed reassurance.

They'd reached her car, still loaded with their luggage from the trip to North Carolina. Seeing it reminded her of all they'd dealt with over the last few days. Her jaw clenched in response to the anxiety, making her head pound.

Chad stopped before opening the door for Alex and pulled her close. He stroked her soft brown hair as she rested her head against his chest, drawing strength from him.

"I believe, without a doubt, that we've come up with the best solution for Miss M., at least for the foreseeable future. After that, God will show us what we should do, okay?" He placed a finger under her chin and tilted her face up.

She saw sincerity and peace in his eyes and felt her own fears melt away. She nodded before standing on her tiptoes and placing a gentle kiss on his lips. "Thanks," she said. "Now hand me the keys, and I'll drive to Miss Matilda's house."

§§§

Dorothy Comstock sat in her car, watching Alex and Chad. *They certainly look very lovey-dovey to have been so rude to me.*

After her confrontation with Terry and the Whites, Dorothy had marched down to the coffee shop to pick up a tray of lattes. She'd then taken the elevator to the labor and delivery floor. In her experience, family members awaiting happy news were willing to open up to strangers, especially strangers who came bearing gifts in the form of sugary caffeine.

By the time she had left the hospital, she'd learned all kinds of stuff about Terry, Alex, and Chad. She'd even gleaned tons of information about her old pal, Matilda Gault. Really interesting information, such as she'd never married and still ran a home for pregnant girls. *Is that even a thing these days?* Apparently, yes.

For the price of a few coffees and a few hours of her time, she'd been able to learn things that could be extremely useful in the future.

Dorothy filed away Alex and Chad's little parking garage snuggle session with the other interesting facts she'd collected today. It really was too easy to snoop in a small Southern town.

Baby News

The drive from the hospital to Together for Good took about thirty minutes, unless Charmain drove. Alex smiled to herself as she recalled the day that Charmain had driven them to the hospital when Alex had gone into labor at the Whites' home. The girl had gotten them there in record time, though they'd questioned several times during the drive whether they'd make it alive.

Thinking of Charmain reminded Alex that she needed to let her sister-in-law know they were on their way so Lydia could be ready to go home with Chad. Her little girl's bedtime was quickly approaching, and Alex wanted to make sure Lydia slept in her own bed tonight. If Alex needed to take one of the residents to the hospital tonight, she didn't want to worry about who would look after Lydia.

"Hey, hon," she said to Chad. "Would you find my phone in my purse? I want to call Char and let her know we're on the way."

Chad groaned, making Alex laugh. She knew he viewed her gigantic purse as a deep, dark cave of mystery and lurking danger. A place that held all the essentials the mom of a toddler and a business woman might need in a pinch.

"I'll just call her on my phone." He punched the button on his phone and groaned again. "My battery is dead. Shoot!"

"Don't be such a baby," Alex said, her tone teasing. "There's nothing in there that'll bite you. At least, I don't think there is." A giggle escaped her as she watched a look of horror cross her husband's face.

"Okay, here goes. Send in a search party if I don't come back." He dug around, his face set in a deep scowl. "Wait a minute. What's this?"

"There's honestly no telling, sweetie. I throw everything in there, and I haven't cleaned it out in weeks." She brought the car to a stop at a red light, looking over to see what he'd found in the depths of her bag. When she saw what he held up in the fading light of the early summer sunset, she felt a pounding in her head as her heart skipped a beat. "Uh-oh."

"What do you mean, *uh-oh*?" Chad held a short plastic stick. He focused on the tiny window at the wide end that clearly displayed a bright red plus sign. "Is this what I think it is?"

Alex nodded, unable to read the expression on his face. Then she pressed the accelerator when the light turned green and eased the car into an empty parking lot before shifting the car into park. Turning in her seat to face her husband, she took his free hand in both of hers. "This isn't how I wanted to tell you."

He still held the stick.

"I had a big speech planned. And a baby-themed dessert for us after Lydia went to bed." She really had wanted to make this special.

"When did you find out? And when, exactly, were you going to tell me?" The hurt in his eyes wrecked her.

I wanted this to be so special.

"I did the test a couple of days ago," she said, letting go of his hand to massage her temples. The pounding in her head was getting more insistent. "Things have been so crazy lately, with the expansion of my product line and the fight with Mother over the will, I didn't even realize I was late. Then we got the call about Miss Matilda, and I just pushed it to the back of my mind until we knew what was going on with her."

She and Chad had agreed after the honeymoon that they wouldn't wait to start a family. Initially, the had prospect made Alex apprehensive. She hadn't known if she'd be able to love another baby as much as she loved Lydia. But her longing for Chad to know the joy of holding his child for the first time overrode any misgivings.

The crazy pace of life had caused her to forget all about the timing of her cycle, something she'd kept careful track of until the past few months. On the ride up to Woodvale, she'd scrolled through her calendar and noticed it had been six weeks since her last period. Once they had settled in at their hotel, she'd made up a flimsy excuse to run an errand, telling Chad that she needed to get milk for Lydia. Her quest, however, was actually for the home pregnancy test.

This time, the purchase had brought a flutter of excitement to her belly, not the waves of fear it had set off when she'd suspected she was pregnant with Lydia. And when the positive sign had appeared, Alex's heart had soared. She had immediately begun making plans for a sweet surprise announcement to her husband, but she never got to carry through with her plan.

Terry's initial call had come as they were getting ready to meet with the lawyers. The meeting had seemed to stretch on forever, and when they had finally finished, Chad and Alex's only thought had been picking up Lydia from Zeke's house and getting back to Burton.

Now, sitting in the deserted parking lot, Chad looked at her. She couldn't read his expression, making her unsure if his eyes were swimming in happy, sad, angry, or hurt tears.

"Sweetie, I'm so sorry ..." she started but didn't get to finish.

"Sorry for what?" Chad reached across the center console and cupped her face in his hands. "For making me the happiest man on earth? Babe, I'm thrilled!"

Alex released the breath that she hadn't even known she had been holding, relieved at his response. "We'll celebrate later. I really did want to make this special, but I think Charmain needs to go home and pack if we expect her to stay at Together for Good for a week or more." She caressed his cheek, wishing they could properly commemorate this milestone in their marriage.

He nodded. "I agree. But I don't know if I'll sleep a wink tonight." His face radiated joy.

Alex felt both humbled and proud to be able to bring him such happiness.

§§§

Alex made it through the night without incident. She'd opted for sleeping on the sofa in the front room of the big house, as it was affectionately referred to by friends and residents, instead of staying in Miss Matilda's little cottage just a few steps away. Once she made sure the six current residents had breakfast preparations underway, she went to the little house that had been Miss Matilda's home for over fifty years.

Knowing Charmain's reputation for being a less-than-stellar housekeeper, Alex ran the vacuum, started the dishwasher, cleaned the bathroom, changed the sheets, and put out fresh towels. Charmain was stepping up in a big way, and Alex wanted everything to be comfortable for her sister-in-law.

Charmain had her quirks—short attention span, lack of commitment to a career, and notoriously terrible timing in social situations—but Alex understood Chad's sister and why she'd made some of the questionable choices she had.

When Chad and Charmain had lost their mother to suicide, Charmain had only been a child. Their dad had retreated into his grief, never providing the emotional stability the kids had so desperately needed. Chad, only twelve years old himself when the tragedy had occurred, tried to take care of his sister by packing her lunch, doing the laundry, and cooking dinner. And, of course, Miss Matilda had provided spiritual and emotional nurturing, doing everything within her power to provide the foundation that they would need to weather life's storms.

Alex believed the deficits Charmain had faced during such formative years, despite Chad's and Miss Matilda's best efforts, had affected her deeply.

After high school, Charmain had tried going to college, but that had only lasted less than a year. She'd launched into an endless cycle of finding the "perfect job," discovering it wasn't so perfect, getting restless, and quitting. To everyone who knew her, her current position as a fashion stylist at the boutique had seemed like the perfect job for her. Alex, however, recognized the signs of Charmain's impending departure and made a mental note to talk to the girl, whom she couldn't love any more if she'd been her sister by birth.

Shaking herself out of her thoughts and setting her mind to the task at hand, Alex found Miss Matilda's suitcase and packed some essentials—a few of her favorite dresses, a nightgown, slippers, undergarments, a toothbrush, and a comb. If she thought of anything else she needed during the cottage swap, Alex or Chad could get it for her.

Satisfied at last that things were in order, Alex lugged the suitcase around to her vehicle before going inside the big house for one last cup of coffee. She expected Charmain any moment. Then again, the girl did have a terrible track record when it came to punctuality.

Alex smiled thinking of the occasions Charmain had shown up at exactly the wrong time, but the grin turned into a grimace as a pain shot through her lower back.

Must've pulled something lifting that suitcase.

Massaging the spot with her fingertips, she stepped onto the porch and took a big gulp of hot coffee. Then she gasped, surprised to see Charmain's car turn into the long driveway, right on time. It was truly nothing short of a miracle.

Alex called through the screen door and let the girls know she was leaving, wincing again at another twinge in her back. A few minutes on the heating pad might be in order, but it would have to wait until they finally got Miss Matilda checked out of the hospital and settled into her new, albeit temporary, living quarters.

"Thanks for doing this, Char," Alex said as Charmain retrieved her bags from the trunk of her car. Alex didn't know what they would've done if Charmain hadn't been able to come and oversee things while they worked out a more permanent arrangement.

"Happy to do it. I owe Miss Matilda so much. This is the least I could do. Oh, before I forget, I was in such a hurry to pack that I didn't quite get everything cleaned up at home. I let Chad know, but I'm not sure how much he'll do."

Alex smiled, knowing if there was anything she'd taught him in the last few months, it was how to get a house presentably clean in short order.

"I'm sure it'll be fine. Miss Matilda's cottage is ready to go for you. I got a feeling she'll be calling you several times a day. If you have any questions about anything, she'll be more than willing to fill you in."

Charmain had spent countless hours at the home over the years, visiting, studying, helping in the garden. Alex didn't think there was much her sister-in-law would need help with.

Alex wasted no time retrieving her overnight bag and stashing it in the back of her SUV, alongside Miss Matilda's luggage. Within minutes of Charmain's arrival, Alex guided her vehicle down the long driveway. She and Chad were meeting Terry at the hospital, checking out their patient and getting her situated in the guest house. The arrangement ensured their patient was close enough to the Whites for them to be able to check in on her frequently and quickly. A girl from the church youth group was watching Lydia, while the adults tended to the business of getting Miss

Matilda home and settled.

Reaching to turn up the volume on the radio, Alex grimaced at the tug in her back and pressed the button for the heated seat. This would be the closest she'd get to a heating pad for the next several hours.

Happy with how all the details were falling into place, she turned the radio up and belted out every song played on the Christian station, letting the seat's warmth permeate her aching muscles.

Arriving at the hospital, she quickly found a parking spot near Chad's truck then hurried to the lobby and tapped her foot impatiently while the elevator made its sluggish descent. Finally, she stepped into the cramped little conveyance and endured its equally slow journey back up. Once the doors crawled open, she rushed as fast as she dared to Miss Matilda's room, peeking around the open door. She grinned at the sight that greeted her.

Miss Matilda sat, fully dressed, on the edge of the bed, her feet dangling far from the floor and her good arm crossed over her cast. Terry and Chad sat on each side of her while a nurse was busy setting the brake on the wheelchair intended to transport the patient to the hospital exit. Miss Matilda's face, however, indicated anything but elation at finally being discharged. Her deep scowl told the world of her extreme displeasure.

"What's wrong, Miss Matilda?" Alex asked.

"I keep telling them I'm not an invalid. I can leave here on my own two feet."

Alex had to suppress a grin at the similarity between the old lady and Alex's own strong-willed daughter. Come to think of it, independent Southern women pretty much dominated Alex's whole group of friends.

I suppose I have to count myself in that group, but I don't have to admit to it.

A gentle knock on the open door broke the tension. Dr. Sheffield, the obstetrician in charge of making sure the girls from Together for Good received top-notch care, popped her head in. Her flawless, mocha-colored skin glowed beneath the hospital-green scrub cap, and she smiled when she saw Miss Matilda.

"Hi, Matilda. Dr. Duncan told me you were here. I wanted to check in and make sure you're doing better. Do you have everything you need?" As she spoke, she crossed the room and sat in the chair in front of Miss Matilda.

The older lady's countenance softened somewhat, but she still launched into her own personal declaration of independence, making it clear to everyone that she had no intention of getting in a wheelchair.

Alex decided to use the time of distraction to visit the restroom before they started the long process of getting Miss Matilda checked out of the hospital and back to their house. She'd had several cups of coffee, and her bladder had reached its limit.

Grabbing her purse, she motioned to Chad that she was excusing herself, and he gave her a thumbs-up.

Stepping out of the tiny restroom a few minutes later, Alex's face was ghostly pale. She stared ahead, unseeing, unable to comprehend what was happening.

Something was terribly wrong.

§§§

Chad chatted with the doctor, who remembered him from the crazy couple of days that had led up to Lydia's birth when he and Char had been Alex's support system during a scary time. He laughed at something Terry said and glanced up to see Alex slip out of the restroom.

Seeing her face, chalky white and almost catatonic, Chad's insides clenched in worry. He tried to catch her eye, but she simply stared ahead of her, seeing nothing.

Chad patted Miss M.'s back, eased off the bed, and crossed the room. Once he reached Alex, he put his hands on her shoulders in an attempt to get her to focus on him.

"What's wrong?" he whispered in her ear.

Her breath caught in her throat, a tiny gasp escaping. She shook her head, and when she tilted her face up to look him in the eye, he saw raw fear staring back at him.

"I'm bleeding, Chad."

She couldn't have spoken more quietly if she tried, and Chad struggled to understand both her words and their meaning. He couldn't.

"What? Are you hurt?"

Dr. Sheffield began saying her goodbyes, but she touched Alex's shoulder on her way out the door. As Alex's doctor, she was aware of their plans to have a baby. She also recognized a distraught patient.

"Is everything okay, Alex?" Concern tinged her voice.

Alex shook her head. "Can we step out for a minute, Doctor?" she said softly, not wanting to arouse concern among the others.

Dr. Sheffield led the way, with Alex and Chad close on her heels.

On the way out, Chad saw Terry look at him with one eyebrow raised in question, but all Chad could do was shrug as he left the room.

The doctor led them into the tiny waiting room that they'd been in yesterday. "So, Alex, tell me what's going on." Dr. Sheffield placed a hand on Alex's arm.

Her kind gesture and gentle tone were Alex's undoing. She dissolved into heaving sobs and garbled, incomplete sentences. "Six weeks, so … did the test … Positive … Vacuumed this morning … heavy luggage … back hurt. Used the heated seats …." Each pause was punctuated by a hiccupped breath. After the last word, she collapsed, spent and sobbing, against Chad, who held her and rubbed her back.

He wanted to do nothing more than protect her from all harm. He failed miserably.

"Do you have any idea what she's talking about?" Dr. Sheffield asked Chad.

"Maybe. Yesterday, she told me she took a pregnancy test, and it was positive." He left out the part about Alex keeping the news to herself until his accidental discovery of it. "When she came out of the restroom just now, she told me she's bleeding."

Shaking her head, Dr. Sheffield set her mouth in a thin, firm line. "Alex, why don't you come with me?"

"What? Now? I can't. I've got to help them get Miss Matilda home."

Chad could see the emotions warring within Alex. She wanted to find out what was happening to her, but she felt responsible for getting their dear friend settled.

"You go, honey," Chad said, trying to absolve Alex of the guilt that she surely felt, regardless of the choice she'd made. "Miss M. has to be cleared by her doctor, and then there's all the paperwork and discharge instructions. Then we've got to get her downstairs and loaded. It'll be a while before we're on our way home."

"This won't take long, Alex. I just want to draw some blood. We won't have results until later today." Dr. Sheffield led them out of the little room and looped her arm around Alex.

"Do you want me to come with you, babe? I can let Terry know." Chad felt utterly useless.

She shook her head. "I'm just getting some blood drawn. I'll be fine."

She didn't look fine, though. He'd seen her put that brave face on when she actually felt like falling apart. He hoped she wasn't falling apart now.

Shadow of a Shattered Dream

Lying in her bed several hours later, Alex had no recollection of the drive home. She barely remembered kissing Lydia on the way into the house and coming upstairs. Dr. Sheffield had recommended she take it easy the rest of the day, at least until they got the test results.

Alex had cried. She'd prayed. She'd bargained with God. But, most of all, she'd blamed herself for not telling Chad about the pregnancy immediately, for overexerting herself this morning, for using the heated seat in her car, for drinking too much coffee. She thought of everything she'd done in the past forty-eight hours, and she condemned and berated herself for each one, wondering if she'd contributed to the problem, whatever it was.

To complicate matters, with Alex confined to the bed for the time being, Chad and Terry had gotten Miss Matilda settled into the little guest house out back by themselves. Well, they'd had Lydia helping them, but Alex wasn't sure if that was an asset or a liability. Her four-year-old was energetic and inquisitive. If the men channeled her energy in the right direction, she could be helpful. Left to her own devices, however, she'd wreak havoc and cause double the work for them.

The buzz of her cell phone snapped her out of her thoughts, but when she saw Dr. Sheffield's name appear on the screen, her heart froze. Drawing a shaky breath, she tapped her phone.

"Hello, Dr. Sheffield." She wished Chad were with her, but he'd taken Lydia to the supermarket to get something for dinner.

"Alex, are you free to talk?"

"Yes." *But I don't think I want to hear what you have to say.*

"I'm afraid it's not good news." Dr. Sheffield sounded genuinely regretful. "The levels of pregnancy hormone in your blood are very low. Too low, in fact, to indicate the pregnancy is still viable, especially considering the bleeding you're currently experiencing."

Alex thought her heart would stop beating. She listened mutely as the doctor continued.

"I want you to come back tomorrow so we can draw some more blood, just to confirm. But don't get your hopes up. It doesn't look good."

The soothing quality of Dr. Sheffield's voice helped soften the knife to Alex's heart, but only a bit.

Yesterday, she'd wondered if she'd ever be able to love another child as much as she loved Lydia. Now she grieved the baby's loss with a force that shook her to the core.

"Do you understand what I'm saying, Alex?" The doctor sounded so kind, so calm, so … concerned.

"Y-yes. I lost the baby." They were the hardest words she ever had to say.

The worst part, however, was knowing she'd have to say those words again and anticipating the disappointment in Chad's eyes. How would she ever face him? How could she tell him that she'd let him down when he'd been so thrilled to find out she was pregnant? Would he ever forgive her?

Dr. Sheffield continued to talk about the frequency of miscarriages, with many women having no idea they were even pregnant, and about how this in no way indicated they couldn't try again. She said Alex should rest for the next few days and what to expect. Her words seemed to come from the end of a long tunnel, echoing in Alex's head but making no sense.

"I know this is a lot to take in, Alex. I'm going to post some instructions to your online chart. Log in and print them out. Then you can refer to them whenever you have questions. It's perfectly normal to feel overwhelmed. Give your body time to heal and your heart time to grieve. I'm so sorry for your loss. You call me if you need me, okay?"

"I will. Thank you."

After Alex ended the call, she sat on the bed and sobbed, hoping to cleanse herself of the guilt, and pain, and loss. She tried reasoning with herself, telling herself over and over that she'd just found out about the baby, so she couldn't have gotten too attached. But then her heart would acknowledge all the hopes and dreams that she'd already begun to have for their little one.

At their wedding, she and Chad had promised to love each other through the good and the bad ... in sunshine and in shadows ...

We're definitely in the shadows now.

... through hopes fulfilled and dreams shattered.

We're watching a dream shatter right before our eyes.

§§§

Chad lifted Lydia out of her car seat and let her run ahead of him while he grabbed the bags from the back seat of his truck. He heard her little feet stomping on the wooden stairs leading to the kitchen. She'd told him that she wanted to see her mommy and show her the doll that he'd gotten her for being such a big helper today. True to her word, she bounded up, excitement bubbling over.

"Mommy, look at the new doll Chaddie getted for me!"

I'm probably gonna get a lecture about spoiling her.

Stalling to postpone the inevitable chiding, Chad continued to busy himself with the groceries in the truck. He glanced through the windshield occasionally to watch the girls' exchange. When Alex spoke, her voice sounded tight and scratchy, but her body was turned away from the truck, obstructing his view of her face.

"That's great, sweetie. Why don't you take her inside and show her your room?"

"Okay, Mommy." Lydia grabbed the doorknob, but then she turned around before going inside. "Mommy, you look sad. Are you sad because Chaddie bought me a doll?"

"Not at all, baby." Alex smiled and tousled her daughter's hair. "I'm really glad he got you a new doll."

Satisfied at the explanation, Lydia went inside and slammed the kitchen door shut behind her.

Chad nudged the truck door shut with his hip, preparing himself for whatever news Alex might have. Feeling sure she'd heard from Dr. Sheffield by now, he braced for the worst. Then, taking one look at her tear-streaked face as she stood at the top of the same steps that Lydia had just mounted in a joyful frenzy, he knew.

Her eyes were red and swollen, and she had wrapped her arms around her midsection in a posture she'd taken since he'd met her whenever she felt insecure, uncertain, and hurt.

Chad dropped the bags in the driveway and rushed up the steps two at a time, pulling her close and stroking her silky brown curls.

"Chad, I'm so sorry," she wailed into his chest, her body quaking with the force of her sorrow.

"Shh … Listen to me. You have nothing to be sorry for, sweetie." Chad took her face in both hands and forced her to meet his eyes. She seemed to be searching for something, but he didn't know what.

"I … I lost the baby. Our baby. Can you ever forgive me?" She collapsed against him once more.

"Alex, you did nothing to intentionally miscarry. You don't have to apologize." He had to make her understand that this wasn't her fault. She couldn't carry this guilt *and* grieve her loss. It would be too much for her to bear. "Do you want to go up and get a bath while I feed Lydia and get her to bed?"

"I appreciate the offer," she said, sniffing and swiping at her eyes with the heels of her hands. "I'll be okay, really. Besides, I want to be with both of you right now."

He kissed the top of her head, inhaling the sweet aroma of her apple-scented shampoo. "Okay. I picked up a rotisserie chicken and some macaroni and cheese at the supermarket deli."

Normally, she'd chide him for resorting to his bachelor ways and planning a dinner with no vegetable, but tonight, she simply nodded. No doubt, she was glad she didn't have to think about planning or preparing anything. She wrapped her arms around his waist and squeezed.

He hoped she didn't let go too soon. He didn't want her to see the tears in his own eyes.

§§§

Alex had dreaded the thought of having to be a master conversationalist at dinner that night, but Lydia's nonstop chatter let her off the hook. The little girl talked incessantly while Chad put away the groceries and plated their dinner. She rattled on about her adventures over the past couple of days, including gathering eggs with Charmain at Miss Matilda's, helping carry the older lady's flowers into the guest house out back, being allowed to select a doll for all her hard work, and everything in-between ... in no particular order.

Alex smiled as she listened to her daughter's tales, liking how it felt for the weight of sorrow to lift, even just a little bit, simply by spending time with those she loved most.

She wasn't sure if she felt like a slug or royalty sitting at the kitchen table and having her dinner placed before her, but Chad had insisted. He dropped a quick kiss on her cheek before he sat down then reached for both his girls' hands. The three of them bowed their heads for him to pray.

"Father, we thank You for this day and for this meal. We thank You for family and friends who are always willing to help. Be with us, Father, in the coming days. Direct our steps, comfort our breaking hearts, and heal the wounded and grieving among us. Bless this food to nourish our bodies, so we may better serve You. In Jesus' Name."

"Amen," the three voices chorused together.

Alex held on to her husband's hand and gave it a brief squeeze. She mouthed the words, *"Thank you."*

He squeezed back, raised her hand to his lips, and kissed it gently before letting go.

The three of them spent the rest of their early supper listening to more of Lydia's stories, from kindergarten drama to escapades of baking cookies with Charmain at Together for Good. In no mood to talk, or even correct her daughter for speaking with her mouth full, Alex smiled and let Lydia's monologue wash over her, glancing at Chad occasionally to see him hanging on to every word the little girl said.

When they'd finished eating, he rose to clear plates, and Alex joined him. But he put a hand on her shoulder and shook his head. "You stay there. I'm going to put these in the dishwasher and fix Miss M. a plate."

Another wave of guilt washed over Alex. *How could I have forgotten about poor Miss Matilda?*

"Oh, my goodness, Chad," she said, bringing both hands up to cover her mouth. "We need to fix her a vegetable to go with this. I think I've got stuff for a salad in the fridge, or we could steam some frozen veggies."

Standing at the sink, Chad tried to hide a grin as he rinsed the plates.

"What's so funny?" She saw nothing amusing about offering their guest a balanced meal.

"Nothing, sweetie. I was just thinking how hospitable and, um …

predictable you are." When he looked up from his task, Alex saw nothing mean-spirited or accusatory in his gaze. All she saw was his love, his steadfast love, which continued to baffle and elate her all at once.

"Mommy," Lydia announced as she scooted off her booster seat. "I'll get a bag of peas out of the freezer. Aunt Char told me they're Miss 'Tilda's favorite. Chaddie, you can cook them, and then we'll take dinner to her."

Alex and Chad laughed at their girl's take-charge attitude. Neither one doubted where she'd gotten it.

A short time later, the three of them stood at the door to the same guest cottage that Alex and Lydia had called home for several years, knocking softly. They heard their guest call out for them to come in, and then Miss Matilda's face lit up at the sight of them as she closed the Bible in her lap.

Alex was still surprised every time she entered the house to see how different it looked since Charmain had made it her home. She'd rearranged the furniture, hung her own artwork, and painted an accent wall bright red. Whereas Alex had chosen a soft, calming color scheme, Charmain used colors that matched her bold personality, right down to the sunny yellow dish towels and café curtains in the tiny kitchen. Everything about the small space suited Charmain.

"Well, hello," Miss Matilda said. "I'm so happy to see you."

"Thanks, Miss M.," Chad said, placing her dinner plate on the table beside her chair. "You just saw us a couple of hours ago. Did you miss us so soon?"

Alex smiled at her husband's good-natured teasing.

"No. I mean, yes." Miss Matilda was flustered, and it didn't seem to have anything to do with Chad's jokes.

"What's wrong, Miss Matilda?" Alex asked.

"That woman was here. I didn't even know she was back in town."

Alex and Chad exchanged a concerned glance. The doctor had mentioned the possibility for confusion, maybe even mild hallucinations. Alex hoped there was another explanation.

"What woman?" Chad asked, keeping his tone light as he hid the look on his face by retrieving a fork from the kitchen drawer.

"Dottie Smith. Or Comstock. Or, whoever she is now. I'll tell you *what* she is. She's a gossip and a troublemaker, but I can't say that to most folks."

"No, ma'am. I can see how that would put you in an awkward position," Chad agreed.

"Promise me y'all will steer clear of her," Miss Matilda said, her voice emphatic.

"We will," Alex and Chad agreed in unison. Their eyes met, both remembering the heinous woman who had come to the hospital.

Lydia tugged at Alex's shirt and pointed to her new doll. Alex nodded, indicating it was okay to share with their friend.

Alex and Chad had reminded Lydia that Miss Matilda had a broken arm, stressing the importance of being careful around her and not making her tired. Therefore, Alex was proud to see her daughter, who had just minutes ago been racing around their house with her new doll, walk quietly to sit on the sofa facing Miss Matilda.

"Hey, Miss 'Tilda."

Alex smiled at the name Lydia had always called their dear friend.

"Look at the doll Chaddie got me for being such a good helper today. And, watch this, her eyes close when she lays down and open when I pick her up."

"Well, let me see that. My goodness, that's a beautiful doll you picked out. Have you named her yet?"

"Her name is Baby. I'm Mommy's baby, so this doll is my baby." She stroked the doll's face before continuing, "You know, I like being Mommy's baby, but I want to be a big sister like Darnia. She's in my class, and her mommy brought her a little sister. She says being a big sister is a really important job."

"Yes, it is. A long time ago, I had a big sister. She was very good at it, too."

Alex had taken a seat in the comfy chair beside the couch and listened to the quiet exchange. She and Chad had never talked to Lydia about bringing another child into the family, so Lydia's thoughts on the subject came as a surprise ... and a blow.

Feeling her fragile emotions threatening to crumble again, Alex excused herself and slipped down the hall to the bathroom, needing a few moments to compose herself.

After splashing some cool water on her face, she sat on the side of the tub, taking deep breaths and dabbing her eyes with a tissue. When she heard a light rap at the door, she guessed Chad had come to check on her.

"Come in."

She was surprised to see Miss Matilda standing at the door, leaning on the cane that they'd given her at the hospital.

"Miss Matilda, you need to sit down. The doctor doesn't want you up and about. Besides, your dinner's getting cold."

"Alex, quit worrying about others for just a second."

Alex had to smile at the words. Miss Matilda never stopped worrying about, caring for, and loving on others. The irony of her giving that advice wasn't lost on Alex.

She closed her eyes and prayed for the strength to say the words one more time. Then she scooted over, making space for the older lady to perch beside her.

"I had a miscarriage, Miss Matilda."

"Oh, sweetie! I'm so sorry." She reached over and patted Alex's knee. "And here you and Chad are, trying to take care of a feeble old lady. I feel awful for being such an imposition at a difficult time like this."

"Miss Matilda, no! After everything you've done for Chad and me, it's our privilege to get to take care of you for a while. This is just something we've got to deal with and move forward."

Alex had risen as she spoke and helped Miss Matilda maneuver into the little bedroom that would be hers for the foreseeable future. Alex got her settled in the comfortable arm chair in the corner then turned and sat on the edge of the bed. When Matilda shook her head, Alex knew she couldn't hide her sadness, but she didn't feel like she needed to with Miss Matilda.

"I understand about miscarriages, dear. Of course, with as many expectant mothers as I've encountered throughout the years, it's inevitable that a few of the residents have experienced loss." She looked at her good hand clutching the cane and sighed.

"I know how attached you become to the residents. Is it really difficult to watch it happen to them?" Alex thought Matilda seemed inordinately sorrowful over the loss of strangers' babies. Perhaps there was another explanation for her despondency.

Matilda shook her head but wouldn't make eye contact with Alex. "Now is not the time to dwell on my sadness, dear. We need to get *you* feeling better."

Alex knew better than to pry. She'd share when she was ready. Besides, Alex didn't want their dear friend to experience unnecessary stress, especially now when she was supposed to be relaxing and healing.

Slipping off the bed, Alex knelt down and embraced the kind woman who'd been her rock for the last several years, honored to have the chance to reciprocate in some small way.

"I'm going to be fine, Miss Matilda. Thanks for checking on me. You still need to eat your dinner, though," Alex said, her voice taking on the same tone it did when Lydia was being stubborn.

Miss Matilda heard it and bristled. "I know I do. I just wasn't that hungry when y'all got here."

Her look of indignation reminded Alex again of her daughter's strong-willed defiance, rarely exhibited but intensely manifested when it surfaced. All that was lacking was for Miss Matilda to cross her arms and poke her bottom lip out.

Alex was spared any further comparisons by Chad's and Lydia's appearance in the bedroom doorway. Chad held Miss Matilda's dinner plate, while Lydia carried a small lap tray.

"Hey, we thought if the party was in here, we might as well bring the refreshments," Chad said. "I popped your plate in the microwave for a few seconds, so it should be ready for you to dig in."

Alex helped Lydia get the tray positioned on Miss Matilda's lap, then Chad presented her plate with a flourish of his free hand.

"Dinner is served, ma'am." He bowed at the waist as he set the plate down, causing Miss Matilda to giggle at his antics.

"What did I ever do to deserve y'all?" Miss Matilda asked.

Alex smiled. She asked herself the same question every day.

What Next?

"Thanks for helping me, Raven," Alex said to the Together for Good resident who'd agreed to watch Lydia for an hour or so.

Looking at the size of the young woman's belly, Alex knew Raven didn't feel like doing much besides propping her feet up. Even this late in her pregnancy, though, she could read to Lydia and supervise the little girl's marathon coloring sessions. Lydia had already retrieved her crayons and coloring books from the basket and set Baby on the table beside her. It was the spot her beloved blanket, Lammy, had occupied previously, but Baby had nudged out the love-tattered, old fabric for the place of honor.

Alex kissed the top of her daughter's head then slipped out of the front room of Together for Good to join the others in the big, bright kitchen. Chad had a cup of coffee waiting for her, which she accepted as she took her place at the table next to him. The looks on Terry's and Charmain's faces told her that they were no closer to a decision.

"It's been five days," Charmain said, although they all knew how long it had been since Miss Matilda had come home from the hospital. "I have to go back to work soon. What will we do?"

"Well, I guess I could stay here a couple of nights a week," Alex volunteered, but her offer was met with resistance all around.

By now, she'd gotten the results of the follow-up bloodwork, which had confirmed the miscarriage. She'd shared the news of the loss with both Terry and Charmain and, as expected, they'd been kind and sympathetic, promising to pray for her and Chad as they dealt with their pain.

"No," Terry said, shaking his head emphatically. "You have a family to take care of. And you need to take good care of yourself. Why don't I move into the guest house?"

When Charmain smiled behind her coffee cup, Terry looked insulted.

"What? Do I need to remind you I grew up here?" He leveled his gaze at each of them, daring anyone to argue. "You don't think I can handle cooking, gardening, and laundry? I'm a bachelor now, remember? I've acquired some pretty impressive skills."

Alex understood Terry's need to defend both his capabilities and his pride. He'd been one of the first people in Burton to befriend Alex when she'd been little more than a scared, pregnant teenager, running physically and emotionally from her stepfather, J.T.'s, assault. Despite her efforts to hide her attacker's identity, Miss Matilda had somehow figured it out, stunning everyone when she had dropped the bombshell that J.T. was also Terry's biological father, making him Lydia's half-brother. The shock had forced Terry to reevaluate his loveless marriage and, ultimately, divorce his manipulative wife.

Since then, Terry's divorce had been finalized, he'd met and lost his biological father, and he'd gone into semi-retirement from his architecture business. The pressures of helping Zeke, J.T.'s best friend and second in command for years, run the construction company that Terry would soon inherit demanded more of his time than he'd counted on. Although he'd never faltered in keeping his aunt Tilley as his top priority, nobody at the table entertained any delusions of Terry being remotely able to singlehandedly run the home.

"I have no doubt of your skills, Terry," Charmain said, staring into her cup and trying to suppress a grin. "In fact, you're probably way more qualified than I am … in most things. But, would you know what to do if one of the girls came to you in the middle of the night and said her baby was almost here?"

The self-satisfied look evaporated from Terry's face, replaced in an instant by sheer terror. Although Charmain was single and had no children, she'd helped deliver a child in Miss Matilda's cottage, a fact that Alex had discovered shortly before her and Chad's wedding.

"That's what I thought. So, you see why we've got to figure out something more permanent? And appropriate," Charmain said, chugging the last of her coffee then rising to retrieve the pot. She refilled everyone's cups while they all stared into space, deep in thought.

"What about that Dorothy lady we met at the hospital?" Chad asked.

Alex and Terry looked at him like he was speaking a foreign language.

"What? I'm just throwing names out there."

"I know, honey," Alex said, "but that lady kind of gives me the creeps. And remember what Miss Matilda told us? I don't think we can trust her."

"I agree," Terry said before returning to stare into his mug.

They all acted as if the answers would be found in the dark depths of the steaming brew.

A knock at the front door drew them out of their reverie.

"I'll get it," Raven called.

They heard the door opening and the familiar sounds of greeting being exchanged. The group seated in the kitchen listened and tried to catch what was being said, but they couldn't make out the muffled voices. Nobody had the energy to rise and greet the newcomer.

It was several seconds before they heard footsteps on the hardwood as the guests approached the kitchen. Then Yvonne and Marquis Dixon peeked their heads around the doorway.

"Hi, y'all. Mind if we come in?" Yvonne asked.

"Hey. Come on in. It's good to see y'all," Terry said, finally remembering his manners and rising from his seat as he shook Marquis's hand.

"We heard Miss Matilda was ill, so we wanted to come and check on her," Yvonne said, handing a bouquet of flowers to Alex.

Alex put the flowers in a vase before retrieving two more mugs from the cabinet. She filled them with hot coffee then set them in front of their guests before reclaiming her seat next to Chad. Marquis draped his arm protectively around his wife.

Alex continued to marvel at how her relationship with this pair had come full-circle. Initially, this woman who'd broken Chad's heart in high school had fanned the flames of jealousy and ire in Alex's heart. Considering how news traveled in a small town, Alex had been surprised to learn how completely in the dark Chad had remained for years concerning Yvonne. She'd shown up in Burton last year, trying to find the son that she'd put up for adoption at birth. Instead, she'd reconnected with Marquis, her child's father, and the couple soon discovered they were still in love.

On their way to elope, they'd stopped by the home to share their happy news with Miss Matilda, not realizing it was Alex and Chad's wedding day. Alex had shocked everyone when she'd insisted they get married in the beautiful setting where she and Chad had started their lives as husband and wife just a few hours earlier.

Looking at the couple now, Alex thought what a striking pair they made. Fair-skinned and blonde, Yvonne's slight frame stood just over five feet tall. Marquis's ebony skin and closely cropped hair were a startling contrast to Yvonne's fairness. A former football player, his tall, muscular build made him an imposing figure, but Alex knew what a gentle giant he truly was.

"… resting while she stays in our guest cottage, which is where Charmain usually lives." Chad put his hand on Alex's as he finished his sentence, making Alex aware that she'd been lost in thought, something she did a lot lately.

"Wow. We had no idea it was so serious. Who's staying here with the residents?" Marquis asked.

"I am," Charmain said. "But my leave from work runs out in a few days. We were just discussing long-term options."

"How long-term are you looking at?" Yvonne asked, her eyes mirroring her genuine concern for the kind woman who'd helped her get her life back on track. Twice.

"We honestly don't know at this point," Terry said. "The doctor says it could be a few months. Or it might be a permanent situation. It all depends on her recovery and the amount of damage the stroke caused. We should know for sure after a few more weeks of physical therapy."

With both hands wrapped around his mug and his shoulders slumped, Terry looked worn out. The last week had aged him several years. Alex wished she could present a simple answer to the problem at hand, if for no other reason than to relieve some of the pressure that Terry put on himself.

"Mrs. White?" Raven stood in the doorway to the kitchen, her face drained of color and her hand propped on her lower back. "Would it be okay if I brought Lydia in here? I'm not feeling so great. I think I need to lie down for a little while."

Alex was still becoming accustomed to being addressed by her new last name, but it wasn't the use of her name that startled her. Raven's expression proclaimed her agony—eyes narrowed, lips pursed, brow furrowed.

Alex turned to Charmain, gauging her reaction. Yvonne brought her hand to her mouth, her eyes darting between the other two ladies at the table. The three women's unspoken communication spurred them into frenzied action.

"Raven," Alex started, trying to force a calm into her voice that she didn't feel, "how long have you felt badly?"

"This morning when I woke up, I just didn't feel great. But look at me." She gestured to her protruding tummy. "I'm as big as a horse." She moved her hand to the lower part of her belly, wincing as she spoke.

"Raven, why don't you sit down?" Charmain's chair scraped across the kitchen floor as she rose, with Alex and Yvonne close behind.

By the time the ladies crossed the kitchen to stand beside her, Raven was doubled over, grasping the doorframe in a white-knuckled grip with one hand and clutching her mid-section with the other. It wasn't until she began panting, trying to stave off the pain, that Alex noticed the beads of sweat glistening on her brow.

Alex turned to Charmain, now wide-eyed with panic, and tried to speak with all the composure she could muster. "Maybe you should call Dr. Sheffield," she said over her shoulder as she and Yvonne led Raven to a chair.

§§§

Chad and Terry stood watching in stunned silence. Chad couldn't help but remember the evening a few years ago when Alex had joined him and Char for tacos. She'd gone into labor at their house, but he'd known only a few sketchy details of the birth process.

At her request, he'd stayed at the hospital with her through the long night. The next day, Charmain had held her hand during her grueling hours of labor and delivery.

Now, as he watched his wife, sister, and ex-girlfriend tend to this girl, he knew another baby was about to make its entrance into the world. He marveled at how calm the women seemed.

Dr. Sheffield had told Charmain that it would be best for Raven to come to the hospital. With her being as far along as she was, the doctor wanted to check to make sure everything was progressing normally, admitting her if an examination indicated it was necessary.

"I'll take Raven," Alex said.

"No!" a chorus of voices rang out.

Relief flooded Chad's heart. Knowing Terry and Char were on his side gave him the advantage of numbers. He'd argued with Alex until he was blue in the face about taking a step back from her frenetic pace of life, even if only for a few days. She'd balked at his advice, insisting she felt fine. Still, he worried about the stress—physical, emotional, and mental—that constantly barraged her body and mind.

"Okay. So, who's going to take her?" Alex asked, shoving a hand on her hip and challenging them to defy her.

The assembled group heard the front door slam shut. Almost immediately, Marquis, who'd slipped out of the room when the commotion had begun, skidded into the kitchen. Lydia towed along in his wake.

"I've got it running, and the AC is going, so it'll be nice and cool for the drive. I got her bag from her room, and it's in the car. We should be good to go," Marquis panted out, the exertion of sprinting up and down the stairs causing him to huff out his words.

"Thanks, honey," Yvonne said, touching his face tenderly.

"Chaddie, what's wrong?" Lydia asked, her eyes wide as she clutched her doll.

Chad didn't want Lydia to be frightened by the situation, and he knew a surefire way to distract her. So, he fixed his gaze on his sister and tilted his head toward the back door. Charmain understood his suggestion.

"Hey, Lyddie, wanna go see the chickens?" She held out her hand and started walking toward the back door.

"Yay!" Lydia cried, jumping as she waited on her aunt to catch up. "Baby, you're going to see the chickens," she told the little doll that was her constant companion.

"Be careful," Alex called after them. Then she turned her attention back to Raven.

Chad thought Alex would be miffed at Yvonne and Marquis taking the lead on this particular crisis. He risked a sideways glance at her as they followed the mom-to-be and her two escorts to the front door, which Terry had rushed ahead to open. Alex didn't look upset at all, though. Instead, she looked ... What was that look? He'd seen it before.

Uh-oh. She's got an idea.

Alex hugged Yvonne while Terry asked Marquis to call and keep them posted.

Chad stood numbly in the gravel driveway, still unable to comprehend how quickly things had gone from coffee and conversation to impending delivery in a matter of seconds. Although he'd been visiting Miss M. at the pregnancy care home for years, he hadn't considered how deeply the demands of her position ruled her life.

He turned to follow the others inside but stopped when Alex turned around to face the men, holding up a hand to indicate she intended to be heard.

"Now, hear me out before you turn your nose up at an idea I just had." Alex sucked in a deep breath, preparing herself before revealing her suggestion. "What about Yvonne and Marquis?"

"What about 'em?" Chad asked, his head still reeling from recent events.

"What if we asked *them* to run Together for Good?" She clapped her hands in front of her and beamed.

A smile slowly spread across Terry's face. Chad, however, looked at his wife as if she'd just announced she intended to jump off the roof with chicken feathers attached to her arms. In retrospect, he wished he'd responded with a bit more tact. Instead, he'd snorted his displeasure and stomped up the porch steps, basically rejecting her idea.

No discussion.

§§§

Terry looked at Alex, the pain of Chad's dismissal evident on her face. While Terry agreed with the plan to ask the Dixons if they'd like the position, he also knew better than to meddle in marital matters. People had tried for years to tell him Gail was no good for him. He'd never listened, always believing his marriage vows outweighed all else. How wrong he'd been.

There was something else wrong with Alex, though. He couldn't place his finger on anything she'd said or done, but Terry felt a tension in the way she moved and spoke. He'd seen the same wariness in her when she'd first moved here.

"Alex, why don't we go in and discuss it with Chad? I'm sure he'll see the logic in your idea."

But Alex shook her head. "I think I'll just walk around the yard for a bit, Terry."

He watched her trudge away, shoulders drooped, head bowed. Somehow and for some reason, she'd reverted back to the scared, overwhelmed girl whom he'd made a deal with on Aunt Tilley's porch.

Proposed Changes

Miss Matilda had put a bench beneath the arch that Alex had built for their wedding. Alex collapsed onto it and looked up through the branches of the enormous oak tree. Sunlight filtered through the leaves, making shadows dance on the sparse grass around her.

Despite the utter peacefulness of her surroundings, turmoil raged inside her. She stretched her tired muscles, needing to ponder the emotions and thoughts that she could no longer keep at bay, no matter how much she tried.

She'd dealt with plenty of emotional upheaval in her life—when J.T. had assaulted her, when she'd discovered she was pregnant with Lydia, when she'd gone to confront and ultimately forgive J.T., when she'd planned a wedding in a few short weeks. All these events, and others to a lesser degree, had disrupted her life, her peace. But she'd dealt with them and moved on, which, she told herself, she must do now.

This current time of darkness, though, felt different. More suffocating. More paralyzing. If all she had to work through was the miscarriage, she believed she might cope, if only for Lydia's sake. Adding the pressures of finding a caretaker for Together for Good and her mother's malicious legal disputes overwhelmed Alex and made her feel inadequate, consumed with uncertainty, and unfit to be the wife, mother, and the friend she should be.

Tilting her head back again, Alex watched the bright beams that penetrated the thick, leafy branches. They pierced the quiet darkness, bold in their pursuit of reaching the ground below.

Oh, how I wish something could pierce my darkness, break through the shadows I'm in.

"Alex White," she addressed herself aloud, even as the thought still echoed in her mind, "Miss Matilda would be so disappointed."

She bowed her head, ashamed at having tried to handle her crushing problems all by herself again. Sure, she'd prayed over the past few days, but she'd continued to hold tight to the sorrow and pain, believing she could somehow fix her problems all by herself by doing more and more things. Now, however, she poured her heart out to God, laying her burdens at His feet and knowing He would listen to her cries for help and strength.

She longed for Him to wash her in His peace and equip her for whatever she faced. She begged forgiveness, requested guidance, and asked the Lord for the words to talk to those she loved. Alex knew she needed the loving support and sincere prayers of her friends.

The peace she so desperately sought gently seeped into her soul as the weight of her burdens lessened.

When she looked up, she saw Chad slipping beneath the low-dipping branches and walking noiselessly toward her. He rubbed the back of his neck, making Alex smile. The gesture had been a sure sign of jitters since the day she'd met him.

Alex patted the bench beside her, inviting him to sit with her. Chad raised his eyebrows, questions visible in his eyes, even in the dim light. She nodded and held her hand out to him. He took it, kissing it softly, and sat beside her. Neither spoke, not daring to disturb the reverent silence of the outdoor sanctuary.

Alex knew she owed her husband an apology for how she'd stormed off back at the house, for withholding life-changing information this past week, and for retreating into her bubble of self-pity at the first hint of heartbreak.

She prayed she hadn't pushed him away so far that he couldn't forgive her.

§§§

Still holding her hand, Chad slipped his other arm around his wife, enjoying the feel of her relaxing her body against him.

"I'm sorry …" they both spoke at once.

Chad chuckled, but he needed to go first. He needed to apologize for his bone-headed reaction, as his sister had so astutely described it when she'd heard the story from Terry.

"Alex, let me start, please." He felt her nod against him. "Sweetie, I'm sorry I responded so rudely to your idea. It was inexcusable. I know you've got Miss M.'s best interests at heart." The next sentence almost stuck in his throat. "Besides that, you understand what it means to live here. And so does Yvonne. It's just … well, it's still so hard for me to completely trust her after what she did to me years ago."

Alex pulled away, turning her face up toward him. "Honey, I know she made some terrible choices, but I truly believe she's changed and would do an excellent job." Those eyes, like pools of rich, dark chocolate, swam in unshed tears. A lone droplet escaped, and Chad tenderly wiped it away. Alex continued, "But, that's not what's tearing me apart right now. I feel so guilty, Chad, for the grief I've caused. I've dragged you into this messy legal business with Mother. On top of that, I didn't tell you about the baby right away, and now it's gone." She averted her eyes, letting her head tilt forward.

"Alex, I've told you that it wasn't your fault. You have nothing to apologize for." Chad cupped Alex's cheek in his hand, gently lifting her face and stroking her cheek softly with his thumb.

"So, you're not angry or hurt that I didn't tell you right away?"

"No, babe. It was big news. And we were dealing with some heavy stuff with the will and Miss M. I'm glad you wanted to make the news a celebration." He needed her to know he didn't fault her, didn't second-guess the decision she'd made. He also needed her to know he shared in the loss.

"Alex, you know you don't have to bear this alone. I'm sad, too. I'd only known about the baby for a few hours, but I'd already begun to have thoughts of what we'd name him, what he'd look like, teaching him to play ball. You know, dad stuff." He shrugged one shoulder as he spoke these last words.

Alex smiled, but it didn't reach her eyes as she reached up to stroke a lock of hair out of his eyes. An element of sadness seemed trapped within her.

"What if it had been her, not him? Would you have been excited to have a double dose of baby dolls and tea parties?"

"I'd gladly drink tea until my eyes float."

She laughed the first all-out belly laugh that he'd heard from her in days, and it set his world back on its axis. Somehow, he'd managed to coax the sparkle back into her eyes, and he watched them glint in the dappled sunshine. Chad wanted to sit here forever and watch her, entranced by the many facets of who she was—beautiful and strong, funny and keenly intelligent, loving and vulnerable.

He knew they couldn't stay here all day, though. They had responsibilities. There were decisions to be made. But his first responsibility would always be to her.

To remind her of his devotion, he took her in his arms and kissed her, willing the world outside the embrace of the giant oak tree to stay away for just a few moments longer.

§§§

Raven gave birth to her son the next morning. Yvonne never left her side. Once Marquis knew mother and baby were doing well, he called Alex to let her know.

"Thanks, Marquis. We appreciate you calling. Everything went well?"

Alex sat at the table in their modern, spacious kitchen with a cup of coffee, listening to the details of the little boy's weight, length, and birth time.

As Chad flipped pancakes at the stove, he signaled for Alex to set the plan in motion.

She nodded.

"Hey, Marquis, are you and Yvonne busy later? Chad and I thought you might like to come over for some burgers and dogs tonight." She nodded as she listened to him speak. "Okay. We'll see you about six o'clock then. No, you don't need to bring anything. Y'all get some rest, and we'll see you tonight. Bye."

"Well, it sounds like all we've got to do now is ask them," Chad said, launching a pancake into an acrobatic spin before catching it on the plate.

Alex nodded, impressed with her husband's skill but uncertain if he had a realistic view of what still needed to transpire. There were a lot of steps left to take, and many ways for the whole plan to fall apart, leaving them back at square one.

First, they had to ask the Dixons if they'd even be willing to take the position. It could be a few weeks before the doctor decided how long Miss Matilda would be out of commission, but her hand would be in a cast for at least another month or so. If they accepted, their resumes and statements of faith would need to go before the home's board of directors. Of course, Terry was the chairman and held a lot of sway, but the slim chance of their being rejected did exist.

If they received board approval, they'd need to get settled into the cottage behind Together for Good and get into the routine of running the house—taking applications for residents, settling the ladies into their new home, setting up prenatal care, gardening, cooking and, as they'd witnessed yesterday, the occasional emergency. The list of duties that Alex and Charmain had made yesterday seemed daunting, even for two able-bodied, twenty-something people. Alex had no idea how a lady of Miss Matilda's advanced years did it all.

But none of those steps to getting Yvonne and Marquis set up as the home's caregivers scared Alex as much as the initial step. Someone had to let Miss Matilda know their plan. She winced as she thought of breaking the news to their friend, especially considering she was recovering from a stroke and a broken hand.

Chad called into the living room for Lydia to come to breakfast before he set the plate heaped with pancakes on the table. After Chad said the blessing, the family started the now-familiar Saturday morning ritual of pancakes, butter, syrup, and bacon. Lydia regaled them with tales of her new doll, but Alex sat chewing quietly, staring out the kitchen window at the birds.

"Earth to Alex," Chad said, waving a hand in front of her face.

"Oh! Sorry." Alex dragged her attention back to the present.

"What's got you drifting away from us?" Chad asked around a mouthful of bacon.

"You know we have to tell her? Who's going to do it?"

From the look on Chad's face, he knew exactly who and what she was talking about. He set his fork on his plate before chugging a big gulp of coffee.

"Doesn't matter, does it? She's not going to like it." His eyes, cheery and bright a couple of seconds ago, clouded over with the thought of the difficult task as they wandered in the direction of the little house out back where their guest resided.

Alex patted his hand before stabbing a huge chunk of the syrup-soaked stack. "I'll call Terry when we're done with breakfast. Let's not think about it right now."

He nodded, but Alex knew it still simmered in his brain. As it did in hers.

§§§

Although he knew he was the right person for the job, Terry looked forward to the task ahead of him almost as much as a root canal.

On second thought, the root canal might be easier and less painful.

Aunt Tilley had run Together for Good since his parents had died about fifty years ago. She had her way of doing things, and she didn't appreciate anyone trying to change her. Over the years, Terry had fought her on most technological advances, including getting a microwave, installing a dedicated landline for the home, connecting to the internet, modernizing the kitchen, and installing a sprinkler system in the garden. He smiled, remembering how each upgrade had initially met with resistance and complaining, but after she'd become accustomed to the change, she'd embraced each one with gusto. The change he planned to present today, however, might be the exception to the rule.

Terry didn't foresee his sweet but regimented aunt accepting the suggestion to step aside, even if just for a brief time. He'd need to choose his words carefully.

Terry eased his luxury sports car into Alex and Chad's driveway, sending up silent but fervent prayers for the right words. He'd brought flowers, just to be on the safe side. His failed marriage and his successful business had taught him the importance of knowing what the opponent's state of mind was. He hated thinking of Aunt Tilley as an opponent, but today, she might as well be.

Tapping on the door to the little cottage, he entered when he heard his aunt call out. She beamed from her chair, motioning for him to come in.

"Oh my. What have you got there?" Her eyes lit up at the sight of the flowers, although she still had several arrangements from well-wishers following her hospital stay.

"Beautiful flowers for an even more beautiful lady," Terry said, filling a vase with water and shoving them in it. He crossed the kitchen and tiny living room in a few strides before placing a kiss on her cheek. He commented on how nice she looked.

"Aunt Tilley, have you got a date?" he teased.

"Go on, silly," she said, waving a hand dismissively. "I'm having dinner with the Whites and the Dixons. You're invited, aren't you?"

"I am," he said, alarm bells going off in his head.

He knew he was supposed to break the news to her soon, but knowing they'd all be together for dinner increased the urgency of his task. If the whole crowd knew about the plan to have Yvonne and Marquis fill in, or possibly take over, for Aunt Tilley, except for her, she'd pick up on it, and fast!

He groaned inwardly as his cell phone buzzed with an incoming text. Alex.

Lydia invited Miss M tonight. Really must tell her beforehand! Sorry.

He smiled, imagining his little sister chattering about the cookout. He could picture her face lighting up as she invited her new backdoor neighbor, whom the little girl adored. He felt sure Alex had been informed of the addition to the guest list only after the invitation had been extended.

"What's so funny, dear?"

His aunt's question, and her scrutiny of him, snapped his attention back to the mission at hand.

"Nothing, Aunt Tilley. Actually, you know what? There is something I'd like to talk to you about," Terry said, taking a seat on the sofa and facing her.

Before he could launch into his well-rehearsed proposal, she held up her bandaged hand to stop him.

"Wait, dear. I need to talk to you, too. Let me go first, if you don't mind."

He nodded, worried about what scheme she'd cooked up in that razor-sharp mind of hers.

"I'm not as young as I used to be," she started. When Terry started to protest, she shook her head. "No. Don't try to butter me up. It's true. This incident with the stroke and my hand have made one thing perfectly clear to me." She took a deep breath before continuing, "I can't run the home forever."

Terry's jaw dropped open. He sat gawking, unable to speak.

"Now, before you get upset, I've bathed this in much prayer. But I think it's time for me to start training a replacement. I want the home to continue its work, with or without me. And, let's face it, one day, it'll have to be without me. I'm not saying that day has come, mind you, but ... well ... Maybe I need to slow down a bit. Pass on everything I've learned over the years."

Terry rubbed his hand down his face, stalling for time as he processed her announcement. As it sank in, he began to chuckle. Then the chuckle turned to laughter. Soon, tears rolled down his face from the force of his guffaws.

"Terry Lovell! Have you completely taken leave of your senses? Settle down, young man." Aunt Tilley sniffed, her righteous indignation at his extreme response causing her nostrils to flare.

Terry tried to compose himself, gasping for breath as his mirth subsided. "I'm sorry, Aunt Tilley. Really, I'm not laughing at you, I promise. I'm laughing at the situation."

"Well, I don't know about that. But ... I forgive you." She reached out and patted his knee, just as she'd done when he'd been a little boy. "Now, what was it you wanted to say?"

Terry felt the weight of dread, like a thundercloud hanging over his head since Alex had called earlier that morning, evaporate. The sunshine broke through to his heart, encouraging him that things would work out fine.

"You know what, Aunt Tilley? How 'bout I make us some tea? Then we can discuss what I came to talk about. I think you'll like what I've got to say."

He filled the kettle and set it on the stove, feeling foolish for all the energy that he'd wasted in fear of this confrontation.

When am I going to learn God always has a better plan than I could ever dream up?

Dropping tea bags into the mugs, he texted Alex.

Have I got news for you!

The Decision

As the friends relaxed and watched Lydia chase lightning bugs around the yard, Alex and Chad broached the subject of running Together for Good with Yvonne and Marquis. The terms were clear. The couple would be needed for an undetermined amount of time. A scary prospect, to be sure, but one they didn't appear uncomfortable with. Alex was impressed with how composed they'd remained throughout the proposal, even as they learned of the weighty responsibilities the position demanded.

Charmain had retrieved many of Miss Matilda's files, and the older lady tried to summarize each document as it was heaped on Yvonne and Marquis. Finally, she recommended they peruse them all later while weighing their decision. Terry pulled the couple aside to discuss privately the compensation package the board was authorized to offer.

As the evening drew to a close, Yvonne and Marquis walked to their car, both loaded down with big binders full of notes, history, and procedures from Together for Good. They also carried the profound burden of a monumental decision; a decision that affected not only them and their young marriage, but also all of the people surrounding them. Not to mention who knew how many expectant mothers and their children.

"Alex," Yvonne said, stowing her tome in the back seat before turning to face her hostess, "there's no denying I treated Chad badly, but I want you to know I'm a different person now. You'll never know what an honor it is to be asked to do this after what I put everyone through."

Alex smiled, understanding a bit of the journey this woman had taken—from brokenness to wholeness, from hurting to healing. Alex had walked a similar road. If she were honest with herself, she was still walking it.

"Yvonne, if we allow God to work in our lives, He changes us. It happened to me. I can see it happening to you, too. Y'all make sure this is what He's calling you to do." Alex hugged Yvonne and felt an unlikely alliance forming.

The Dixons promised to pray about the request.

Everyone at the cookout understood what an enormous leap of faith they were asking the couple to take. A career move was stressful for anyone under any circumstance, but for both the husband and the wife to take a new job, with no previous experience in the field, could be considered madness. Yvonne hadn't been with the local accounting firm for long, but she'd already received a promotion. And Marquis loved his job coaching at the high school. Additionally, they'd have to move out to the Together for Good's premise, uprooting their entire existence. And it all had to happen within a few days.

It was in God's hands now. Alex knew He'd provide for the ladies and babies who relied on the services that Together for Good offered. She just wished she knew for certain what that provision would look like.

God doesn't clear His plans with you.

The thought brought a smile to Alex's lips.

"Do you think they'll do it?" she asked Chad as they waved goodbye from their driveway.

He shrugged and took her hand. They walked up the steps leading up to the kitchen.

"I'm not sure," he said, opening the door and letting her go inside first. "I think it's safe to say, though, that the biggest surprise of the evening was Miss M." His wide grin indicated how pleased he'd been at the older lady's acceptance of the plan. In fact, Miss Matilda's enthusiasm for the Dixons being offered the caregiver position had shocked and pleased everyone.

Alex returned his grin as she scooped coffee into the filter in preparation for the mayhem that ensued in their home every Sunday morning.

"I completely agree," she said. "And we were all so concerned she'd put up a fight. She never ceases to surprise us. I do worry about one thing, though."

"What's that?"

"Does she see this as a temporary situation, or is she prepared to step aside for good, if necessary?"

"I think that's another thing we've just got to hand over to God," Chad said before he tiptoed into the living room and scooped Lydia off the couch. She'd sacked out long before the festivities had ended.

Alex nodded, stroking the soft brown curls on her daughter's head as it rested against Chad's shoulder.

Yes, let's just leave it all in His hands.

§§§

Chad convinced Miss M. to watch the morning service online. Not yet trusting her stability in the crowded worship center, she'd agreed, but she insisted it was just for today. And she made it clear she had no intention of missing Sunday dinner at Together for Good. Chad agreed to the ironclad terms of her negotiation, set up his computer for her to stream the service, and kissed her cheek before he left.

The Dixons slipped into the pew next to the Whites a few minutes after the service had begun. Chad tried to decipher the looks on their faces, to no avail.

Tired, definitely. Happy, possibly. Anxious, maybe.

Chad saw Terry on the platform, singing with the praise team. He watched the couple's late arrival closely then fixed his gaze on Chad and raised one eyebrow. Chad gave him a barely detectable shrug. The whole exchange took less than a couple of seconds and went unnoticed by most of the congregation. But not by Alex.

As she watched the exchange across the packed sanctuary, she pressed her hand against Chad's leg and drew her brows together, shooting daggers from her eyes in Terry's direction.

Chastised, the men attempted to focus on the worship service without further raising Alex's hackles.

Throughout the songs, the sermon, and the invitation, Chad found his mind wandering to what the Dixons' answer would be and all the potential ramifications of their decision. If they agreed, would they be able to leave their current jobs and apartment on such short notice? Could they move in time to allow Charmain to go back to work? And if they did move in, what would happen if, or when, Miss M. was healthy and ready to go back home?

Conversely, what if they'd decided it was all too much, too fast? Chad knew everyone involved would understand, but they had no backup plan. How could the home continue to run if there was nobody there to keep it going?

Chad dragged his attention to Reverend Drummond, stunned to discover he was saying the benediction.

Wow, I really let my mind wander. I missed the whole service. I hope Alex doesn't want to discuss the sermon highlights.

As soon as the pastor pronounced the final "Amen," Chad watched Terry make a beeline for them, weaving his way through the crowd. Chad reached around Alex and Yvonne to shake Marquis's hand, trying not to appear over-eager, although he caught the ladies' attempts to stifle a grin. The foursome exited the pew with the flow of the crowd.

"So," Terry said, out of breath after his sprint up the aisle, "have you made your decision?" His face shone with expectation and a bit of trepidation.

"Terry!" Alex swiped his arm. "Could you give them a break? We just asked them last night. This is a big decision, and they don't need pressure from us."

Terry shuffled his feet and hung his head, reminding Chad of Lydia when she'd been reprimanded.

"Sorry," Terry said, clapping Marquis on the back and hugging Yvonne. "Y'all take your time."

"As a matter of fact," Marquis spoke up, "we have made our decision."

Chad's jaw dropped. He watched Terry cross his arms, schooling his features, as if preparing for bad news. Alex, though, smiled calmly, nodding as Yvonne spoke next.

"We think Miss Matilda should be with us when we give you our answer."

Chad and Terry both threw their hands up, sighing heavily.

"Are you kidding?" Chad asked.

While he loved planning surprises for others, Chad had never enjoyed the suspense engendered by this kind of "expected surprise." So much hung in the balance for so many, yet the Dixons alone knew whether they'd all soon be celebrating or scrambling for another answer.

"I completely agree," Alex said, leading the group out the church doors so she could hurry over to the pre-school area.

A shrill voice halted her progress.

"Yoo-hoo! Alex! Terry!" Mrs. Comstock ran down the aisle, waving both hands, her flowy skirt billowing behind her.

Yvonne and Marquis raised their eyebrows, and Alex shot them a look that warned them to keep quiet.

"Mrs. Comstock, what a surprise," Alex said, shaking the lady's hand when she reached their group.

"Please, call me Dot. Who do we have here?" Dot raked her gaze up and down the Dixons, who stood holding hands. "Are you together?" She waved a pointy red fingernail back and forth.

The woman's audacity infuriated Alex. She clenched and unclenched her hands, trying to rein in her ire.

"Mrs. Comstock," Terry stepped in, "allow me to introduce Mr. and Mrs. Dixon, friends of ours and fellow members of the church."

"Oh my." Dot brought her hand to her chest. "Things certainly have changed since I was here."

"Thank goodness," Terry said, ever the picture of smoothness.

Alex smiled at his ability to handle awkward social situations and still manage to put people in their place.

"If you'll excuse us, please. Have a blessed afternoon, Mrs. Comstock."

With his dismissal, Terry led their group toward the exit, leaving Dorothy Comstock staring after them.

"What the ...?" Marquis began, looking back at the unpleasant congregant as they departed.

Terry shook his head. "Later," was his only answer.

"Charmain and the residents fixed lunch before they came to church," Alex said, glad to be free of the worrisome woman. "Chad and I will stop off and pick up Miss Matilda and dessert, then we'll see you at Together for Good. I'll meet you at the car in a few minutes, sweetie." Alex kissed Chad's cheek then waved before disappearing into the quickly thinning crowd to retrieve Lydia.

Chad and Terry shared one final look before Terry turned and got in line to greet Reverend Drummond.

"Well," Chad said to the Dixons, trying to hide the disappointment at having to wait still longer to hear their answer, "I guess I'll see you at lunch."

§§§

Terry sat in a rocker on the front porch of his childhood home, awaiting his aunt's arrival. Today would be her first time back since her stroke, and he wanted to make sure things went smoothly. He'd been banished from the kitchen for asking too many questions of Charmain and the three ladies who currently lived here, prompting him to seek solace in the spot where he'd spent so much time as a boy.

As soon as Alex's beat-up, older SUV pulled into the driveway, he smiled. She'd be quite well off when they got the details of J.T.'s estate settled, but she hesitated to give up her trusty, rusty vehicle. She'd confided in him, not long after they'd learned about the extent of the wealth J.T. had left them, that she didn't want it to change her or how she lived.

While Terry understood the sentiment, wisdom borne of experience had taught him that, when God blessed someone abundantly, He expected them to use it wisely. Alex and Chad had some important choices ahead of them, but those decisions could wait for another day. Today was about Yvonne and Marquis and the decision they'd reached. Whatever it was.

Terry descended the porch steps, watching Alex free Lydia from the confines of her car seat. The girl bounded out of the car and bolted straight to him. Within seconds, she launched herself into his waiting arms.

He never tired of the wonder that flooded his heart every time he thought of the blessing his little sister was to him. Holding her tightly, he spun around several times, making her giggle with delight.

"Why don't you go see if Aunt Charmain can use any help?" he said, gently setting her feet on the gravel. His hands lingered on her shoulders for a second, making sure she wasn't too dizzy from spinning. And then she was off, her patent leather shoes clomping as she clambered up the steps and rushed across the porch.

Terry turned his attention to his aunt Tilley, who hung tightly onto Chad's arm as she carefully stepped across the uneven gravel.

"Hello, dear." She beamed, love shining in her eyes.

"Hey, Aunt Tilley," he said, kissing her cheek and offering his arm. She handed her cane to Alex and looped her other arm through Terry's.

Together, Terry and Chad got her safely into the house and settled in her usual seat at the head of the table, which, within minutes, was groaning under the weight of a huge spread. The aroma of fried chicken, green beans, macaroni and cheese, and homemade biscuits filled the dining room, making Terry's stomach growl. Everyone quickly took their seats and held hands, waiting for Aunt Tilley to say the blessing.

Before she began, however, Marquis cleared his throat and looked at Yvonne. When his wife nodded, he spoke.

"Miss Matilda, Yvonne and I have some news."

All eyes were on the couple, no one daring to even breathe as they awaited the announcement.

"We'd be honored to run Together for Good for as long as you'll have us."

Cheers erupted.

"Well," Aunt Tilley said as she signaled for everyone to settle down, "seems to me like we've got quite a lot to thank the Lord for. Let's pray."

Her "Amen" didn't have time to die on her lips before everyone around the table broke into excited chatter. Platters were passed, tea was poured and, before long, the clink of silverware against dishes replaced the conversation.

"So, Marquis," Terry started between bites of chicken, "when do y'all plan on getting started?"

Charmain, who'd been about to take a bite of beans, held her fork in mid-air, not wanting to miss this crucial piece of information.

"Well, we'll actually be ready to move by next weekend, if that's okay with everyone?" Marquis looked around the table, trying to gauge reactions on the faces staring at him. "Our apartment is pretty small, so there isn't that much to pack. Plus, with it being the long Memorial Day weekend, maybe we can get a couple of folks from church to help out."

"Now that tax season is over, it's actually a great time for me to leave," Yvonne added. "But ..." She looked at her husband, nodding for him to speak up.

"Well, if there's any possible way, we could eventually work it out for me to get back to coaching. You know, like part-time. That would be really great. It's just something I'd like for y'all to consider." Marquis was generally a quiet man, so for him to boldly speak up for something he wanted let the others know how important it was to him.

"I think we can work with that," Charmain said before stuffing the beans into her mouth and chewing with a smile.

"That's great news," Terry said. He folded his napkin and stood. "If y'all will excuse me for just a few minutes ..."

"Terry, what in heaven's name are you doing? We're not done here." Aunt Tilley put great emphasis on mealtime manners.

"I'm sorry, Aunt Tilley. May I be excused? I'm going to call the other board members and see if they're available for an emergency meeting this afternoon. If so, we can get this ball rolling."

"In that case," Aunt Tilley said, pulling herself up into the prim posture of a proper Southern lady, "I think you're justified in leaving the table. You're excused, young man."

As Terry walked out of the dining room, feeling like he was ten years old again, he caught the smile Yvonne and Marquis shared. Could they possibly be as excited about this change as the rest of them were?

Move-In Day

Alex parked her car in front of the little cottage behind Together for Good. The people carrying the Dixons' boxes from pickup trucks to the little place they would now call home resembled a line of industrious ants. She smiled at how God had orchestrated this move.

"Hey, guys," Alex greeted the new occupants, holding Lydia's hand as they approached the cottage's front porch steps. "What can we do to help?"

Before Yvonne or Marquis could answer, one of the Together for Good residents came out the back door of the big house, carrying a plate of cookies and inviting Lydia in for a snack. Alex nodded, but set a two-cookie limit. Within seconds, Lydia had disappeared, obviously excited to get a better offer than unpacking boxes.

Turning her attention back to Yvonne and Marquis, Alex noticed the brief look that passed between them before Marquis kissed his wife's cheek and went inside. The screen door slapped shut behind him.

"Um, Alex ... Chad said you can't ... I mean, he thinks maybe it's a good idea if you didn't carry boxes." Yvonne's gaze wandered as she spoke. Her long, blonde hair was pulled back into a loose French braid, but wisps escaped and formed a halo of humidity-induced curls around her face.

"I'm not sure what he's stressed about, but he seemed pretty insistent."

"Yvonne, I'm perfectly capable of carrying some boxes. But, if it'll keep my husband from worrying, at least let me go inside and clean the kitchen and bathroom before you get your things unpacked."

Alex knew Charmain had probably let the place go in the brief time she'd been in residence, and she dreaded to see what condition the house was in, even after such a short time of neglect.

Yvonne smiled at Alex's offer, her eyes sparkling. Obviously, she'd already assessed the need to do some housework, but her first priority was getting their belongings moved into the place.

"Actually, that would be great," Yvonne admitted. "I'd love to help these guys from the church get everything unloaded and in the correct rooms. What a blessing we're doing this on the long weekend. I had no idea so many folks from the church would come out to help."

Smiling, Alex went in the front door and left Yvonne to deal with the volunteer workforce. It truly was a blessing. And not just having the help, but the couple's decision to make this jump headfirst into the unknown at a moment's notice.

"Hey, Marquis," she called out. Following the sound of his voice, she found him in the hall beside the little bathroom, pulling cleaning supplies out of a box. "You must have read my mind. Those supplies are exactly what I was looking for. Now, let me do this and you go help Yvonne."

Holding both hands up in surrender, Marquis voiced no argument as she shooed him out of the way.

Given the almost dollhouse-sized scale of the rooms, Alex had the kitchen and bathroom sparkling from top to bottom in less than an hour. Her face glowing with the exertion of a job well-done, she went in search of the Dixons to see what she could do next.

Her mind had wandered a million miles away when she rounded the corner coming out of the kitchen and ran head-on into Chad.

Chad laughed as he pulled her close, and she relaxed her head against the familiar strength of his chest.

"You haven't been working too hard, have you?" His voice rumbled against her ear as he spoke.

"I'm not an invalid, you know? This kind of thing happens to women every day." She kept her head resting against him, not sure she'd be able to convince him if he looked into her eyes.

"I know that, babe. But it's you I'm concerned about, not other women." He rubbed her back as he spoke, relaxing the tight muscles.

"Thanks for your concern," she said, standing on her tiptoes to kiss his cheek. "By the way, what are you doing here? I thought you and Terry had some errands to run."

"That's why I was looking for you. We put in a huge order at the barbecue place out on the highway so we could feed all these folks some lunch." He offered his arm, and she looped hers through it. "Oh, and we stopped and picked up Miss M. I thought she'd like to get out of our guest house and join us here."

This man. He thinks of everything.

"What a great idea. Let's go. I'm starving."

§§§

Lydia lay napping on Terry's shoulder as he rocked on the front porch of the big house. Alex often told him he spoiled her by letting her do it, but he couldn't help himself. Although he was her brother, he often felt God had gifted him with the unexpectedly sweet role of surrogate grandparent, made to love, spoil, and dote on her. It was a role he took seriously and enjoyed immensely.

Most of the volunteer movers had lingered over lunch before leaving, possibly heading home to take naps themselves following their morning of hard work. It seemed like an excellent idea to Terry, so he let his eyes drift shut.

Right as he felt himself succumb to sleep, a soft touch on his shoulder startled him awake.

"I'm sorry, dear. I didn't mean to wake you. I'll come back." Aunt Tilley began the cumbersome process of navigating an about-face with her cane, but Terry put his hand out to stop her.

"No, no. It's fine. I'm just enjoying the breeze out here while Lydia dozes. Join me."

Aunt Tilley lowered herself into the nearest rocker, wincing as she did. Terry noticed with alarm how much older she looked than she had before the stroke. He couldn't recall ever seeing her as pale and fragile as she looked now.

He reached over and covered her hand with his. "Aunt Tilley, are you feeling okay?"

"I feel fine ... for a washed-up, old fool." Tears pooled in her eyes, which were normally lit up with joy.

"Are you kidding? You're not washed-up, or old. And you're most definitely not a fool. What's this all about?" He tried to remain upbeat and encouraging, even as his insides churned with concern. She didn't often descend into a melancholy outlook. "What's this really about, Aunt Tilley?"

"This place is all I've ever known." She picked at her cast, evading his eyes. "And, although I'm so pleased that Yvonne and Marquis will cover for me while I'm convalescing, I've got this feeling in my bones that I'm done." Finally, she faced him, the sadness and fear obvious in her drawn, pinched features. "And it scares me." Her admission came out as barely a whisper.

What am I supposed say? They'd all known this was a possibility. Faced with the reality of it, however, Aunt Tilley was having difficulty giving up the role she'd known her entire adult life.

An idea struck Terry as he watched his precious aunt, a woman who had been more like a mother to him for most of his life, spiral deeper into despair. He didn't want to build her hopes up, but he had it in his power to ease this transition for her.

"What if it didn't have to be either them *or* you here at Together for Good? What if it could be the Dixons *and* you?" he asked.

"I don't understand what you're talking about. There's only room for two in the caregiver's cottage. You know that from growing up there, dear."

"Right. But what if there were two cottages?"

"Don't be silly, Terry. There's only one cottage. I don't know what you're talking about."

"Aunt Tilley, I've got the original plans for the cottage. Mom and Dad saved them, and I found them when I was moving out of mine and Gail's house. What if I built the mirror image of the cottage that's back there now? I could connect the two structures with a little courtyard, equip yours with senior-friendly features. How 'bout it?" His enthusiasm for the project grew as the idea blossomed in his mind. He hadn't been this excited about an architecture job since ... well, he couldn't even remember when.

"So, what you're saying is"—Aunt Tilley leaned forward, no longer evasive but fixing him in her piercing, gray-eyed gaze—"you don't think I'll ever run the home again. Is that right?"

Terry had to choose his words with great care. He needed her to know that her experience and expertise were invaluable, while also making her understand that her physical capabilities were no longer what they used to be. And, as difficult and humbling as it was, she needed to accept this reality.

"Maybe. But at this stage of your life, maybe you'd be better suited to an advisory role."

She seemed to consider his suggestion, so he forged ahead.

"Think about it, Aunt Tilley. You could lend your advice and share your experiences ... pass on your knowledge at your own pace ... but you'd get to sleep through the night whenever a girl went into labor in the wee hours of the morning."

"Do you think Yvonne and Marquis would go for it?" She seemed to be warming up to the idea.

"We can ask, but think about it. They've been thrust into a completely unfamiliar role. Why wouldn't they want some advice and guidance right next-door?"

Lydia began to stir in Terry's lap, and Aunt Tilley slipped her hand out from beneath his. She rose slowly from her chair and patted his shoulder on her way back inside.

"I love you, dear. Thank you for making this old lady feel needed."

"I love you, too, Aunt Tilley. And, for the record, I'm not making you feel anything. You're a crucial part of the ministry of this home. You always have been. We all need you."

As she left, she had a spring in her wobbly step that hadn't been there before.

§§§

By late afternoon, the Dixons were well on their way to being settled, Miss Matilda had found a spot to catch a nap on the sofa in the front room of the big house, and Chad was pushing a giggling Lydia in the swing under the oak tree. Alex and Terry relaxed on the front porch with glasses of tea, rocking and letting their thoughts wander.

"When do you think this business with J.T.'s estate is going to be settled once and for all?" Alex asked.

"Hard to say." Terry shook his head. "I thought we would've heard from one of the attorneys by now."

"I guess Mother is putting up a bigger fight than anyone expected." Alex had locked horns with her mother before, and it was neither easy nor pleasant. "I'd hate to be the one trying to reason with her on this. She feels entitled to everything J.T. had. To tell you the truth, I still have mixed feelings about the whole thing."

She'd talked to Chad about her misgivings at accepting such a huge sum, and he'd assured her of his support with whatever decision she made. Alex knew, however, that her decisions now had to consider the best interests of not only herself, but also of Chad and Lydia. If she and Terry prevailed in the legal battle over the estate, she felt sure she could secure her little family's future. She wanted more than that, though.

Alex wanted to reach others, believing and hoping the pain from her past could be used for good in a meaningful and tangible way. She hadn't decided on a specific means of accomplishing such a monumental, albeit obscure, feat, but she continued to pray for guidance and inspiration on this front.

"Who's that?" Terry asked, interrupting her thoughts and pointing to the spot where the long driveway met the road.

Alex watched the fancy convertible slowly wind its way toward Together for Good. She found it odd that the top was up on such a gorgeous day. A fact which, when paired with the dark window tinting, made it impossible to discern who drove the sleek vehicle.

Please don't be Mrs. Comstock.

The car pulled to a stop in front of the house, and neither Terry nor Alex moved. They also never took their eyes off the new arrival.

When the driver's door was opened and a long, slender leg ending in a stiletto emerged, the pair on the porch looked at each other, questions in their wide eyes.

"Do you recognize that car?" Alex asked, specifically avoiding reference to the shapely leg.

Terry shook his head but continued to watch the action in the driveway.

A tall, red-headed beauty unfolded herself from the low-riding car, her attention trained on the phone in her hand. She glanced at the house numbers affixed above the porch then back again at her device. With a satisfied look, she placed the phone in her sizable designer tote bag and carefully picked her way across the gravel, trying not to scuff the finish on her towering heels. When she made it to the first step, she finally looked up, startled to see Alex and Terry watching her.

"Can we help you?" Terry asked, finally remembering his manners and standing at the lady's arrival.

Seeing this beautiful, well-dressed woman made Alex self-conscious of her sweaty, dusty clothes and messy hair. This lady could have stepped right out of the pages of a fashion magazine.

"Hi, I'm Meredith Rouse," she said, extending her hand.

Finally able to assess their guest up close, Alex guessed her to be in her late thirties, maybe early forties. Everything about her communicated understated elegance and undeniable wealth—the skirt that hugged her toned body, her flawless makeup, and her tasteful manicure. But, her beautiful blue eyes, as pale as the Southern sky, held warmth.

Terry shook Meredith's hand while he nudged Alex with one foot. Roused from her gawking, Alex jumped up and greeted their visitor, sliding a third rocker over for her.

"What can we do for you, Meredith?" Alex asked.

"Actually, I'm here to see … Oh, shoot, let me look one more time to make sure I get it right," she said, retrieving her phone from the big leather bag. "I just got this case yesterday, so I haven't had much time to familiarize myself with the parties. Here it is. Alex White, née Powell, and Terrence Lovell. Can you let them know I'm here?"

Terry smiled before replying, "I think you just did."

Meredith's smile faltered before she understood what Terry was telling her.

"Oh! I'm terribly sorry. How do you do? Did they call to let you know I'd be here today?"

"Well, that depends." Alex was growing more confused by the minute, but she hoped Meredith would get to the point soon. "Who, exactly, was supposed to be calling?"

"I'm with the Baker and Monford law firm in Clairdon, North Carolina. We're handling the estate of a Mr. James Terrence Wickham. I'm here to apprise you of the current situation and go over some details. Is now a good time to talk?"

Big News and Little Kittens

Meredith sat at the kitchen table, where Terry had led the trio shortly after her arrival, and sipped from the tall glass of iced tea that he'd poured for her. She'd recounted the latest details of the estate settlement, producing page after page of legal documents for them to review and sign.

Terry admired Meredith's thoroughness, professionalism, and ability to explain the details of each document so folks with no legal background could understand. Still, both he and Alex were dazed by the sheer volume of information that she had hurled at them.

"And Mother accepts these terms?" Alex asked, leafing through the pages too fast to digest any of the information.

Terry knew Karen had blown a gasket when she had learned that the bulk of J.T.'s estate had been bequeathed to Alex and himself.

Meredith nodded, but Terry noticed the attorney's brow furrowing almost imperceptibly.

"She does, Mrs. White." Her words conveyed Karen's assent, but the hesitancy in her voice sent another message.

"Please, call us Alex and Terry. We don't stand on formality around here." Alex briefly placed a hand on Meredith's, the friendly gesture an attempt at putting the attorney at ease.

"Very well. Actually, Alex, may I speak candidly?"

Alex nodded, encouraging Meredith to continue.

"Your mother was initially, um ... let's just say she was, as you know, quite unhappy with the contents of Mr. Wickham's will."

Terry and Alex looked at each other and smiled, knowing Meredith had seriously understated the situation. Unhappy. Someone was unhappy when the coffee shop got their order wrong. Karen had been *livid* and had spared no expense mounting a legal battle to retain what she believed was rightfully hers.

Meredith caught the glance. "What?" she asked, caution ringing in the word she drew out to two syllables with her silky Southern drawl. "Do y'all know something I don't?"

"Do you want to tell her, or should I?" Terry asked Alex, who held her hand up to her former business partner.

"I'll start," Alex said before launching into an edited version of how she'd ended up in Burton.

The details of Karen's drive to advance her career at all costs stayed in the narrative, but Alex omitted the part about J.T.'s assault. Terry picked up on Alex's hesitancy to provide certain information. He and Alex had long ago talked about what she'd say when Lydia began asking why she didn't call Chad her daddy. Alex didn't want rumors and half-truths floating around town that could hurt her daughter, and Terry knew firsthand how long-held secrets could shake a person to the core.

Alex sipped her tea and raised her brows, giving Terry the go-ahead to step in and finish the story. She'd made no mention of the fact that J.T. was Terry's biological father. He'd figure out if Meredith already knew later.

"Alex and I drove up to see J.T. last summer. We led him to faith in Jesus during that trip. A couple of months later, Karen showed up here, with remarkably bad timing, actually, and told us that J.T. had died. As you mentioned, to say she was unhappy about his will is putting it mildly.

She had no idea he'd changed it, and she announced in no uncertain terms that she meant to contest it."

Meredith nodded, sipping her tea slowly. Terry noticed she wore no ring on her left hand.

Where did that come from?

After his divorce, Terry had decided the life of a bachelor suited him. While he saw the younger crowd trying their hand at internet dating or letting friends set them up, he relished the freedom he now enjoyed. He had nobody to criticize his every move, dictate his social schedule, or question his massive expenditures on Together for Good. He also had nobody to share dinner with, take walks with, or bounce business and personal ideas off of.

Terry realized he'd let his thoughts wander when he saw both ladies staring at him, obviously waiting for him to continue.

"Anyway," Alex said, rescuing her friend while casting a suspicious sideways glance his way, "Chad and I went up to meet with your firm a couple of weeks ago. When we had to leave due to an emergency, we were told someone would be in touch. Honestly, we were just expecting a call."

"Oh, I hope it was nothing too serious that called you away. Anyway, I joined the firm about six months ago. I'm currently licensed in both North and South Carolina, so the partners decided I was best suited to wrap up the final details on the case. I wanted to explain everything to you and make sure you understood what you were signing."

"We appreciate that," Alex said.

"Plus"—Meredith grinned—"I can visit my parents in Greenville on my way back to Clairdon."

"Oh, I've done some work for clients in Greenville," Terry said. "A beautiful city. Growing so fast."

He and Meredith launched into an in-depth discussion of the pros and cons of the population boom into what used to be the quiet suburbs of the city.

Alex listened as she slipped away from the table to put on a pot of coffee, needing a bit more of a caffeine jolt than a glass of tea could provide. She took several mugs out of the cabinet, certain Chad would appreciate a cup, before sitting back down and waiting for a lull in the animated conversation.

"So, Meredith, once we've signed all of this legal stuff, what's next?" Alex asked. "I mean, what do we need to do now?"

"Oh, I'm so glad you reminded me. Of course, there will be some banking and investment details you'll both need to deal with, but we'll send all of those instructions to you at the addresses provided. I wanted to go over the final terms of the estate. Basically, once you've signed everything and it's filed with the court, here's an estimate of what you'll inherit." As she spoke, Meredith reached back into her bulging leather bag, removing just two sheets of paper this time. She pushed one to Alex and one to Terry then gave them time to absorb what they read.

Terry gasped when he saw the numbers. He looked at Alex, who had wrapped her arms around her mid-section and rocked.

"And, um, ... well, Karen is aware of these terms?" Terry asked again.

"She is." Meredith nodded. "Quite honestly, she didn't have any recourse. Mr. Wickham's revised final instructions were quite clear, very specific, and perfectly legal."

Alex released the breath that she'd been holding with a *whoosh*. "Is Mother provided for?"

Terry marveled that Alex could be benevolent under the circumstances.

Again, Meredith nodded. "She is. As my associates specified earlier, she'll receive a generous monthly stipend, as well as the life insurance and the house."

Meredith's answer was vague, but Terry said nothing.

"Okay, then," Alex said, rising to pour the coffee that now filled the kitchen with its enticing, smoky aroma. Her voice shook as she filled their cups. "I guess Terry and I have quite a bit to think about, don't we? Where do we need to sign?"

§§§

Dorothy patted the tie-dyed scarf that almost tamed her crazy hair as she unbuckled her seat belt. Reverend Drummond had asked for volunteers to arrive at nine o'clock, but Dottie simply didn't "do" mornings that early. *I'm sure they can still use my help a little bit later.*

Glancing at her watch, she saw it was already three in the afternoon. Then, looking around, she saw none of the trucks that she'd expected. The porch on the little cottage behind the house was piled with boxes and crinkled newspaper. A man was pushing a little girl in a swing under the big oak tree.

Well, I can tell when I'm not wanted.

As Dottie turned in a huff to get back into her non-descript, beige sedan, she noticed a North Carolina license plate on the expensive convertible that she'd parked next to. Curious, she walked onto the front porch of the main house to get a look inside.

To Dottie's surprise, the only thing between her and the inside of the home was a screen door. She heard voices coming from the direction of what she remembered was the kitchen. Maybe it still was, but everything in the home looked as if it'd been updated. Dottie could clearly see Matilda sacked out on the sofa in the room off the foyer.

The snooping woman didn't hesitate. Quietly, she squeezed the handle and opened the door, thanking the Lord they lived in a place where people saw no need to lock their doors. The comfortable sneakers that she'd worn made no sound as she tiptoed across the wood floors. If someone caught her, she'd act lost and pull her confused old lady act. In the meantime, she learned as much as she could about Meredith, J.T., and a will, the main topics being discussed in the kitchen.

When Matilda began to stir, Dottie trotted to go out the way she'd come. Then she had an even better idea.

§§§

Terry offered to show Meredith around the property, leaving Alex alone with her coffee and her thoughts. She'd grown up knowing her family had plenty of money, but she'd never guessed J.T.'s fortune to be so vast. His family had been in the real estate development business for a long time and had obviously invested the profits wisely. Alex now understood her mother's fury.

Karen had watched J.T. wither away in the last years of his life, and as he did so, Karen's opportunities for and invitations to lavish parties and extended vacations had dried up, too. Gone was the familiar and comfortable lifestyle that Alex knew her mother had worked hard to attain. But, from what Alex had been able to gather from Zeke, Karen comforted herself with the belief that she'd be a wealthy woman once her husband was gone. She'd even told Alex as much at the attorney's office a few weeks ago.

The fact remained, however, that J.T. had wanted Alex and Terry, not Karen, to carry on his legacy. They'd nurtured and supported his late-in-life salvation. Alex believed he'd want them to honor his memory by helping others to come to know Jesus as their Savior. She and Zeke had discussed this when she and Chad were in Woodvale recently.

"Hey, sweetie."

Alex jumped at Chad's greeting.

"Whoa. I'm sorry. You were a million miles away, babe. What's up?" he asked, taking a mug out of the cabinet.

Alex watched Chad pour himself a cup of coffee, refresh her cup, and carry them both to the table. As he performed the familiar task, she contemplated how to best break the news to him. How did she express her doubts in the face of receiving such wealth? Would he think she was crazy for being unsure if they were competent enough to use the money wisely? This wasn't a couple of thousand dollars they were talking about.

"Where's Lydia?" Alex asked, using genuine concern for her daughter to buy some time.

"She asked if she could stay outside and join Terry and his visitor. He was giving her a piggy back ride when I tapped out."

Alex nodded. *Here goes nothing.*

"Chad, I wanted to talk to you about the lady with Terry. She isn't really a visitor." Alex reached across and held Chad's hand in hers.

"Oh, wow," he said. "She looks kind of fancy and ... well, old to be a new resident."

Alex saw the confusion in his expression and giggled.

"No, it's not that. She's an attorney from North Carolina. She came to finalize the details of J.T.'s will so that, once probate is finished, everything will be good to go."

Understanding dawned in Chad's eyes seconds before the questions started.

"So, is this whole mess almost over? Is your mom still furious? What do you need to do next?"

Alex's heart swelled to realize he had asked nothing about the amount she'd inherited, though she knew it was precisely what they needed to discuss. As her husband, he had a right to not only know the details but also to help her decide how to proceed. The choices they made, if done properly, could have far-reaching, eternal implications.

Without speaking, she pulled the piece of paper out of her pocket and unfolded it, carefully smoothing out the creases before pushing it across the table.

"What's this?" he asked, pulling it toward himself as he took a sip of coffee.

"It's a list of assets that comprise my portion of the inheritance, including the mountain house and the truck."

Chad scanned the page for several seconds before his eyes bulged and he choked on his coffee, sputtering and spraying it everywhere.

Laughing, Alex jumped up and grabbed a handful of paper towels to clean up his mess. Stealing a sideways glance, she tried to gauge his true reaction to the obscene sum.

"Alex, is this a joke?" Chad's face had gone ghostly pale, and his hands shook, causing little ripples in his coffee.

She shook her head, never taking her eyes off his.

He blinked several times. Then he closed his eyes and drew in a deep breath, holding it for a second before releasing it through pursed lips. When he opened his eyes, they were bright with mischief. "You know what this means, don't you?"

Alex shook her head, confused how he could go from shell-shocked to playful so quickly.

"It means ... I'll be married to a millionaire!"

Alex rolled her eyes as her husband scraped his chair back, took her by the hand, and waltzed her around the huge kitchen. They were both giggling by the time he dipped her, reminding Alex of their wedding day. He'd done the same thing immediately following their vows. He'd left her breathless then, and he did so now.

"You're so crazy," Alex said, fanning herself as she dropped back into her seat. "Honestly, though, what do we do now?"

"Whaddya mean? We can do whatever we want." Chad looked at her as if she'd sprouted another head.

"Chad, I'm completely unprepared to responsibly manage this kind of wealth. I want to be wise ... make Godly decisions ... you know, plan for our future, for Lydia's future. But I also want to honor J.T. Not the man who hurt me, but the man who took care of me most of my life. Most importantly, the man he became at the end of his life." With her eyes, she pleaded with her husband to understand the dilemma raging inside her heart. The distress triggered by the day's revelations showed in her tense face.

"You're right, of course," he said. "I'm sorry to have been so flippant. Why don't I ask a few of my customers who they recommend as a financial advisor? We can talk to a few and see if their suggestions suit your goals."

"That's just it, sweetie. J.T. may have left the money to me, but we're a team now. Our path forward has to meet *our* goals, not just mine. I need your input. We've got some big decisions to make."

Sobering, Chad stood and pulled Alex up and toward him, wrapping his arms around her.

She tilted her head up, trying to decipher the look in his eyes. His next words gave her the clue she needed.

"How is it that you're so much younger than me yet so much wiser?" He finished his question with a kiss on her forehead.

"Oh, I wouldn't say I'm wiser," Alex answered, feeling more relaxed now that she'd voiced her concerns and knew he'd prayerfully consider their next moves. "I would say that I recognize a fact you haven't faced yet, though."

"Yeah? What's that?"

"I'll be married to a millionaire, too." She giggled as she stood on her toes to place a gentle kiss on his smiling lips.

§§§

Alex retrieved a notepad and pen from the junk drawer and, together, she and Chad started making a list of all they wanted to accomplish but had thought they'd never get to do and all the causes they wanted to support. They listed both immediate and long-term goals. Lydia's college topped the list, a list that grew as they embraced their capacity to be benevolent.

"Will you close your business?" Chad asked, although he thought he knew the answer.

Alex shook her head. "I've worked really hard to build it up to where it is. I'd hate to just walk away."

Chad understood. He had no intention of closing his auto repair business, either. The folks of the town needed the service he offered, and he loved working with cars. Besides, it was one of the few parts of his dad that he held on to and remembered fondly.

"You know what I'd love to do?" Alex chewed on the pen cap, deep in thought.

"What's that?"

"I'd love to offer Charmain the chance to go back to school. If she'd like to, of course." They'd talked about how much greater Charmain's options might be if she had a degree, but they understood her wanderlust and how it played into the equation.

"What are y'all working on so intently?" Miss M. asked, moving slowly into the kitchen with the help of her cane.

Chad jumped up to pull a chair out for her, and Alex poured her a cup of coffee.

"Did you offer Dottie anything to drink?" Miss Matilda asked.

Alex and Chad looked at each other then at Miss Matilda. Alex was fairly certain their friend's cognitive abilities hadn't been severely affected by the stroke, but her question made Alex wonder.

"Dottie wasn't here, Miss M.," Chad said.

"She most certainly was. She was sitting in the chair, staring at me as if I were some monkey in a cage at the zoo when I woke up."

Chad watched as the color drained from Alex's face.

Why was she here? What did she overhear?

If Miss M.'s assessment of Dorothy Comstock was accurate, and her judgment usually was, Dottie would distort and spread whatever information she'd gleaned from her visit with Miss M. Worse, anything she'd picked up by eavesdropping—nobody knew when she'd arrived—could be all over town by tomorrow morning.

"Where is she now?" Alex asked, her voice sounding strangled.

"As soon as I woke up and saw her there, I knew that woman was up to no good. She wanted to 'chat, catch up, talk about old times.'" Miss M. used air quotes to indicate the ridiculousness of Dottie's suggestions.

"What did you do?" Alex and Chad asked in unison, making the older lady smile.

"I invited her out on the porch. You know, beautiful day, lovely breeze, blah, blah, blah. As soon as we got out there, I looked at my watch and told her I was so sorry, but I was late to a meeting." She beamed with pride as she finished her story.

"Basically, you lied and threw her out." Chad's summary of the situation earned him a swat on the arm from his wife.

"What I did, Mr. White," she said, sitting up straight and assuming an air of superiority, "was remove an intruder from my home then safely extricated myself from the situation."

She's been watching way too many crime dramas.

"So, what's that y'all are working on?" Relaxing, Miss M. deftly changed the subject by gesturing to the growing list Alex and Chad had been working on.

"Alex and Terry got news about the estate." He respected the privacy of the people involved by keeping his response brief and vague.

"I see." She took a dainty sip from her mug, shifting her gaze from Alex to Chad and back.

"It's … considerable," Alex said, pushing the crinkled, coffee-stained paper toward the older lady.

To her credit, Miss M. didn't flinch at the amount shown on the page. She simply raised her eyes and patted Alex's hand.

"No amount of money will undo the hurt you've suffered, dear."

"No, ma'am, it won't. But it will allow us to help many people."

Alex had impressed Chad from the moment she'd walked into his shop years ago. Today, however, he was prouder of her than he'd ever been.

He sat watching as Alex shared their recently-developed and still-evolving list with Miss M. Before she could explain the third item on the list, however, the back door flew open and Lydia stormed in.

"Mommy! Chaddie! Come quick. It's kittens!" The little girl's feet ran in place, so great was her excitement.

"Uh-oh," Miss M. said, drawing curious stares from Alex and Chad. "I completely forgot about the mama cat that was hanging around before my accident. I'd been feeding her."

Chad noticed how she still frequently refused to acknowledge she'd had a stroke, often referring to it as "her accident."

"That's been well over a week, Miss Matilda," Alex pointed out. "What's she been eating since then?"

Miss M. shrugged.

"Mice from the barn would be my guess," Terry said, coming in the open back door. "That's where we found her. She's nestled in a corner with her five babies. Do y'all want to come see them? They're adorable."

"Please, Mommy, come look at them. Can I have one? Please, Mommy. Please, Chaddie. I'll take good care of it, I promise." Lydia clasped her hands in front of her chest as she begged.

Alex shot Chad a look. Ever since Lydia's friend, Darnia, had become a big sister and gotten a puppy within the space of two weeks, Lydia had held up that family as a standard to be emulated.

Chad shrugged, warming up to the idea of having a pet.

"Come on, sweet pea. Let's take a look at those babies." He swept the little girl into his arms and left the kitchen. He heard Alex sigh and Terry chuckle before he reached the bottom of the steps.

I guess everyone knows what a soft spot I've got in my heart for this little girl.

"Looks like you're getting a kitten." Terry laughed.

A Production and a Proposal

The summer days melted away, and Alex felt as if she'd melt with them. Having grown up in the blistering, humid Southern heat, she was accustomed to scorching temps from sunup until well into the evening. The residents of Burton, South Carolina sought respite where they could find it—air-conditioning, snow cones, and pools, anything to relieve the crankiness brought on by having one's clothes drenched in sweat simply because the car was parked all the way across an asphalt-paved parking lot.

Alex sat at her desk, sipping iced tea and giggling while Midnight nipped at her bare toes. The little, snow-white ball of fluff had brought so much joy to this household in the few short weeks she'd been there. Most times, the sweet little mischief-maker followed Lydia around the house and yard like a puppy. Alex had been firm, however, about the kitten not joining the little girl during afternoon rest time. A four-year-old without a bit of downtime was a recipe for a meltdown, and Alex wasn't taking any chances.

Despite several failed attempts to concentrate on creating shipping labels for her latest orders, Alex gave in to Midnight's playfulness, abandoning all pretense of working to play with the kitten. They'd both almost reached the end of their energy when Alex's phone rang.

"Hello."

She didn't recognize the number, but with clients all over the Southeast, this wasn't an unusual occurrence. When confronted with a telemarketer, she requested not to be called again and clicked the button immediately, not bothering to listen to the annoying sales pitch.

"Miss Powell?" The woman's voice sounded tentative, uncertain.

"It's Mrs. White," she corrected. After almost a year, the name had finally begun to feel natural.

"Oh, I'm terribly sorry. Let me make a note of that." The unfamiliar voice paused, giving Alex the opening she needed.

"Listen, if you're selling something, I'm not interested. Please put this number on the do-not-call—"

"No, no. It's not like that," The voice grew stronger, almost desperate. "I'm not selling anything. I'm calling about your work."

"What can I do for you?" In truth, Alex had all the business she could handle for now. Still, her upbringing dictated she be civil and cordial, even if she knew the phone call to be a waste of her time. She'd learned folks' paths could cross at the most unforeseen times, and burning bridges never helped anyone.

Supplying shops in Asheville, Atlanta, Columbia, and St. Augustine was a full-time job. Alex also juggled the responsibilities of motherhood, wife, friend, and active church member. Add to these roles was her newly acquired responsibility of managing the mountain house rental property, and Alex sometimes felt she barely kept her nose above water. When her head hit the pillow at night, she felt as if she'd blinked and the day had evaporated, leaving only exhaustion in its wake. Alex didn't see how she could take on one more client, not right now, with all that was going on in her life. But she'd listen to the woman before politely declining.

"My name is Jaclyn Jones. I have a YouTube channel called Kingdom Kreatives. That's kreatives with a K. Have you heard of it?"

"I'm sorry, but no. My friends try to get me to listen to podcasts. Honestly, I'm not sure I even know what a YouTube channel is."

Without a doubt, Alex had the talent and drive to succeed as an entrepreneur. The world of social media, however, had never figured prominently into her life, for self-preservation and safety. She'd learned how to build a website in her high school computer programming class. It was how she'd been able to upgrade Chad's online presence. From the time she had left Woodvale, though, Alex had gone dark online. Her best friends had her cell phone number, so she stayed in touch, but she'd decided early on not to make it easy for her mother or J.T. to track her down via pictures of what she had for breakfast or her daughter's potty training. Now that they were no longer a threat, Alex saw the wisdom in professionally engaging with thousands of people in order to advance her career. But she had a husband, a four-year-old, and a business. Where was she supposed to find the time for such luxuries?

"Oh. Okay … Well, I feature up-and-coming artists—painters, photographers, sculptors, you name it. We chat for about an hour. You show some of your latest work, maybe give the viewers a peek into what your plans are for future projects, and I always make sure the artists share how their Christian faith inspires, motivates, and encourages them in the creative process. It's like a TV show that people can subscribe to and get updates when new episodes are posted."

She sounded sincere and passionate, but Alex didn't see how she could possibly squeeze one more thing into her hectic life. She did appreciate Jaclyn explaining her show, though, in terms even her tech-challenged mind could understand.

"Miss Jones, it sounds great. It really does. I just don't think I can commit to anything else right now. How did you find me, if you don't mind my asking?"

It turned out that Jaclyn lived outside Asheville, known for its burgeoning art community and home to Penny Wyse Interiors. Through a series of God-orchestrated events last year, Alex had met Penny in a greasy spoon diner in North Carolina. She later recommended her best friend, Brittany, as the new acquisitions coordinator for Penny's store. Brittany loved her job, and Penny thanked Alex whenever she called to check on pieces for her showroom.

"Brittany's one of my most loyal followers," Jaclyn gushed. "She lets me put ads for my channel in the shop. And she recommends the show to folks she talks to. I just love Britt."

Alex smiled. Brittany had been her best friend since they were little girls. She'd stuck by Alex through everything, even helping plan Alex's escape from Woodvale years ago after Alex had discovered she was pregnant. If anyone understood Britt's magnetic personality, it was Alex.

"I'm sure she's told me about your show. I'm just not much of a podcast person. Or a YouTube person. Whatever. I really wasn't joking when I said I don't even know how to get to one—"

"Don't worry!" Jaclyn interrupted her before she could continue. "I'll just text you the link to the latest episode. Why don't you watch it before you decide for sure, okay?"

Alex sighed, wondering for the thousandth time how she got herself sucked into new commitments without even trying. Her phone dinged, indicating the message containing the link had come through.

"Fine, I'll watch. But I'm not making any promises. I'll be in touch in a couple of days."

"Perfect. Talk to you then. And, Mrs. White?"

"Actually, you can call me Alex."

"Thanks. You won't regret it, Alex!" *Click.*

Alex stared at her phone, not sure whether to be impressed with the girl's tenacity or angry with herself for possibly taking on yet another task to accomplish.

Rising to fix a cup of tea before Lydia's rest time was over, Alex clicked the link to Jaclyn's show.

§§§

When Chad opened the kitchen door, the sound of his girls' laughter greeted him. Smiling, he reveled in what a blessed man he was. He hoped Alex would still be laughing, or at least smiling, when he brought up his latest idea. It had the potential to either thrill her or go terribly sideways, but he had to try.

"I'm home," he called when nobody rushed to greet him.

"We're in here," Alex answered from the living room.

He found Alex and Lydia snuggled up on the sofa, watching something on Alex's laptop. Midnight snoozed in Lydia's lap as the little girl stroked her fluffy white fur. The girls giggled again. Whatever they were watching obviously had them hooked.

"What's so funny?" Chad asked.

"We're watching videos on YouTube." Alex smirked as she delivered the news.

He was only too aware of her resistance to such things. What could be so interesting and funny that it had sucked in his die-hard, anti-technology wife?

He parked himself on the couch next to them and started watching. Soon, he was also laughing along with the girl on the screen as she and her guest talked and painted.

"Who is this?" Chad asked.

He was immediately shushed by the girls.

The sound startled Midnight, who raised her head, yawned, and then halfheartedly licked a paw before curling back up and closing her eyes.

A few minutes later, the lady was saying goodbye and upbeat music accompanied the screen fading to black.

Alex sent Lydia to wash up then turned to kiss her husband. "How was your day?"

"It was good. Tuesdays are when the deacons bring in the single ladies' cars for oil changes, so we were pretty busy."

Chad was happy he'd found a way to serve through his business. Given the hours he worked, he couldn't help out much around the church campus on weekdays, but he was happy to provide complimentary oil changes to the widows and single moms.

Alex smiled. She didn't rush him, but the look on her face made it clear she had news.

"So, how was your day?"

"Actually, it went better than I expected." She rose from the couch then helped him up. "We've been watching that show for almost two hours. Can you believe it?"

Chad followed her to the kitchen, where they easily settled into their dinnertime routine. The pot roast cooking in the slow cooker had smelled delicious the minute he'd stepped in the door, so he knew he didn't have to wait to eat dinner.

He grabbed plates and silverware while she filled glasses with iced tea for them and milk for Lydia.

"It must have some amazing guests to hold your attention for that long." Chad knew Alex wasn't one to sit still long enough to watch TV or a movie.

"That's what I wanted to talk to you about. She wants me to be a guest. I told her that I was too busy, but she convinced me to just watch an episode before deciding." She scooped roast, carrots, and potatoes onto plates as she spoke, concentrating her attention on her task.

Chad had the distinct impression she was avoiding looking at him.

"That's great, babe," he said.

"Is it, though? I'm so swamped with everything going on around here, how will I fit one more thing into my schedule? It'll soon be time for Lydia to start kindergarten. Managing the mountain house is taking up way more time than I'd expected, from interacting with guests to cleaning and maintenance. It's just so much at once."

Chad took the slotted spoon out of Alex's hand and put it back into the slow cooker before turning her to face him. She still avoided his eyes, so he placed a finger under her chin and tilted her face up.

"Listen, sweetie. You do what you feel is best. And tell me what I can do to help." He ran his fingers through her silky hair as he spoke, inhaling her lavender perfume. "Have you contacted any property management companies about handling the mountain house?"

She shook her head. "I guess I should have done that today instead of falling into the rabbit hole of Jaclyn's videos."

With just a few minor details left to wrap up with the estate, Alex and Terry had each assumed control of the business ventures that J.T. had left them—the mountain house for Alex, and the construction company for Terry. It had turned out to be more time-consuming than Alex had imagined.

Zeke had used a service to manage the property for J.T. for years, and he'd only lived an hour away from the place. Chad wished Alex had taken Zeke's advice about the day-to-day care and booking of the place.

"Let me do that for you," Chad offered. "Get all the information about the property together, and I'll make some calls tomorrow, starting with Zeke. He can probably give you some good advice. Also, maybe it's finally time to consider hiring some help around here. Think about it, huh?" Chad truly wanted to lighten her load, but he also wanted to free her mind to consider his plan. "Hey, I've got something kind of important I want to talk to you about."

"Okay," Alex said, searching his eyes for a clue as to what he was cooking up.

Before he could begin, however, Lydia's little feet beat a rhythm on the wooden floors down the hall. His life-changing suggestion would have to wait.

§§§

The pot roast was delicious, but Alex had a hard time concentrating on the meal. Chad's announcement that he had something important to discuss could be anything from buying a new dress shirt to firing an under-performing mechanic. She tried to wait patiently for him to broach the subject, yet it was clear he didn't feel comfortable doing so with Lydia around, so Alex assisted her daughter in her after-dinner routine.

After clearing her dishes and feeding Midnight, Lydia asked to take the kitten for a visit to Miss Matilda. Alex was only too happy for her daughter to have a bit of a distraction to give Chad a chance to bring up his big news.

Together, they watched the little fluff ball jump down the steps, close on Lydia's heels, as she carried a covered bowl full of pot roast to their recuperating friend.

Alex rinsed the last dish and handed it to Chad to put in the dishwasher. She pushed the coffee pot button, looking forward to their evening mugs enjoyed on the back porch.

Alex and Chad worked in silence for a few minutes, but she was about to explode to know what he wanted to discuss with her. Finally, she couldn't take it any longer.

"Okay, mister, out with it."

Chad chuckled and looked at his watch as he closed the dishwasher. "Wow! You lasted a lot longer than I expected. Five whole minutes." He then moved out of the way as she playfully snapped the dishtowel in his direction.

Alex tried to school her features into a scowl, but failed miserably. His cute grin disarmed her every time.

"Stop teasing me. What did you want to talk about?"

"Let's take our coffee out back and talk."

They poured mugs of strong, hot coffee then went to the screen porch where they could hear the crickets chirping and the cardinals sing.

Chad rubbed the back of his neck, a sure sign of nerves. Releasing a deep breath, he then dropped his head backward briefly before looking into her eyes. "Alex, I want to adopt Lyddie." He watched her carefully, gauging her reaction.

Tears sprang to Alex's eyes, and she covered her mouth with both hands. "I thought you'd never ask," she whispered.

"What? For days, I've stressed over how to ask this, and you've already been considering it?" Chad's mouth hung open as he struggled to understand. "I thought this was going to be a sales job. I've got all my points laid out and ready to explain."

Before she'd miscarried a few months ago, she'd considered the right time to approach her husband about adopting Lydia. It would be so much easier for the little girl, and for Chad and Alex, if her last name were the same as her parents and siblings. Alex had every intention of telling her daughter about the circumstances surrounding her conception and birth, but that day was in the distant future, beyond what Alex could think about right now.

Alex smiled, an act that still didn't feel natural following their loss. Chad, however, had a way of coaxing from her a belief that things could one day be happy again.

"You can still give me your sales job, if you want," Alex said, trying to keep her tone teasing and light. "But I'd love for Lydia to call you Daddy."

She didn't have the last syllable out of her mouth before Chad had leaned over to shut her up with a kiss.

§§§

What neither Chad nor Alex knew was that Dorothy Comstock, who was deathly allergic to cats, had fled Matilda's house when Lydia had arrived with Midnight. As she pulled Matilda's cottage door shut, she heard the couple make their way to the back porch to enjoy their evening coffee.

Dorothy stood in the driveway, mere feet from the Whites' screen porch, fanning herself and trying to recover from exposure to the beastly feline, when she heard Chad say he wanted to adopt Lydia. She lingered in the shadows of nearby shrubbery, taking mental notes throughout the whole exchange. When it became obvious the pair were kissing, Dorothy thought it in bad taste to continue her reconnaissance mission and turned to leave.

Smiling, she walked down the driveway, her sneakers not making a sound in the quiet night, to her car parked on the road, out of sight from both houses.

Except for the brush with death from anaphylaxis, that was certainly a useful excursion.

Difficult Things

Work on Aunt Tilley's cottage had moved slower than Terry would have preferred. He wanted to get it built as quickly as possible, but the old plans used for his parents' original cottage required several upgrades to meet current building codes. While he made the necessary modifications, he threw in specifications for the senior-friendly features that he'd promised his aunt, like extra-wide doorways, smooth flooring throughout, and a ramp at the side of the porch.

Progress had also been slowed by Terry's frequent trips out of town. It had begun when he'd gone to Woodvale shortly after Meredith's revelatory visit. With Zeke's help, he'd taken stock of J.T.'s—now his, he constantly had to remind himself—business holdings, current projects, and staff. Trying to get a handle on this kind of information long-distance had proven too difficult.

On his first trip to Woodvale, Meredith had invited him to have dinner with her. Terry knew he should have declined Meredith's offer—the last thing he needed was to become involved with a woman who lived six hours away—but she'd assured him that it was strictly professional, and he'd let himself believe it.

They'd ended up talking for hours. Terry smiled when he recalled the young waiter who had hovered over their table after they'd spent two hours over appetizers, dinner, and dessert. Terry had made it worth the young man's time, tipping him three times the expected rate.

He and Meredith had then strolled around the downtown area, stopping occasionally to sit and watch the late-night passersby go about their evening. When Terry had looked at his watch and saw midnight had passed, he'd apologized for monopolizing Meredith's evening. She'd laughed him off and asked when he'd be back. He had silenced the alarm bells going off in his head and promised he'd see her soon.

Thus began Terry's every-other-week treks to Alex's hometown. Nobody in Burton knew why he was gone so much, or who he went to see. Most folks from Burton believed he'd thrown himself back into his work, like the old day, but nothing could be further from the truth.

Meanwhile, the owners of the little bed and breakfast on the outskirts of Woodvale knew him on a first-name basis. The lady who worked the drive-thru at the local burger shop knew exactly how he liked his burgers fixed. And Zeke had grown accustomed to having Terry stop by jobsites occasionally to discuss the weather, the future of the company, or the congregation Zeke pastored.

While Terry wrestled with modifying Aunt Tilley's house plans, his heart longed to be with Meredith. It had been a long time since he'd felt like this.

Come to think of it, have I ever felt like this?

Gail had never made him feel this way—like a kid who was ten-feet tall, interesting beyond comparison, and ... what was it, exactly, that Meredith made him feel?

Important. That was it.

Several times, Terry had planned on calling her to say he couldn't make it for the weekend, but once he heard her voice, he wanted nothing more than to be with her. Make her laugh. Watch her cook dinner. Discuss the movie that they'd watched together or the latest book they'd read during their time apart.

Contemplating his predicament, Terry wiped his hand down his face, staring with unseeing eyes at the computer screen in front of him. Now that Aunt Tilley's plans were at the county office for approval, he'd moved on to his latest project—a new house for himself. It wasn't going well, however.

All he ever thought about was what Meredith would think. How would she decorate this room or that one? And she wasn't even going to be living there!

They'd resisted putting labels on their relationship. Both had been burned by previous relationships, although Meredith had kept the details of her love life failures to a minimum. They were intelligent adults, supposedly capable of proceeding with caution. However, Terry found it increasingly difficult to be cautious about anything when it came to Meredith. If it weren't for the one huge red flag in their relationship, he'd throw caution to the wind. But, that one thing was enough to hold him back.

Meredith didn't know the Lord.

Terry remembered the conversation from early in their relationship clearly.

"I tried calling you this morning," she'd told him one Sunday evening when he'd stayed in Burton.

"I was at church," he'd said. Trying to assess the situation, he'd asked as lightly as he could, "Where do you go to church?"

"Psshh!" She'd dismissed his question. "I haven't been to church in years. I've seen so many things as an estate attorney. It's made it really difficult to believe the whole notion that faith really helps anyone."

"Well, my faith is very important to me." Terry had known he needed to make his position known.

"And that's fine ... for you. It's just not for me."

He'd let it drop.

The closer he got to her, though, the more he regretted not making more of an issue of it from the beginning. He'd let his growing feelings silence his spiritual voice.

Terry knew the problems that could arise from being with someone who didn't share his faith. He'd often wondered about Gail's true grasp of Christian beliefs, but he'd never said anything to her.

Regardless of his ex's principles, or lack thereof, Terry knew his faith in Jesus had given him the strength he'd needed when he'd lost his parents, learned of his adoption, endured a brutal divorce, met his biological father, and sat by his aunt's bedside. He often prayed Meredith would see something in him that would make her ask questions, something that would turn her heart around. So far, though, it hadn't happened.

The chirp of Terry's phone pulled his attention back to the present. Seeing Meredith's name on the screen, he smiled as he answered, "Hey, you," trying not to let the concern from his recent thoughts creep into his voice.

"Hey, yourself. What're you doing this weekend?" Her voice was smooth and rich.

"Um ... I'm staying in Burton, working on my house plans." Terry winced as he made the admission. He hadn't told her about his own house yet.

"Ooo ... Impressive. I'm going to see my family this weekend. I thought I'd drive down from Greenville for the day on Sunday." Her voice had changed from throaty and confident to tentative and questioning. She'd never invited herself to Burton.

Terry wasn't sure he was ready for this step in their relationship. He'd just been considering the wisdom of pursuing this thing any further because of their differences in belief.

"Sure, sure," he said, trying to stall. How did he tell her all he'd been thinking about? This was definitely a topic for a face-to-face conversation.

"What time will you be here? We have Sunday dinner at Together for Good around one o'clock."

"That sounds good. I was thinking I'd leave Greenville around eight, so I'll get to Burton by ten or so. Wanna meet for coffee somewhere?"

"I've got a better idea," he said. "How about you join me at church?"

The silence on the line was deafening.

"Look, Terry." Meredith sighed. "Maybe this wasn't a good idea. I mean, I've told you the whole *church thing* isn't for me."

Terry could imagine her twirling her long red hair as she chose her words.

Terry's heart shattered in that moment. She was right. As difficult as it was, he knew what he had to do. He couldn't pursue a relationship with someone who didn't share his love for, and commitment to, the Lord. What he didn't know was how he'd ever find the strength to walk away.

He swallowed hard and cleared his throat. He didn't trust his voice, but he forced himself to say what needed to be said.

"I understand, Meredith. I hope you know how much I'll miss you."

"Terry, wait. What are you—"

"Let me finish, Mere." He couldn't stop himself from using the familiar version of her name, which he'd become accustomed to doing during their time together. It rhymed with "air," which was what her presence gave him. "This is so hard for me." He took one more deep breath before continuing. "I've enjoyed our time together, more than you can ever know, but my faith is everything. I can't be with someone who doesn't share that." Terry felt himself starting to ramble, so he clamped his mouth shut. His eyes stung, and his throat constricted.

Through the ringing in his ears, he thought he heard Meredith's voice catch as she said, "I understand. I'll miss you, too, Terry. Bye." *Click.*

Terry looked at the phone in his hand. *If it was the right thing to do, why was it so ridiculously painful?*

§§§

With the Dixons settled into the cottage behind Together for Good, Charmain and Miss Matilda now shared the Whites' guest house. Until Terry got his aunt's new home built, Miss Matilda would stay put. She was never more than a phone call away whenever Yvonne or Marquis had a question or needed anything.

Charmain, Alex, and Chad checked on their friend often, but they gave her the space she needed to feel independent. Alex knew they'd all miss the dear lady when she finally did move back to the pregnancy care home, but she also knew it was where Miss Matilda's heart longed to be.

One late summer morning, Alex delivered breakfast to Miss Matilda before disappearing into the guest cottage garage where her workshop awaited. Chad had taken Lydia to pre-school at the church, giving Alex a head-start on her day's work. Shipments needed to go out to three stores in a few days, and a lot of work had to happen to ensure everything was ready in time.

Finding her groove, Alex was applying a coat of sealant to a coffee table when her watch buzzed with an incoming call. Glancing at the number, she saw it was a North Carolina area code and decided to let it go to voicemail. The only things important enough to interrupt finishing the piece she was working on were calls from either Chad or the pre-school. Besides, it was probably Jaclyn wanting to finalize the date and time for Alex's interview. She didn't want the show to distract her today.

Alex had fretted and lost sleep over whether to go on Jaclyn's show. One morning during her quiet time, the Lord had dispelled her doubts. She'd been studying Paul's letter to the church at Colossus, and when she had read verses twenty-three and twenty-four of chapter three, a peaceful calm had flooded her spirit. She'd written the verse on a note card and taped it to the bathroom mirror to remind herself that whatever she did, it was her act of worship to the Lord. She thought of the verses she'd now committed to memory.

Whatever you do, work heartily, as for the Lord and not for men, knowing that from the Lord you will receive your inheritance as your reward. You are serving the Lord Christ.

She may have received an earthly inheritance from J.T., but when she worked with her heart, focused on God, her true inheritance came from Him. Part of that work included taking a break from her business to tell others how God had directed her steps and set her on the creative path that she pursued today. Maybe someone could be encouraged by her story.

In the workshop, Alex worked and let her mind wander to all the things currently vying for her attention—miscarriage, Miss Matilda, inheritance, videotaping. She was glad she'd chosen today to complete some of the more mundane, mindless tasks on her list. Things that didn't require a great deal of concentration.

Before she knew it, her alarm for lunch buzzed.

When she got in the zone, she could work all day without stopping for much more than a granola bar. But, while Miss Matilda was convalescing, Alex made a point of fixing lunch, even if it was just a sandwich and fruit, for their guest. More often than not, Alex joined the older lady. The pair shared a closeness and kinship unlike any Alex had ever known, and she intended to enjoy their days together as long as she could.

Alex tapped her phone to silence the lunch alarm and noticed the caller from North Carolina had left a voicemail. She quickly closed up her can of polyurethane, placed her brushes in the cleaning bucket full of mineral spirits, and washed her hands in the workshop sink.

Alex rapped three times on the door leading into the cottage kitchen, the signal she used to let Miss Matilda know lunch would be ready soon. After pushing the button on the wall to raise the huge garage door, she tapped her phone again to listen to the message.

It wasn't Jaclyn. It was Meredith. And the call wasn't from the office phone that Meredith always used when she called. This had to be her personal cell.

At the sound of Meredith's voice, Alex felt a knot form in her gut, her mind spinning with questions. *Has Mother prevailed? Has J.T.'s will been overturned?*

It shouldn't make much difference, but she and Chad had made some pretty significant plans to help a whole lot of folks. It saddened Alex to think they might have to wait before pursuing those dreams ... if they ever could.

Meredith's message played all the way through, but Alex was so caught up in her own thoughts that she didn't hear a single word after the greeting. She replayed the message, focusing her attention on Meredith's halting and tentative words that were totally out of character for the polished, confident attorney whom Alex had come to genuinely like.

"Alex, it's Meredith, the estate attorney. So ... um, well ... I was wondering if we could talk. Not about the case. Don't worry; everything's almost wrapped up with that. No ... I, uh ... well, I was wondering if we could talk about Terry. Oh shoot, I probably shouldn't have called you. Never mind. Don't call me. Or ... you can ... if you want. Whatever. Well ... bye."

Her curiosity piqued, Alex knew she'd call Meredith back. First, though, she needed to get lunch to Miss Matilda.

It was a beautiful day, unseasonably mild for the last week of July, so Alex decided they'd eat outside. Within a few minutes, the two ladies sat at the table on the patio between the two houses, enjoying a slice of quiche and a wedge of honeydew.

"Do you have anything special going on today, dear?" Miss Matilda asked.

Mealtime was still a slow process for Miss Matilda as she attempted to retrain the muscles in the hand that, until last week, had been in a cast. Since her days were mostly consumed with physical therapy, slow walks down the driveway, and an occasional baking day, she often inquired about how the young people were spending their time.

Alex usually shared freely with her friend. Before answering today, however, Alex questioned the wisdom of mentioning Meredith's call and ultimately decided against it. She needed to respect Terry's privacy. And she definitely didn't need to upset his aunt. Instead, she launched into a description of the pieces that she'd finished that morning, pausing only to chew.

"What about you? Have you gotten hooked on any soap operas yet?" Alex grinned as she asked, knowing Miss Matilda's opinion of day-time programming.

"Pshh." Miss Matilda waved her hand at Alex, dismissing the suggestion. "That stuff's just garbage for the brain. And I understand Dottie Comstock has started stirring up her own little soap opera in Burton. Some of the girls at church have been listening to her, but I don't have time for that woman's foolishness. I have found some very interesting podcasts and YouTube videos, though."

Alex almost choked on her melon. How could this woman, who was old enough to be her grandmother, possess a level of tech savvy so far beyond Alex?

"Miss Matilda! You're a podcast fan? How did you get into that? What are some of your favorites?"

"I've got skills, you know." Miss Matilda smiled and dabbed the edges of her mouth daintily with her napkin. "I really like some of the Bible study programs. I've discovered some great teachers. But I listen to all kinds of stuff. Whatever sounds interesting."

"So, you watch YouTube, too? Have you heard of Kingdom Kreatives?" Alex asked. She was surprised by her friend's new-found interest.

"Oh, I love that one! Brittany texted me several weeks ago and suggested I watch it. I love how Jaclyn ties in the artists' creativity with their stories of faith. Have you seen it? Probably not, huh, since you don't even listen to podcasts while you work, much less take time to focus on watching an episode."

Ouch! Who's the dinosaur here? Not Miss Matilda, that's for certain!

"Actually, I'm going to be one of Jaclyn's guests. We're still trying to get our schedules to sync up."

"Oh, Alex, I'm so excited for you! What a wonderful opportunity." Miss Matilda's face lit up as it did whenever something truly delighted her.

Alex wished she shared her friend's enthusiasm for the project.

She smiled, glanced at her watch, and began clearing plates.

"You wait right there. I'll put these in the sink then come help you back inside," she told Miss Matilda as she climbed the stairs to her kitchen.

"Actually, dear, the weather's so nice I think I'll sit out here for a bit. If that's okay with you?"

"Sure. Can I bring you anything before I get back to work?"

"If you wouldn't mind bringing me my Bible and the notebook sitting next to it on the kitchen table, that would be lovely."

"Yes, ma'am. I'm on it."

"And, Alex." Miss Matilda paused until she had Alex's undivided attention. "Whatever has you so fretful, remember Who is in control. Hm?"

Alex nodded, amazed for probably the thousandth time how this wise lady could perceive her thoughts and feelings.

Or maybe I'm just that transparent. Nah!

§§§

Matilda enjoyed the gentle breeze and blue sky as she read her Bible and took notes on points she wanted to remember. What she enjoyed most, however, was her quickly returning ability to use a pencil and flip through pages, like before. The difficult days of physical therapy, both to regain her mobility and to rehab her hand, had been hard work. But it had also been worth the effort.

Not that I'd ever admit it to anyone.

She smiled as she thought how the young folks would preach an "I-told-you-so" sermon if she acknowledged the benefits of the PT sessions that she had so vehemently grumbled about.

"What's so funny?"

The question startled Matilda, causing her to spill the last of her iced tea. At first miffed with herself for being so clumsy, even as she'd been extolling the rewards of her hard work, her ire soon found a new target.

Dorothy Comstock.

"Dottie, I wasn't expecting you." Matilda meant it as an accusation. *The woman knows my cell phone number. She could have at least texted.*

"Let me help you, Matilda dear," Dottie said, ignoring Matilda's comment as she let herself in the cottage door and emerged with a roll of paper towels.

The women made quick work of cleaning up the spill. Soon, after Dottie had returned the paper towels to Matilda's kitchen and deposited the dripping used ones in the trash can, she lowered herself into the seat that Alex had recently vacated.

"So, Dottie, what brings you out this way?" Matilda tried to be cordial, considering Dot had helped clean up the mess. *The mess she caused.*

"Oh, you know, I just go around and visit people, chat, pick up on the latest town news."

You mean work the gossip circuit.

Matilda kept the thought to herself, replying with a simple nod.

"Well, your little crew's been busy, huh?" Dottie's eyes sparkled, giving her the look of a hungry cheetah on the prowl.

"I suppose." Matilda refused to feed the woman's appetite for secrets and speculations.

"Well, I was just telling Evelyn about that young bi-racial couple who's booted you out of a job, and your house. And that cute nephew of yours." Dottie rolled her eyes heavenward and fanned herself with one hand. "That pretty girl who lives here must be pretty upset about Terry being gone so much lately. I mean, they're both loaded now, with the inheritance and all, but maybe she's trying to get back at Terry for stepping out on her."

The shock of Dorothy's accusations rendered Matilda speechless, which Dottie apparently took as license to continue.

"I mean, why else would she want someone, other than her daughter's father, to adopt the little girl? Don't look at me like that, Matilda." Dottie wagged a finger at her dumbstruck hostess. "Everyone in town knows Terry is that little girl's daddy. Why, just look at them! They look exactly alike."

Something in Matilda snapped. Decades of being the sweet Southern lady evaporated in an instant as she prepared to go to battle on behalf of those she loved most.

She rose from her chair, vaguely aware of and thankful for her steadiness as she leaned over the vile woman. An anger unlike any she'd ever felt coursed through her veins, emboldening her and causing her to tremble with fury.

"Dorothy Comstock, you wicked, contemptuous woman. How dare you come to the home of this lovely girl and her husband, both of whom have cared for my every need during my recovery, and spew your baseless, venomous accusations. And you should know I will tolerate no falsehoods being spread about Terry. I don't know where you've gotten your hurtful gossip, but I suggest you cease and desist this instant." Matilda drew two long breaths, sitting down as she felt the adrenaline rush subside. "Leave, Dot. Just leave. Now. And don't ever come back." She looked Dottie square in the eye and was met with a practiced defiance.

"I'll leave, Matilda. Remember, though, you didn't deny a single thing I said. That's all I needed."

Matilda watched Dottie walk to her car—a four-door, foreign thing somewhere between the color of sand and baby poop—and bowed her head.

Lord, what have I done?

know where to begin." Meredith lost her grip on the last fragile vestiges of her self-control.

Alex knew the feeling too well, so she sat quietly and allowed Meredith to sob and sniffle, babble and blubber. She wished Meredith was sitting beside her, instead of in another state. A hug would be good for both of them right about now.

When Meredith regained a bit of composure, her voice sounded flat, as if her spirit itself had been ripped from her. Gone was the confident, upbeat, accomplished woman who Alex had met a few weeks ago. She'd been replaced by a quiet, tentative, almost robotic-sounding girl, hurt and confusion ringing in every word she spoke.

"I met Scott in my sophomore year of college."

Alex didn't make a sound, not wanting to intrude on the memory or give Meredith a reason to stop sharing.

Meredith took a deep breath before continuing. "We dated. Fell in love. Had plans for our future. Big plans. I was a criminal justice major getting ready for law school. He was going to medical school after completing his biology degree. We had everything figured out."

Alex had to remind herself to breathe. Breathing, however, might make noise and cause her to miss part of Meredith's quietly-told tale.

"Everything was perfect. We both graduated with honors, took a year off to study for our entrance exams, applied to several schools, and we even started to talk about marriage. Then ..." Her voice broke, and she stopped talking.

Meredith's grief was palpable, even over the phone. Alex's heart ached for the woman whom she'd come to admire. At the same time, her curiosity begged to know what horrible, life-changing event had plunged Meredith into such despair. She didn't have to wait long for an answer to her unspoken questions.

Meredith's voice grew even quieter, which Alex hadn't believed possible. She strained to hear the rest of the story, plugging her other ear with her finger.

"Then I found out I was pregnant." It had taken Meredith several attempts to get the words out.

Dread crept up Alex's spine as she thought of all the possible outcomes for the situation that Meredith had experienced. She understood all too well the mixed emotions such a discovery could ignite in the heart of a woman. Ironically, if Alex received the same news today, it would have only one effect—to make her happier than she'd been in quite a while.

"What did you do?" Alex whispered when Meredith didn't continue, scared to speak in a normal tone, lest she spook her hurting friend.

"I told Scott about the baby. I was so happy. I thought we could modify our plans, get married, raise our child. It would have been so wonderful. I tried to make him see it my way …"

Again, silence.

Alex guessed Meredith was trying to gain control over her emotions as she dredged up this painful memory. This clearly wasn't something Meredith allowed herself to contemplate often. Her pain was too raw, too intense. Too fresh to have been eased at all by the grieving process.

"And then …?" Alex prompted.

"Scott was livid. He didn't understand how I could have let it happen. I reminded him it wasn't a situation I'd gotten into alone, but that just made him angrier. That night … the night I believed would be one of the happiest in our lives was the first time he …" She choked on her words.

"Did he hit you, Meredith?" Alex thought she might be sick at the thought of someone hurting this woman who'd become a friend.

"Yes."

Alex barely heard the whispered reply. She heard something else loud and clear, though, and she understood it well—shame, self-loathing, desperation. Alex had been there, and she'd survived. Flourished, even.

She knew the sweetness of grace and forgiveness that Meredith so desperately needed, but she also knew she couldn't force Meredith to understand, to believe.

Alex kept listening, letting Meredith speak at her own pace.

"He insisted I terminate the pregnancy. I tried to reason with him, but he became furious when I did. So, I did it, Alex. I killed my baby."

It was several minutes before Meredith was able to continue. Still, Alex waited. She understood. She'd almost made the same irrevocable decision. But God had put Miss Matilda in her life, and now her precious Lydia brought more joy than she'd even known was possible.

"I went back to him after that. The day I had the abortion, I received my law school acceptance letter. The next day, Scott received rejection letters from his top two med school choices. It was the final straw for him. He kept yelling about how it wasn't fair that I would be accepted when he was the one who deserved to be given the opportunity. That was the last time he hit me. I packed my stuff and left while he was at the bar that night. I never heard from him again."

Alex let her mind conjure images of a young, scared, devastated version of the woman whom she knew. This younger version of Meredith must have felt hopeless, alone, broken.

"Mere, you went through an awful trauma. I don't know if you ever sought counseling, but you may want to consider it. It doesn't matter how long ago it happened, you need help sorting through those memories and feelings." Alex had benefited enormously from her counseling with Reverend Drummond.

"You may be right. I'll think about it." Meredith's lifeless voice didn't indicate any enthusiasm for the prospect.

"I've got one last question for you. What does this horrible time in your life have to do with your feelings about church?" Alex didn't want to make any assumptions about Meredith's thought process and experiences, but she needed to know why Meredith had such a strong aversion to the Christian faith. And why she'd told Alex this story when asked about church.

"Alex, I've heard about Christians' views on abortion. I'm smart enough to know they consider it a sin. That makes me a sinner. And I've heard God can't tolerate sinners. I don't want to spend my time praying to a God who won't listen to me. Or, worse, Who will only punish me because of the horrible things I've done."

Meredith had gone from despondent to belligerent. Alex knew she'd have to make her appeal with a gentle touch, giving Meredith what she understood best—facts.

§§§

Terry didn't sit on the platform with the praise team on Sunday morning.

From his seat at the back of the worship center, he saw Aunt Tilley in the pew next to Alex. It was his aunt's first time back in the worship center since "her accident," and she was thrilled to return to the place where she drew such joy, such strength and solace. He thanked the Lord for letting them keep her a while longer.

Once the benediction and final Amen were spoken, Miss Matilda and Alex sat back down in the pew, allowing the crowds to dissipate a bit before trying to navigate the sloping floor.

Chad kissed Alex on the cheek before scooting out the side door. Terry knew he'd return soon with Lydia.

Alex and Aunt Tilley chatted with friends who stopped by to welcome the older lady back and inquire about her health. Aunt Tilley was radiant, hugging her closest friends and talking animatedly to everyone else.

Terry noticed Dottie glance in their direction several times, but she never made a move to come over and greet her.

"It's good to see you back in your usual seat," he said, slipping into the pew behind them.

Both ladies snapped their heads around, surprised to see him sitting down as he wrapped his aunt in a one-armed side hug.

"Terry, dear! I didn't see you on the platform singing. I thought you'd gone out of town again." Delight shone in Aunt Tilley's eyes.

"Nah. I was just running a bit late this morning." He darted his eyes around the room, not meeting his aunt's stare.

Alex raised one eyebrow in question, but he pretended not to notice. He knew what Alex was wondering. Why had he been late? Terry was never late.

But, this morning, he'd been waiting, hoping Meredith would change her mind and join him. Hoping she would somehow understand how important his faith was to him. Hoping she'd be willing to open up to him about her reluctance to seek solace and strength and comfort in the Creator of all things.

But she hadn't come.

His heart felt like a lead lump in his chest as he attempted to put on a happy face for the others' sakes.

"Bubba!" Lydia's high-pitched squeal pulled the adults' attention to the little girl running ahead of Chad.

Terry pasted on a smile that didn't reach his eyes as he moved into the aisle to catch his little sister when she leaped into his arms.

"Hey there, Lyddie Bug. What did you learn in Sunday school?"

Lydia launched into the story of the men building houses, one on sand and one on solid rock.

"I told Mrs. Drummond my Bubba builds houses. Right? Bubba, you don't build your houses on the sand, do you? They'll fall if you do."

Terry swallowed hard, his mind racing as he floundered for the words to answer the little girl. He hoped the other adults wouldn't notice how uncomfortable he was answering the simple question.

What have I built my life on? Right now, it feels like I'm swimming in quicksand.

"Sweetie," Alex said, rescuing Terry from his inability to formulate an answer to a simple question, "why don't we let your Bubba go so we can get over to Together for Good for lunch?"

"You'll be there, won't you?" Lydia asked him as she squeezed his neck in a tight hug.

"Absolutely."

Sitting in his car a few minutes later, the air conditioning blasting on high, Terry sighed and let his head drop back against the leather headrest. After a few seconds, he put on his seat belt and eased the car onto the highway.

His mind was so occupied on his sadness that he never saw the little sports car with North Carolina license plates parked across the street from the church. And, by the time the tall redhead had stepped out of the car, Terry was well on his way to Sunday dinner with his family.

§§§

Alex wasn't sure she should tell Terry about her conversation with Meredith. What the lawyer had told Alex was deeply personal. If Meredith wanted Terry to know those details of her past, it was her information to share, when she wanted to share it. Alex prayed Meredith could find healing, peace, and a life shared with someone she loved.

She held Chad's hand for several seconds after he finished saying the blessing. Plates and silverware clinked all around them in the frenzy of Sunday dinner at Together for Good, but today, Alex felt especially thankful for the kind, thoughtful, loving man God had placed in her life.

Scattered and Gathered

Terry realized how foolish he'd been to hold out hope of Meredith showing up at church. His latest relationship debacle only served to strengthen his resolve to remain a bachelor ... forever. It also gave him the time to throw himself into his work without having to remember to take a break to make a phone call. Or make a six-hour trip, each way, every other weekend. Zeke was more than capable of running the business, a fact Terry had refused to admit while he'd been getting to know the beautiful Meredith.

During his self-imposed isolation, Terry avoided a few topics of thought, scared that acknowledging these things might paralyze him. Like how much he still missed Meredith. Or how much he prayed she'd discover the Truth for herself. Or how the loneliness engulfed him. He'd never felt this way, not even when he and Gail had split. Quite the opposite, in fact. After the divorce, he'd felt liberated, free. But Gail had been a manipulative, controlling narcissist. He saw that now. Meredith was sweet, and kind, and thoughtful.

Terry rubbed his hands over his face and felt two days' worth of stubble as he tried to concentrate on the drawings in front of him. Now that he'd gotten all the necessary permits and approvals, he really wanted to finalize the three-dimensional rendering of Aunt Tilley's new house for her to take a look at. He also needed to file the plans and permit applications for Mrs. Kirkland's addition. His concentration just wasn't what it had been a few weeks ago.

What am I doing? I've never been this absentminded and distracted.

Pushing back from the desk, Terry rose and walked out the back door of the little brick house he'd converted into his office years ago.

He'd always loved this location, nestled in the woods just outside of town and overlooking a little pond. It provided him the backdrop of tranquility that he needed when work got crazy. It was also where he'd been living since selling the huge house that he and Gail had shared. Although not an ideal living situation, he'd been able to save a considerable amount that he would have normally spent on rent, while being able to work whenever the mood struck.

He stepped onto the back deck and sucked in a deep gulp of warm summer air, closing his eyes as sunshine bathed his face.

His ears perked up when he heard gravel crunch in the driveway out front. Then his heart and mind raced in alarm. He didn't remember scheduling any appointments for this afternoon. He hadn't even showered or shaved, and it was … Looking at his watch, he was shocked to see it was after two o'clock.

Where has the day gone? Did I even eat lunch?

He couldn't decide whether to greet his visitor out front before whoever it was had an opportunity to invade his space or go back in the way he'd come out and try to act as if everything was fine. The decision was made for him when he heard Alex calling his name from the foyer.

"You look fabulous." Her voice dripped with sarcasm, but her look held both astonishment and concern at his disheveled appearance.

Normally, he was the kind of guy who ironed his jeans. The wrinkled, holey T-shirt he now wore, complete with a ketchup stain from last night's fast-food French fries, was completely out of character.

"Yeah, I've been kind of busy." Although he tried to speak normally, his high-pitched voice sounded defensive, and he knew it. He avoided her critical stare, turning toward the kitchen. "Would you like a water? I can get you one from the fridge."

"Sure. Thanks."

He felt her gaze on his back as he opened the refrigerator door. Peering inside, he discovered one partially consumed bottle of water and an almost-empty jar of mayo. Nothing else. Terry's head pounded as he tried to remember exactly when he'd last been to the grocery store.

Striding into the reception area, where Alex had taken a seat, he handed her a glass filled with tap water, trying not to notice her questioning glance as he took the seat across from her.

"So, what brings you out this way?" Terry fought to keep his voice modulated, but the question came out forced, abrupt. He prayed he hadn't forgotten some important appointment. Or worse. "Is anything wrong with Aunt Tilley?" Panic clutched his heart at the thought of another health scare.

"No, no. She's fine. Actually, I'm worried about you, Terry. I've tried to call you for a few days, but your phone keeps rolling over to voicemail." Alex sipped her water but kept her eyes trained on him. He'd seen her watch Lydia the same way when she thought the little girl was up to something naughty.

"Shoot. My battery must've died. Sorry. To answer your question, though, I'm fine. Just really in the zone, working. You know, Aunt Tilley's place. The Kirkland addition. My house." According to his way of thinking, the more projects he listed, the less troubled Alex had reason to be.

She didn't buy it for a second. He should have known better.

"Cut it out, Terry. I'm not stupid. And, FYI ... I know about you and Meredith."

Alex had never been one to beat around the bush, so Terry didn't know why her abrupt declaration surprised him. He could make the effort to deny it, putting on a great show of indifference, but he simply didn't have the energy needed to keep up the sham of denial.

He slumped over, placed both elbows on his knees, and hung his head. He and Alex had been through a lot together; why not let her in on the latest episode in his dramatic life?

"Who told you? I thought I'd been pretty discreet."

"Ha! You're a funny guy. You go around floating on air for weeks, you're gone almost every other weekend and, despite that little project list you rattled off a second ago, you've all but quit working on plans for your own house." Alex held up a finger for every point she made. "And ... here's the thing that finally tipped me off—you have a Burger Bonanza wrapper in your car."

Terry winced. Of course, Alex would know about Burger Bonanza. When they'd stopped there together last year on the way home from seeing J.T., she'd told him her friend's parents owned the place. How could he have been so careless?

"Okay. So I went to Woodvale. I needed to check in with Zeke on the business, convince the clients their projects will be completed with the same level of quality and attention to detail they expect."

She might have nailed him on his travel destination, but she couldn't possibly know about him and Meredith ...

"She called me, Terry."

And ... there it was. His love life had become fodder for his half-sister's mother and their attorney.

Ire boiled up within him. Then he looked into Alex's eyes. The sadness and concern he saw there silenced his protest and doused his anger.

"What did she say?" He hadn't spoken to Meredith in almost a week.

"I think it would be best if *she* told you what she shared with me."

Terry's brows drew together in question. *What?*

"What I will tell you," Alex said over her shoulder as she took her glass to the kitchen, "is that y'all need to talk." She put one hand on his shoulder while hoisting her giant bag off the floor. "Also—and I'm saying this as your friend—get a shower and go to the grocery store. Preferably in that order."

Terry chuckled for the first time in days. It felt good. And a little bit strange.

Maybe she was right. Where was his phone charger, anyway?

§§§

Alex took deep breaths on the drive home, trying to calm her nerves and steady her heartbeat. Seeing Terry in that condition had seriously rattled her. She'd had no intention of mentioning her conversation with Meredith, but it was obvious Terry needed to be shocked out of his stupor.

It was up to him now whether he called Meredith or not. Alex hoped he did and that it went well. She wanted so much for Terry to find someone who loved him. Meredith, too. Still, Alex understood where Terry's thoughts were, and she didn't blame him one bit.

Glancing at the dashboard clock, Alex noticed she had a few minutes before she had to get in the carpool line at the church pre-school. She decided to pop into Reverend Drummond's office to get his advice on what else she should do, if anything, about the situation with Terry and Meredith. Or if she'd already done too much.

Chrissy, the church secretary, was on the phone, so Alex waved and motioned she was going to wait outside the pastor's office. Chrissy gave her the thumbs-up as she continued to talk.

"I know, Dottie, but did you see it with your own eyes?" Chrissy said into the phone softly.

Alex didn't slow down, so she didn't see Chrissy watch her head down the hall.

Alex had had plenty of turns in the big, comfy chair inside the office, but there were a couple of reasons she had no intention of staying long today. First, she didn't have an appointment—she knew Reverend Drummond's crazy busy schedule could become jam-packed with staff meetings, sermon preparation, and counseling sessions. Second, Alex didn't have a concrete problem she needed help with. She simply wanted the Reverend's sage advice.

Alex put down the magazine that she'd been flipping through when she heard Reverend Drummond's booming voice approach the other side of the door, indicating a meeting was winding down. Suddenly, Alex's palms began to sweat, and her mouth went dry as she rethought the wisdom of her decision to show up unannounced. If he was conducting counseling, waiting here might violate some kind of confidentiality rule. Or, at the least, proper decorum.

Why didn't Chrissy stop me on my way in?

Panicking, she grabbed her purse and turned to attempt a hasty retreat. She didn't move fast enough, though.

"Alex?"

She definitely heard two voices call her name, and she cringed at having to encounter the pastor and his client.

She turned slowly to face the preacher and whoever had just finished their counseling session.

"Meredith?" Alex's knees went weak with surprise. *What in the world is she doing here? When did she get here? How does she know Reverend Drummond?*

The questions tumbled around in her head, but Alex couldn't find her voice. She stood, paralyzed in the position they'd caught her in, opening and closing her mouth like a beached fish, unable to articulate her embarrassment or pose her many questions. When she finally recovered her voice, the eloquence of her explanation left much to be desired.

"Meredith, Reverend Drummond, I'm so sorry. I shouldn't have waited

… Got to go pick up Lydia … Won't breathe a word …" Alex stammered her abject apologies, backing away from the pair, even as Meredith and the preacher smiled at her, both seemingly unrattled by Alex's presence.

"Alex," Meredith said, crossing the small waiting area to hug the dumbstruck girl. "It's fine. I've been in Burton since last Sunday. Reverend Drummond has been kind enough to meet with me several times." Meredith turned to look at the white-haired man. "Thank you. You've made a world of difference."

Reverend Drummond beamed. "It was my pleasure, dear. Let me know if I can be of any additional assistance."

"I'm so confused," Alex said, continuing to look at both people for clarification. She got nothing but more Cheshire cat grins.

"Let's walk to your car, Alex. I'll explain on our way out." Meredith hooked her arm through Alex's and led her to the exit. They waved at Chrissy, who was still on the phone, speaking in a low voice.

By the time they got to her car, Alex had heard the story of Meredith's longing to understand what drew Terry and Alex to God. Reverend Drummond had given Meredith several large chunks of Scripture to read each day, and they'd discussed her questions and observations, the truth each passage presented, and how to begin applying all of it to everyday life.

"So …?" Alex asked, obviously wanting to know if Meredith had accepted Jesus as her Savior, her conscience still stinging from her recent intrusion on the privacy of the counseling session.

Meredith maintained her poker face. Her years as a lawyer had obviously taught her not to crack under interrogation. Alex was impressed … and frustrated.

"I think I'll give Terry a visit," Meredith said, waving as she walked across the parking lot to her sleek, expensive sports car.

Alex stood beside her trusty, beat-up SUV, waving as Meredith drove off.

What a strange and eventful day it had been. First, Terry and his disheveled—

Oh no!

Alex dug her phone out of her purse and frantically texted, hoping the man had put his phone on the charger.

Get shower. NOW. You're welcome.

§§§

"Meredith," Terry said as he opened his front door, trying desperately to school his features. He couldn't let her know how thrilled he was to see her, nor could she know what a wreck he'd been while trying to figure out a way to make their relationship work. "What a nice surprise."

That, of course, wasn't the complete truth. Thanks to Alex's succinct text, he'd known something was up. He trusted Alex, so he'd complied with her command. He had to remember to thank her later. For now, though, all he wanted to do was concentrate on the woman on his front porch.

"Won't you come in?" Terry said, wincing inwardly at the formality of the invitation. He tried to relax a bit, keeping his tone conversational. "So, how'd you find the place?"

"I have been mailing documents to you for a couple of months now," Meredith said. "This is lovely," she continued, perusing the house's spacious foyer, which served as the reception area for Terry's architecture business. "So, is this your home or your office?"

It was Mere's first visit, and Terry had always been vague regarding his current living situation. He'd shared his plans to build Aunt Tilley a cottage at Together for Good. He'd also briefly mentioned his plans to design his own home. What he hadn't told her, however, was how distracted he'd been since she'd shown up the day the Dixons moved in. She had no idea she was the reason he couldn't concentrate on his work, preferring instead to constantly plan and anticipate his next trip to Woodvale.

She turned to face him and focused on his eyes with her steady gaze, seeming to ask thousands of unspoken questions.

Flustered, Terry cleared his throat, closing the front door behind them.

"Well, it's been my office for about fifteen years, but I started living here a while back." He didn't see the need to share the details of renovating the home that he and Gail had shared and the legal battle that had ensued over the profits from the home. Best to keep it simple and keep his ex-wife a distant memory.

"I like it. From the outside, I thought it was going to be a … you know, what do they call it? Shabby chic kind of place. But you've made it so open and contemporary in here. And I love these tables," she spoke as she walked around the reception area, admiring the furnishings, the vaulted ceiling, and the custom millwork.

"Thanks. The, um … the tables are Alex's work. They were some of her earliest pieces." Terry swiped his fingers through his still-wet hair, trying to relax.

The small talk felt awkward, but Terry had no idea why Meredith was here. What did she want from him? He thought he'd been clear in their final conversation. And yet, he still hoped …

"Is there somewhere we could sit and talk, Terry?"

Terry's senses went on high-alert. "Sure. Have a seat. No one will disturb us in here."

The area off the foyer was elegantly furnished with a sleek sofa and several comfortable arm chairs. Meredith lowered herself into one of the chairs, and Terry positioned himself on the couch, facing her, but well out of arm's reach. He couldn't trust himself to be close to her. His resolve would evaporate, and he'd be kissing her before they could draw their next breath.

Leaning forward with his elbows perched on his knees, Terry hoped he looked relaxed and open to what Meredith had to say. In reality, his insides felt as if they'd turned to jelly. He remained silent, waiting for her to begin.

Finally, Meredith closed her eyes and drew a deep breath before speaking.

"Terry, I've made a decision. But I'm going to need some help."

New Life

Matilda dozed in the recliner, her Bible opened in her lap. Somewhere—she couldn't tell where, but it seemed far away—an insistent knocking threatened to dispel the fragile haze that separated sleeping soundly and being wide awake. She wasn't expecting anyone, though, so she ignored the sound and tried to continue to drift in her half-sleep. When the banging became more insistent, she reluctantly roused herself from her nap, disoriented as she looked around the tiny room.

"Come in," she called in a gravelly voice, lowering the recliner and grabbing her cane. Hadn't she and Alex just finished breakfast? It was too early for lunch. Besides, Alex hadn't even tapped her code on the kitchen door, announcing lunchtime.

Maybe I slept through it. Or maybe I'm so spoiled that I sit around napping until lunch is announced and served to me, like some royal lady. Matilda Gault, you should be ashamed of yourself.

Terry peeked his head in, stopping Matilda's harsh self-criticism in its tracks while her heart soared.

Although he visited every few days, she was always thrilled to see him. She worried so about his well-being. Did he eat well? Was he getting enough sleep?

A lifetime of knowing the boy, and then the man, had equipped Matilda with the instincts and concerns of a mother. She'd raised the boy since he was ten years old, for heaven's sake. She'd devoted much time and energy to making sure he was healthy and happy. Well, until Gail had come barreling into the picture.

If she were honest with herself, she'd never liked Gail. Still, she understood Terry's commitment to his vows. Now all Matilda wanted was for Terry to be at peace with the decisions he'd made in his life and to be happy as he moved forward.

"You got a second, Aunt Tilley?"

"For you, dear, I've got all the time in the world."

Terry opened the door wider and ushered Meredith into the cottage.

Matilda hid her surprise, but curiosity coursed through every inch of her being. Using her most genteel Southern manners, she tried to determine what was going on without prying.

"Well, what a lovely surprise. To what do I owe this unexpected pleasure?"

Terry's eyes sparkled.

Meredith looked up at him, but not as his attorney. That was love shining in her eyes. Matilda would bet her last dollar on it.

"Is Alex around?" Meredith asked.

"Yes, I believe she's back from taking Lydia to pre-school. She should be in the workshop." Matilda waved her hand in the general direction of the garage as she answered, not sure what Alex's role in this unannounced visit could be. She hadn't mentioned anything at breakfast.

Terry crossed the room in a few long strides to poke his head into the garage. Within a few seconds, Alex was in the tiny living room, wiping her hands on a paint-spattered towel.

Terry motioned for everyone to have a seat.

Why would Terry, Alex, and a lawyer want to speak with me? Matilda felt certain the others could hear her heart pounding in her chest. *Are* they going to put me away in some old-folks home? That's not what they call it now, is it? If so, how does that explain the look on Terry and Meredith's faces? They look positively smitten.

Terry took Meredith's hand, and Matilda knew they had important news to share. She glanced sideways at Alex, trying to gauge the situation from her reaction. However, Alex sat on the edge of the ottoman, her gaze darting between the pair, obviously as confused as Matilda. Knowing she wasn't the only one who didn't have a clue what was happening gave Matilda some strange sense of satisfaction.

"Aunt Tilley, we've got a few things to tell you." Terry looked at Meredith and smiled. "The first thing, before I forget, is that I have the 3-D rendering of your house, ready for you to look at. After you've had a chance to give it a final review and approval, we'll be ready to break ground really soon."

"Oh, Terry, that is excellent news. I can't wait to see it!" Matilda clapped her hands as she looked at her nephew with pride and excitement. She'd enjoyed her stay with Charmain, but she looked forward to living on her own again. She continued to get a bit stronger every day. And knowing that Yvonne and Marquis would be just a few steps away gave Matilda confidence she could make the transition to living alone again.

But Terry had said he had a few things to tell them. His announcement about her house was short and to the point. What else did he have up his sleeve? Matilda didn't want to play some silly game where she had to guess his intentions.

"That's not all, though," Terry said, glancing over to Alex, who still looked as confused as Matilda felt.

"Right," Meredith said, taking a deep breath. "I just wanted y'all to know, I've asked Jesus to be my Savior." Her voice was soft and timid.

The other women's reactions, however, were neither soft nor timid.

Alex jumped up and fist-bumped the air before plopping back onto the ottoman, beaming at the couple. Almost immediately, she popped back up and leaned over to hug Meredith, who now had pools in her eyes.

Matilda dropped her head and raised her hands. She didn't know Meredith well. What she did know was that the woman hadn't been to church with Terry. She also knew her dear nephew had been happier than she'd ever seen him in years, maybe ever, and then he'd sunk to depths that she hadn't seen since his divorce. She suspected Meredith was the source of the two extremes.

"So ... fill us in on how this wonderful news came about!" Alex gushed, thanking the Lord over and over in her mind while trying to maintain a composed exterior.

"Well," Meredith began, "maybe I should start at the beginning for Miss Matilda."

She looked at Terry, who nodded and patted her hand that rested on his knee.

Matilda leaned forward in the recliner, not wanting to miss a single word.

§§§

Alex put the teacups in the dishwasher while Miss Matilda continued to visit with the couple. Meredith's story hadn't been any easier for Alex to hear the second time, knowing what a difficult time Meredith had faced as a young woman. What had been easier this time was knowing that Meredith had begun to forgive herself and to seek the Lord's forgiveness, as well.

"Guys, I'd love to stay and chat, but my shipment absolutely has to go out in the morning. I'll be packing things until midnight if I don't get a move on." Alex waved from the door to her garage workshop, but Meredith stopped her.

"Would you like some help?" she asked. "I can't make amazing works of functional art like you do, but I've packed boxes before. Put me to work."

"Oh, Mere, are you sure? That would be amazing. Thank you."

The women stepped into the workshop, where it looked as if a packing peanut bomb had exploded. Next to the big garage door sat several boxes, neatly stacked and addressed.

"Where do we start?" Meredith sounded overwhelmed by the sight in front of her, but Alex, who had a system, wasn't alarmed in the least.

"Let me show you the method to my madness. Then we can divide and conquer. Sound good?" Alex asked, shuffling through the scattered packaging materials to the shipping spreadsheet on her computer.

The ladies soon found their rhythm, and Alex marveled at how much more efficient the process was with two people than one. Maybe she should take Chad's advice and hire some part-time help. Her shipments went out on a fairly regular schedule, so she could advertise at the local college, or at Together for Good. She filed the thought away for further consideration.

As Alex put the shipping label on the final box, she thanked Meredith for about the hundredth time since they'd started.

"Alex, really, I wanted to help," Meredith said as she placed the box on the stack. "This is totally out of my comfort zone, but it's so interesting. And impressive."

Alex snorted as she laughed. "I can't imagine what's impressive about this mess." The workshop looked more like a disaster zone than her usually-tidy workspace.

"I'm not talking about all this stuff." Meredith looked at the floor covered with Styrofoam. "I mean you. What you've accomplished. What you've overcome."

"You know, I don't really look at it that way." Alex reached for the broom to start the process of returning the shop area to the neat and orderly condition she preferred. "I've done what I needed to do to provide for me and my child. Most importantly, though, I've been massively blessed along the way. It's God Who's impressive."

"You make some good points," Meredith said as she bent over to hold the dustpan.

Does she ever get out of lawyer mode? Alex smiled as she tried to imagine Meredith in a T-shirt, no makeup, and no shoes. *Nope, I can't see it.*

Meredith returned the dustpan to its place before gathering the shipping papers, stacking them, and tapping the edges to align them perfectly, unaware of Alex's scrutiny.

"My advice to you, Mere," Alex said, even though she hadn't been asked, "is to start recognizing how God has orchestrated the details of your life. You've been through some terrible stuff—there's no arguing that point—but how have you dealt with your trials? What unexpected twists and turns has your life taken that's brought you to where you are today?"

Meredith looked pensive, considering Alex's words but not responding.

"Look, I'm sorry if I overstepped …" Alex started, regretting her outburst of unsolicited guidance. Meredith was a grown woman, perfectly capable of making decisions and weighing information. It was what she did for a living, for heaven's sake.

"Alex"—Meredith reached over and placed a well-manicured hand on Alex's arm—"please don't apologize. I've got so much to learn about being a Christian. I know I'm not the first person to make this decision as an adult, but it all feels so new and different. I'm going to need a lot of wisdom and counsel from others who are further along in this journey. Thanks for sharing."

Relieved, Alex patted Meredith's hand, noticing the grime under her own chipped nails as she did.

Maybe I should get a manicure before I go on Jaclyn's show.

She smiled, knowing she and Meredith could learn quite a bit from each other.

Welcome Aboard

That night, Alex slathered lavender lotion on her hands before sliding between the cool sheets. With all the painting, sanding, and cleaning she did every day, her skin needed a little TLC each night. At least on the nights when she wasn't so exhausted that she simply collapsed into bed. "How was your day?" she asked Chad, at the exact moment he put his toothbrush in his mouth. He relayed his day's events anyway and, surprisingly, she understood most of what he said.

This is marriage, she thought, contentment washing over her like a warm summer breeze. *The trivial, everyday things that add up to a lifetime. Lord, please help us to get it right.*

Alex and Chad prayed together every morning, often asking the Lord's blessing on their marriage. They'd both seen examples of broken relationships, vows not honored, detrimental choices made. But they'd also witnessed beautiful examples of what it looked like to pursue both the Lord and one's mate. Their prayer was to one day be an example of the latter to those around them.

Chad wiped the stray toothpaste from the corner of his mouth then tiptoed out the bedroom door. He returned within a few seconds.

"Lyddie's out like a light."

Alex loved how he'd embraced his role as Lydia's dad. His love for both of them motivated all he did. She made a mental note to enquire about the adoption process. Tonight, however, she had other matters to discuss with her husband.

"Have I told you lately how thankful I am for you?" she asked, bouncing onto her side so they could spoon and talk.

He nuzzled her hair, making her giggle, then kissed her neck before whispering in her ear, "Mrs. White, I'll never get tired of hearing you say that."

Alex reached over and turned off the lamp, and then they lay there, discussing what errands needed to be run, what chores needed to be done, and other mundane daily things which, when strung together, created the ebb and flow of life.

"I never asked how your day was. Did you get your shipment ready to go?" Chad spoke slowly, slurring his words the slightest bit, indicating sleep would soon claim him.

Alex had too much to tell him to let him fall asleep now, so she nudged his ribs with her elbow. "Don't go to sleep yet. I've got so much to tell you."

Knowing he had to wake up early, she relayed an abbreviated version of Meredith's story of brokenness and salvation. It felt good to finally share her tale of devastation and pain, but it felt even better to end it by celebrating her rescue and redemption. Then Alex tried to casually slip in the next piece of news.

"Jaclyn can fit me in on her recording schedule the first of next month."

She waited. No longer did she feel the steady rise and fall of his chest, which would have indicated he'd nodded off to the sound of her voice.

Rolling over to face him, she could barely make out his features by the glow of the hall nightlight. His feelings on the subject, however, were indiscernible.

"Chad, I know that's the weekend of our first anniversary, but maybe we could celebrate late. Or I could postpone the interview. She has an opening after the first of the year."

"You sure know how to spoil a surprise, Alex White." He smiled and kissed the tip of her nose.

Alex scrunched her face in confusion.

"I asked the company that manages the mountain house to make sure that week is open. I was going to whisk you away for a surprise anniversary trip to the place we spent our honeymoon."

"Oh, Chad! What a wonderful idea. But you know how much I hate surprises," she said, trying to look stern in the dim light. "We can still go. My appointment with Jaclyn is on Tuesday. We can drive up to Asheville on Monday and spend the day window shopping. We'll head over to the cabin as soon as I'm finished on Tuesday. Maybe Wednesday morning, if the session goes long." Placing a hand on his cheek, she kissed his lips lightly before pulling back with a gasp.

"What about Lydia? Oh my, I had planned on her staying here with you. Now I'll need to figure out whether to let her come with us or find someone—"

Chad put a finger on her lips, silencing her outburst. "I've got it covered. Terry's going to watch her. He's thrilled to have her all to himself, and I've got a feeling she'll be spoiled beyond fixing when we get home."

Alex smiled, knowing how much truth he spoke.

Rolling back over, she snuggled close to him as she recounted how much fun she'd had working with Meredith packing boxes. Within seconds, she heard the gentle rumble of his soft snoring.

Smiling, Alex closed her eyes. Her final thought before she drifted off was one more drowsy prayer of thanks for her husband.

§§§

As excited as she was to get away for their anniversary, Alex had to force herself to be disciplined in her preparation for Jaclyn's interview. She wanted to make sure the best pieces she'd made recently were complete and packaged for the trip. Jaclyn liked to have her guests show their creations on camera while explaining the creative process, describing what difficulties or surprises they'd encountered along the way, and sharing what they learned in the creation of the pieces on exhibit. Alex had plenty of before and after photos of the things she planned to take, which she felt would make her discussion more meaningful and easier to understand. Sometimes when she told people she made home décor from discarded items, the glazed look in their eyes indicated they had no idea what she was talking about.

She also had to verify her contact information for Jaclyn to display during the broadcast, notify her miniscule band of Instagram followers of the upcoming episode, and make sure she had enough business cards to leave behind. She took great pleasure in crossing things off her lengthy to-do list, but it was times like this she could really use a bit of help.

On a whim, Alex found Riker's number and tapped her foot while waiting for the girl to answer. It had been months since she'd talked to the brilliant young woman who'd catered Alex and Chad's wedding. At the time, Riker and her friend, Blakely, baker extraordinaire, had been Together for Good residents in their final stages of both their pregnancies and their culinary education.

"R and B's Café. How can we make your life more delicious today?"

Alex smiled when she heard Riker's cheery voice.

Encouraged by the success of the wedding, the pair had gone into business following the births of their sons, which occurred within two weeks of each other. Alex had both encouraged and invested in their fledgling business, eager to see other residents pursue their dreams.

"Hey, Riker, how's it going?" Alex asked.

She had to pull the phone away from her ear at Riker's shrill scream of delight.

"Alex! It's so good to hear from you. How are you doing?"

"Great. Tell me all about little Killian."

Alex laughed as Riker regaled her with the latest milestones her baby had achieved, including sitting up and cutting his first tooth.

"How about you? And Chad and Lydia? Everyone's doing well?"

"We're all fine. I really need to make some time to sit down with you ladies and just check in. But I'm wondering if maybe you can help me with something."

"Anything. Just name it."

Alex explained how her life had gotten so crazy lately, with Miss Matilda's recuperation, the upcoming interview, and the growing business. She left out news about the miscarriage, still unable to bring it up in a normal conversation.

"So, I'm looking for someone to help me a little bit. Nothing full-time, really. Just a few hours a week." Alex went on to explain the kinds of things she needed help with, hoping Riker might know someone from her school who would fit the bill and welcome the experience.

"Actually, I may have just the person for you. He's still a student, but he's a super hard worker. I'll send you his contact info and let him know you may be reaching out to him." Before Riker finished describing the young man, Alex's phone dinged with his phone number.

"Thanks, Riker. Tell Blakely I said hi. And y'all figure out a time that would be good to have coffee and chat. Bye."

Alex looked at the phone number. Did she have the guts to make the call and potentially give up some small level of control over her life and business?

A few hours later, Alex sat across from Landry Kline on the patio that she and Miss Matilda had recently vacated after lunch. Riker had hit the nail on the head. Landry's impressive resume, professional appearance, and intelligent questions pegged him as a standout in the school's soon-to-be graduating class. The same school Alex had graduated from last year.

He appeared to be quite young; maybe twenty-one or so. He wore his blond hair short, and Alex could see comb marks in the liberal amount of product he applied. His green eyes were wide and bright against his tanned, unlined face. Alex worried, though, that despite his youth, he might be overqualified and, thus, underutilized in the position she had available.

"So, Landry, your grades are excellent. And I see you've been working with some local businesses on their email marketing campaigns." Alex looked over the description of Landry's work in digital business marketing, and her head spun.

Have I ever done any digital business marketing? I don't think so.

"Yes, ma'am. And, may I say for the record, I'm so honored to have this opportunity. You're practically a legend at school, Mrs. White." He gazed at her like a star-struck teenager, rendering Alex speechless.

"Um ... Okay. I can't imagine why, but—"

"Mrs. White! So accomplished and modest, too. Everything the instructors have said really is true." Landry folded his hands on the table in front of him, leaning slightly toward Alex.

She shook her head, her eyes inviting him to continue.

"You did it all, Mrs. White. Top grades in your class, started your own wildly successful business, had a baby ... all in record time. Really impressive."

Alex wiggled under the praise. She'd done what she needed to do to support herself and her child and had never seen anything exceptional in it.

She tried to redirect the conversation to Landry's interview.

"Well, I appreciate the compliment. And you may call me Alex."

He blushed.

"So, Landry, you understand I only need someone to help me get my pieces ready for shipment a couple of times a month, right?"

"Yes, ma'am. And that shouldn't be any trouble at all. I'm sure you've got everything set up to automatically generate your labels and notify the courier service of a pickup."

Alex's expression went blank. *What is he talking about?*

"What I wanted to suggest, if I may," he continued, "is that you coordinate your social media posts with your shipments. You know, shoot some live footage of you packing your pieces, and then post it for your followers. Create a buzz."

What? Buzzing was for bees.

Alex felt positively ancient. This had to be some more of the high-tech approach to business that she'd avoided for so long. Initially, the avoidance had been out of a need for privacy and safety. Now, years later, she only wanted to pawn it off on someone else. It looked as if she'd found the ideal someone, too.

"Um ... Landry, I don't have any idea what you're talking about. Besides word-of-mouth, my marketing plan consists of business cards to put in some of the local stores. I designed a website, but it's pretty basic. And I've got a few followers on my social media ... I think." She felt as if she were now the one being interviewed and Landry was assessing her performance.

"Don't worry, Alex," Landry said, patting her hand. "I can help you. Riker said you're absolutely swamped with all your work and personal commitments. We can sync your business and personal calendars for peak efficiency. And, of course, I'll create social accounts specifically for the business." He was taking notes now. "May I see one of those business cards, please? I want to make sure your branding is consistent across all media."

When she handed him one of the little cards that contained her name and cell number, his face fell. He turned it over. Blank.

"Where's your logo? Your tagline? Business email address? Website?"

"I don't have the first two. And, I do all of my business from my personal email. Is that a problem? And ... um ... my website is pretty sparse. I can send you the link, and you can see what you think ..." Alex trailed off lamely.

She could see Landry was schooling his features, trying to act as if he weren't about to speak to a child.

"What I'm about to ask is not meant with any disrespect, but what did y'all cover in the online marketing course in school?"

Alex wrinkled her nose and shook her head. She explained she'd been signed up for it during the pandemic. The instructor had become ill and had to be hospitalized for several weeks. When the school couldn't find anyone else to teach the course on such short notice, they waived the class for Alex's group.

"I never really had the time to backtrack and pick it up. And, to be perfectly honest with you, Landry, I kept my online presence to a minimum out of safety for Lydia and me. But things have changed now. I'm ready to take on the internet."

Landry nodded, the corners of his mouth twitching as he tried to keep from smiling. "All the more reason to let me help you. I'll handle your branding and online presence. You concentrate on your beautiful creations."

"Thank you. But, do I really need those things? And, if so, why?" Alex thought she was doing just fine the way things were. She could feel herself resisting what this bright young man was suggesting.

"You do need them. For consistency, recognition, building trust among your customer base."

"But, shouldn't my work speak for itself?"

"Absolutely. And, this way, if you find yourself considering branching out, you'll be set. People will already be acquainted with the quality and imaginativeness associated with your designs."

"Branching out into what? I'm happy doing what I do." She prickled at the thought of her life changing course again.

"You mentioned you've already booked an interview spot, right?

That's likely to lead to other appearances—TV and radio, podcasts. And, what if you find yourself wanting to capture your great ideas in a book? You'll be instantly recognizable, which, of course, in business translates into marketable."

Alex's head spun with all of Landry's ideas, but the more she considered what he proposed, the more wisdom she saw in finally moving her successful business into the current century.

Reaching across the table, she extended her hand, and he gripped it in a firm handshake. "Welcome aboard, Landry. When can you start?"

Old Friends

With about ten days left to prepare for the recording of her Kingdom Kreatives' episode, Alex spent the morning hard at work, sawing, gluing, and nailing. She felt good about the pieces she'd take with her and decided to treat herself by breaking for lunch a bit early.

She'd invited Landry to join her and Miss Matilda later today. He'd called yesterday to let her know he'd finished with three logo proposals for her review and needed her decision before proceeding. Alex thought Miss Matilda would enjoy being a part of the selection process.

Setting her phone on the counter beside the workshop sink, she saw she'd missed a call. Easy to do when power tools were in use. She'd had her noise-cancelling headphones blasting her favorite Christian radio station. Her watch and rings sat safely tucked into her little mint box-turned-jewelry box she'd made for the workshop. When Alex worked, she was unplugged. Just the way she liked it.

Alex picked up the phone and glanced at the caller ID, her heart racing. Dr. Sheffield.

In an instant, the omelet she'd planned on making to surprise Miss Matilda didn't seem so appetizing. She dried her hands and tapped her phone to listen to the message.

"Hi, Alex. Dr. Sheffield here. Hey, I'm just following up to make sure you're feeling okay. We talked about waiting three months to start trying to get pregnant again, and you're safely in that window of time now. Let me know if there's anything I can do or any questions I can answer. Bye."

Alex closed her eyes as Dr. Sheffield spoke. Three months. Not a day went by that Alex didn't think about the baby who could have been growing within her now. And not a day went by that she didn't feel some level of responsibility for the fact that it wasn't.

She could honestly say, however, that, with time and Chad's love and encouragement, she'd begun to experience true healing. Not just physically, but emotionally and mentally, too. She felt as if she could finally see the end of a long, dark tunnel, looking forward to basking in the glorious sunshine as she emerged. She'd always remember the darkness, but she had every reason to revel in the light.

Three months sounded like a long time, but she and Chad had been so busy this summer that it had flown by. Moving the Dixons into Together for Good, making sure Miss Matilda kept up with her exercises—old ladies could be surprisingly stubborn—adopting a kitten—what were they thinking?—researching and brainstorming wise and productive ways to invest the inheritance and, of course, both Alex and Chad worked hard keeping their respective businesses going strong, which for Alex meant taking on Landry as an employee.

Alex remembered how busy last summer had been when she'd graduated, visited Woodvale, and gotten married within a few short weeks. It had felt like a whirlwind then, but this summer, with all its ups and downs, seemed even crazier somehow.

Am I insane for wanting to add another baby into the mix right now?

She tucked the question away and rapped on the door between the cottage's kitchen and her workshop, smiling when she heard Miss Matilda give a little shout in answer.

Midnight unfolded her fluffy white body from her bed tucked under Alex's workbench and strolled toward the garage door, yawning and stretching as she went. It hadn't taken her long to learn the knock meant Alex was heading for the kitchen and, potentially, a little treat.

Alex continued smiling as she scooped the kitten up, marveling at how she'd grown since they'd gotten her, before turning her thoughts to lunch preparation.

She couldn't wait for Landry and Miss Matilda to meet each other.

§§§

"Where did you learn to make such wonderful omelets?" Matilda asked after she had cleaned her plate.

"Chad taught me. He says it's one of his best bachelor skills." Alex smiled as she carried their plates from the kitchen table to the sink. "I like to keep our lunches interesting, Miss Matilda. Can't have you getting bored with your accommodations, can we?" Alex chatted as she rinsed the plates and loaded the dishwasher.

Knowing Alex wouldn't let her help clean up, Matilda vacated her chair and walked toward the door at a careful pace, her cane tapping with each step. She saw Alex check her watch before pushing the button to start the coffee pot.

These kids are always in such a rush to go places. To do things. They should slow down a bit.

"You could let me fix lunch occasionally, you know?" Matilda bristled, growing more uneasy every day with the idea of being waited on for such an extended time. She felt more like a burden than a guest now. She was more than capable of doing basic tasks, like fixing lunch.

"I enjoy doing it, Miss Matilda," Alex assured her, holding the door open for the older lady to spend some time outside in the gorgeous weather. "But, if you want to talk about taking over lunch duty a couple of days a week, I guess I could live with that."

"That sounds fine," she said, patting Alex's arm. "Let's start when y'all get back from your anniversary trip."

Alex agreed and hugged her friend, but not before Matilda caught her looking down the driveway. Matilda wondered what had the girl so distracted.

With a shrug, she concentrated on good posture as she and her colorful cane, a gift from the even more colorful Charmain, made slow but steady progress down the steps and to the patio table that sat between the house and the cottage.

"I've got a favor to ask," Alex said, getting the older lady settled in her seat.

"Anything, dear. You know I'm always available to help out however I'm able."

"I have a new employee stopping by to show me some things he's been working on. I'd really love your opinion."

"What kinds of things, dear? You know I don't know anything about how you make those beautiful pieces of yours. I'm all thumbs."

Alex shook her head and giggled. "No, ma'am. Nothing like that. He's got some logo designs. Although, for the life of me, I have no idea why I need a logo. And he's got some marketing ideas." Alex sighed, clearly frustrated. "I know I need some help, Miss Matilda. I'm just not sure how practical, or necessary, all of Landry's grandiose ideas are."

"Where did you find him?" Matilda narrowed her eyes as she racked her brain to associate the familiar name with a face.

"He came highly recommended by Riker. She said he's done amazing things for their business."

"Well, dear, I know you trust Riker. Why not give the young man a chance? Hm?"

Alex nodded, but her attention was quickly redirected to the little compact car pulling into the driveway. She squeezed Matilda's hand before walking out to meet her new assistant.

Matilda sat at the table, watching Alex's retreating back.

§§§

"Landry," Alex said, shaking the young man's hand. "Thanks for coming back out. I should probably set up a space for you somewhere."

The thought hit Alex out of the blue. She'd never had to worry about anyone else when she went into work mode. As a mom, she constantly had Lydia on her mind. As a wife, she tried to care for her husband and be by his side whenever he needed her. But as a business owner, she'd always gone it alone.

That was about to change.

"Thanks, Mrs. Wh—"

Alex held up a hand to stop him.

"I mean, thanks, Alex." His perfect smile gleamed against his tanned face. "I can work remotely, but I'd love to have a little space close by. It would allow me to get pics of you in action."

Is all of that really necessary?

Instead of voicing her question, Alex smiled and led Landry to the patio table where Miss Matilda waited.

"Landry, I'd like to introduce you to—"

"Miss Matilda!"

"Landry! I thought your name sounded familiar when Alex said it. How's your mom?"

Alex stood back and let the impromptu reunion run its course. The pair before her—a tall, tan, blond, professional-looking young man and a tiny, gray-haired, aging lady—chatted like long-lost friends.

I should have remembered everyone in Burton has some kind of connection to everyone else. Or, at least, what everyone else is doing.

"So, exactly how do you two know each other?" Alex waited for a lull in their conversation before trying to remind them that she was indeed still there.

"Oh, Alex, I'm so sorry. I've known Miss Matilda my entire life. In fact, you could say it was because of her I'm even here at all." He looked at their mutual friend with adoration.

Miss Matilda waved him off, blushing at his praise. "Landry's mom came to Together for Good. She was young and scared, had nowhere else to turn. I just helped her see past the fear. Like I try to do with all my girls."

Landry hugged her one last time before taking a seat and pulling out his laptop. Alex excused herself to get coffee, leaving Miss Matilda to chat with the young man as he got set up.

When they were all settled with their coffee and situated around the screen, Landry showed them his ideas for Alex's business. He pitched logos and slogans. He showed her plans for a slick new website, with capabilities for online sales direct to the consumer. He proposed ditching the business cards for QR codes. He typed notes and made adjustments as the ladies gave their comments and suggestions.

"How about QR codes on the business cards?" Alex asked. "It's so hard to completely give up something I'm so attached to."

"That's a great idea," Landry agreed, typing furiously as he spoke. "That way, the old schoolers—um, no offense, ladies. Anyway, those who prefer a business card can still have one. And the techies can scan the code and access your website."

An hour later, the coffee was long gone, and Alex felt good about the marketing strategy Landry planned to implement. She also felt good about Landry. He'd listened to her input, helped her get over her hesitancy, answered her questions, and incorporated her ideas.

Lord, thank You for this energetic, young genius You sent my way.

§§§

As Matilda watched Landry work, a sense of awe and pride swelled within her.

So confident and skilled. Thank You, Lord, for showing me the difference my work makes. And thank You for his mama's decision to give him a shot at life.

When their al fresco meeting was over, Matilda knew she'd need to start on her four trips up the driveway and back. She took a certain pride in the fact she was finally able to achieve a mile-long walk. She'd worked hard all summer to build up to that distance, and she felt stronger than she had in a long time.

Maybe her accident—*oh, call it what it was, Matilda!* Fine … Her *stroke* was God's way of getting her attention. Maybe it truly was time to take a step back from the work that she'd done so faithfully her whole adult life.

The problem was that she didn't know if she could take her hands off the day-to-day operation. Could she be content watching the Dixons change the way she'd always done things? And, most importantly, would there even be anything to keep her busy, make her feel useful and needed, once she moved back?

One thing Matilda knew for certain, though, was if God was calling her to do something, He'd surely reveal it, in His time.

Lord, give me strength and patience to wait on You.

Going on a Trip

"Will Bubba take me to see the chickens at Miss 'Tilda's?" Lydia almost popped with excitement as she grabbed her favorite toys and nightgown before shoving them into her miniature suitcase.

"I'm not sure, sweetie." Alex didn't want to commit Terry to anything he wasn't prepared to deliver. "You'll just have to wait and see. But, what did we talk about?"

"I know, Mommy," Lydia said. Alex was shocked her daughter had perfected the eye-roll at her young age. "I have to say *please* and *thank you*. And no back-talk. And brush my teeth. And don't in … What's that word, Mommy?"

"Insult. Don't insult your Bubba's cooking." Alex smiled at the last directive she'd given her daughter in an attempt to spare Terry's feelings. He was a terrible cook.

"Yep. And use my manners with Miss Meredith." Lydia scrunched her face, as if trying to remember something. "Is that all, Mommy?"

"Be sure you say your prayers."

"Oh yeah! Bubba wouldn't let me forget that one." Lydia pulled the zipper around her sparsely packed luggage and tugged it off her bed.

"We've got about an hour before we need to go. Why don't you leave that here, and I'll bring it down when I bring mine?"

Alex shooed the little girl downstairs to play with Midnight while she gathered the necessary clothing and toiletries that her daughter would need for her several-day stay.

She'd wisely asked Charmain to check in on the pair a couple of times to make sure all was going well. Of course, she hadn't let Terry know. He really would be insulted to think Alex didn't find him competent to care for his little sister.

After cramming all Lydia's essentials into her tiny suitcase, Alex leaned on the top with her elbow as she slid the zipper around. She placed the bulging pink bag at the top of the stairs then went to finish her own packing, which included a few special items that had to make it to their anniversary trip, undetected by her husband. A knock at the front door halted her progress.

"Ugh. Who could that be? Today, of all days." Alex sighed before calling to Chad, who was downstairs, eating breakfast, oblivious to the frantic preparations that were going on above his head.

"Honey, would you see who that is, please?" She hoped it was a salesman or someone Chad could easily send packing, because packing was exactly what she needed to finish doing!

Hearing Chad invite the visitor in, Alex ran her fingers through her hair and checked the mirror to make sure she didn't have mascara rings under her eyes.

I still need to shower, do my makeup and hair, load the bags, get Lydia to Terry's ... How am I going to make it all happen in less than an hour?

Alex's frantic thoughts raced through her head as she turned the corner into the kitchen. She put the brakes on when she saw Terry and Chad talking.

§§§

"Terry! What are you doing here? I thought I was bringing Lydia to your place?" Confusion clouded Alex's face, but Chad and Terry just grinned at her like they knew some secret. Finally, Terry spoke.

"Chad called. He said you were freaking out—"

"Terry's words, not mine. I said you were a little stressed," Chad clarified for his wife.

"Anyway, I offered to pick Lydia up on my way back from town. Blakely asked me to drop the cake off." Terry motioned to the clear plastic cake container on the counter.

At Alex's puzzled look, Chad answered her unspoken question. "I asked Blakely to recreate the top layer of our wedding cake for our anniversary."

Alex felt tears threaten. What a ridiculously sweet gesture. Last year, as Blakely had been preparing the top tier of their cake for freezing, to be enjoyed on their first anniversary, Alex had decided to make it Marquis and Yvonne's wedding cake. With the hectic pace of life recently, she hadn't given a second thought to Blakely's promised replacement for them to have when celebrating their first year of marriage. Even though their actual anniversary had been yesterday, they'd agreed to postpone celebrating until after the show. The fact that Chad had the foresight to plan for a cake spoke volumes.

Alex turned away from the men, pretending to inspect the gorgeous, intricate details of the confection. When she felt she had a better grasp of her emotions, she turned and threw her arms around her husband.

"You're the absolute best. Thank you." She stood on her tiptoes and planted a kiss on his lips, totally taking him off guard.

Terry squirmed on the other side of the kitchen. "Well, I'll just go find Lyddie Bug, and we'll get going."

"Sorry, Terry. Yes, of course." Alex stammered, a bit embarrassed by her open display of affection in front of Terry. For the most part, she and Chad were pretty reserved in public. "I think she's in the living room with Midnight."

Terry's face blanched. "Am I taking Midnight, too?" He had little experience caring for a young child, but he had even less knowledge of how to care for a pet.

"No," Alex managed around a laugh. "Midnight's moving to the cottage for a few days. Charmain and Miss Matilda have agreed to watch her. Lydia may want to come visit, though."

Alex saw Terry relax before she left the kitchen in search of her daughter.

Chad retrieved the over-stuffed luggage from upstairs, and then Terry and Lydia were soon on their way.

Alex watched them both as Terry maneuvered the car out of the driveway and saw the sheer joy on their faces. And, why not? With the top down on the car, music blasting, and slices of cake carefully packed for them to enjoy later, life was good for them.

What a blessing they were to each other.

And to me.

"So, Mrs. White," Chad startled Alex out of her reverie, "are you all packed and ready to go? Let's get this anniversary trip started."

"Yes, I'm packed. No, I'm not ready to go." Alex took his hand as they walked back inside. "Give me a few minutes, though, and I'll be all set."

"Cool. That should give me plenty of time to pack."

Again, Alex marveled at the seemingly simple life her husband led.

§§§

In all their bustling to get Lydia's belongings stashed in the car, get her safely buckled in her car seat, and say their endless goodbyes, nobody noticed the nondescript beige car drive by the house. Slowly. Three times.

Dottie Comstock smiled a triumphant grin. She loved when she gleaned a juicy tidbit of gossip without even trying.

Not wanting to be too conspicuous, Dot found a spot across from the house where she could park her car and continue her stealthy observations.

I knew Terry was Lydia's father! Matilda Gault can deny it all she wants, but I know the facts when I see them. He and Alex must have a shared custody agreement. Wait until the girls hear about this.

She'd have to be careful, though. She didn't want it getting back to Matilda. That woman scared Dottie, even in her convalescent state.

Matilda kept insisting Terry and the little girl were not father and daughter, but that made absolutely no sense. Dottie wasn't a fool. She knew about things. And she felt it her duty to ensure other folks in town knew them, too.

Dottie's vantage point, parked behind a dense clump of bushes, provided the perfect place for her to watch and learn. Terry never saw her car sitting on the side of the road as he eased his convertible out of the Whites' driveway. He and Lydia were too engrossed in singing along with whatever song played on the radio.

Well, isn't that just the coziest little daddy/daughter date you've ever seen?

§§§

Alex fidgeted as Chad took his time folding and refolding shirts, placing everything neatly into his luggage and moving back and forth from the dresser to his bag every time he forgot an important item—socks, a belt, a swimsuit.

"Well, that should do it," he finally announced. "You ready for me to take yours down with mine?" he asked as he picked up his suitcase.

"Um, not yet. I need to put a bit of makeup on, then I'll pack all my toiletries. You go ahead."

"Okay. Don't take too long. Remember, we've got dinner reservations in Asheville. Britt will kill us if we're late."

"I remember. Hey, why don't you get Midnight's things and take her out to Miss Matilda while I finish up? She should be up and dressed by now."

"Will do."

Within seconds, Alex heard his heavy footsteps cross the kitchen, followed by the door closing. She ran to their bedroom window and peeked out. When he finally knocked on Miss Matilda's door and stepped inside, she raced to her dresser.

Nestled beneath her paint-smudged work shirts was the little white bag that held Chad's anniversary gift. After peeking inside and ensuring everything was still intact, she tucked it carefully away among her clothes, not visible at first glance. She wanted to make sure Chad couldn't see it on the off-chance he decided to open her bag.

Her heart fluttered at the thought of giving her husband the gift.

"Hey," he called. She hadn't heard him come back inside, so the sound of his voice made her jump. "You 'bout ready to go?"

"Um ... Gimme five minutes! I promise!" For once, Alex was grateful for her mommy beauty regimen, which required her to brush her teeth and apply eye makeup at the same time, swipe on lipstick and deodorant simultaneously, then slip on sandals and fluff her hair as she headed out the door. She was downstairs with her suitcase in three minutes.

Chad whisked the case out of her hand and carried it to his truck. She grabbed her purse, a monstrosity only marginally smaller than her suitcase, and verified she had her phone, tablet, and sketch pad.

Glancing at her phone, she saw a message from Jaclyn and froze, praying nothing had gone wrong at the last minute. She tapped the screen, scanned the message, and heaved a huge sigh of relief.

Received the shipment Landry sent. Love the pieces and can't wait to meet you. See you soon. J

In just over a week, hiring Landry had proven to be one of the best decisions she'd ever made. Already she felt more relaxed. He'd taken so much pressure off her.

Making a mental note to make sure he received a generous Christmas bonus, Alex hauled her purse over her shoulder and locked the door behind her.

Chad was waiting beside his freshly-washed truck, holding the passenger door open for her.

This was going to be a great trip.

Sleepy

The valets for the chic French restaurant scanned their phone code then disappeared to retrieve the cars. Alex hugged Brittany, whispering her desire to hear more about the new boyfriend, Derrick. He didn't hear the girls discussing him as he raved to Chad about the new sushi restaurant in Asheville. Brittany watched his every move with adoration, the way Alex hoped she still looked when she saw Chad.

"Next time y'all come to town, we'll have to meet at the raw bar for dinner," Derrick said.

"Well, Derrick"—Chad chuckled, glancing at Alex—"you see, where I come from, we tend to prefer our fish cooked. I'm not much of a sushi person."

"I get it. It's kind of an acquired taste," Derrick agreed. "We'll figure something out."

Alex tried to stifle a yawn.

Where are those valets? I'm about to fall over I'm so tired.

"Hey," Brittany said, noticing Alex's sleepy eyes. "You better get back to the hotel and rest. We've got a busy day tomorrow."

"*We*? You're coming to Jaclyn's for the recording?" This was the first Alex had heard about Brittany accompanying them to the Kingdom Kreatives' studio.

"I wouldn't miss it. Plus, I've never been invited before, so I'm kinda dying to see how it goes down." Excitement shone in Britt's big brown eyes, the expertly applied smoky eyeshadow exaggerating their size. "Are you ready?"

A huge laugh exploded from Chad, and Alex lowered her eyes.

"I may have spent the entire drive up here going over the questions Jaclyn sent me. I know it's not a scripted show, but I want to be prepared for whatever she asks. I'm pretty exhausted now, though. I've been fretting over getting us all ready for this trip for days. Not to mention all the preparation for the show."

"I think you may be missing the point of a casual interview," Brittany said, reaching out to touch Alex's arm.

"And an anniversary trip," Chad said, but his voice held no rancor, only a gentle teasing and immense patience.

These two people, the ones who knew her better than anyone and loved her anyway, would be with her tomorrow. The thought calmed her nerves a bit but did nothing to revive her bone-tired body.

The cars arrived, and the couples took possession of their respective vehicles.

"See you tomorrow!" Brittany called from the open window of Derrick's BMW.

Alex settled into the seat of Chad's truck, and they drove through the velvety darkness with the windows rolled down. The chill of early fall hadn't quite set in, but the furnace of mid-summer had definitely retreated, providing some much-appreciated relief.

"That was nice," Chad said.

"Mmhmm." Closing her eyes, Alex let her head relax against the seat. The huge king bed in their hotel room beckoned to her.

"What do you think of Derrick?"

Chad's voice sounded as if it was coming from down a long hallway, distant and distorted. No matter how hard she tried, though, she couldn't form a response to send back down the endless corridor. Strange, water-colored images floated before her field of vision of Terry walking Midnight on a leash, Chad eating sushi, cameras and bright lights.

"Babe," Chad gently tugged at the black fog surrounding her. "Babe, we're at the hotel. Can you walk?"

As Alex slowly surfaced from her stupor, she heard the frantic note in Chad's tone and nodded, trying to remove her seat belt.

"I've already unbuckled you, and I have your purse, which, by the way, the coroner could use as a body bag. Are you sure you're feeling well, honey?"

With her purse slung over his shoulder, he cupped her elbow with the other hand.

"I'm fine. I'm just exhausted. Everything's finally catching up with me, I guess. A good night's sleep will do wonders."

Alex was so thankful they'd stopped at the hotel on their way into town to check in, get their bags unloaded, and freshen up a bit before wandering downtown then meeting Britt and Derrick. The thought of having to carry her luggage right now ... well, it simply wouldn't have happened.

They waved at the attendant at the desk and boarded the elevator. Once the doors whooshed shut behind them, Chad took both of Alex's shoulders in his strong, gentle hands.

"Listen, you draw yourself a bath as soon as we get in the room. I'll get your pajamas out of your suitcase—"

"No!"

Alex was suddenly wide awake. She'd taken too much care with his surprise anniversary gift to let him discover it unceremoniously by retrieving her nightgown.

Shaking her head, she caught sight of them in the mirror that covered the entire back of the elevator. Chad with her enormous pink and aqua embroidered bag hanging from his shoulder. Her with raccoon eyes from her recent nap. And was that dried drool on her cheek? The absurdity of it all was more than she could handle.

Alex giggled, trying to tamp down the hysteria she felt bubbling within her.

"What?" Chad asked, looking at his wife as if she'd finally lost her mind. For real this time.

Alex pointed at the mirror, putting a hand over her mouth to contain her laughter, and hide the drool path. Her sparkling eyes caught Chad's in the mirror, noting the exact moment he recognized what an odd-looking pair they made.

Their laughter had subsided only a little as they stood outside their room. Chad struggled around the bag hanging from his shoulder to reach his wallet and retrieve their key card. The sight set off another round of giggles from Alex, and she reached over and took her purse from him.

"Would you set the alarm for seven?" she asked, kicking her shoes off and collapsing on the bed.

"Really? Your appointment isn't until ten, right?" Chad asked, grabbing his toiletry kit and disappearing into the bathroom.

"Yeah, but I don't want to be late."

"Seven ought to do it, then," he said, squeezing toothpaste onto his toothbrush.

Alex pulled her nightgown out of her bag and had it on in a matter of seconds.

I'll just wait for him to finish in the bathroom before I wash my face and brush my teeth.

It was the last thought she had before drifting back to sleep. She had no recollection of Chad gently draping the extra blanket over her before he eased himself into his side of the bed.

§§§

She awoke a little after two a.m., disoriented and with her mouth tasting like dirty gym socks.

She heard Chad's gentle snuffling. The one tiny moonbeam making its way through the gap in the heavy curtains fell on his face. His strawberry-blond hair poked out in all directions, the result of his typically restless sleep habits. Now, though, he was the picture of peace. She loved that handsome, boyish face so deeply that she sometimes thought it would consume her.

Alex dared not touch him. Deep sleep was a luxury that usually eluded him.

She eased herself off the bed, tiptoed to the bathroom, and eased the door shut behind her. Once her teeth and face were clean and her bladder was empty, she padded back to bed, pulling the covers back and slipping between the crisp sheets.

Chad stirred, so she stayed motionless until his steady breathing resumed. She thought of the gift she had hiding in her suitcase, and her heart jumped with the anticipation of seeing him open it.

Within minutes, Alex fell back to sleep with a smile on her face.

It's Show Time

"**W**hat in the world was I thinking?" Alex's heart raced as she struggled to breathe normally. "This dress is all wrong. I look like a cow. What am I gonna do?"

Chad looked up from his coffee and newspaper, oblivious to the tempest brewing in their hotel room.

"You look beautiful, sweetie. You always do."

"Chad, you have to say nice things about me—I'm your wife. I need the truth."

"Maybe if you call Britt ..." He left the thought hanging in the air, but it was enough to plant an idea in his frantic wife's brain.

"Of course." She planted a wet kiss on his cheek as she strode barefoot across the room to grab her phone. "You're a genius sometimes, Mr. White."

Chad grinned. "I like those words coming from you."

But Alex wasn't paying attention to Chad basking in his stroke of brilliance. She already had Brittany on a video call.

"Britt! Help." Alex panned the phone up and down her body, displaying the unacceptable choice of attire. "This is the only dress I brought, but I have no idea what I was thinking. It's all wrong for the show."

Alex waited while Brittany, her mouth puckered and drawn to one side, inspected her friend. She tilted her head back and forth. Finally, she snapped her fingers.

"Did you bring any leggings?"

"Yes." Alex's voice held some hesitation.

"A jean jacket or a cardigan?"

"Yeah."

"How 'bout a cute pair of boots?"

"Britt, I don't see how inventorying my entire vacation wardrobe—"

"Shh …" Brittany held up a hand in front of the phone screen to halt Alex's ranting. "Bring everything I just mentioned with you to the studio. I'll take it from there."

The screen went black.

"You need me to help get any of that stuff while you finish getting ready?" Chad asked before chugging the last of his coffee.

"Um … No, thanks. I'll get it. Besides, I'll take my makeup with me and let Brittany do it, so I'm almost ready to go."

That was another close call. I'm giving him his present tonight or the secret's liable to be ruined.

While Chad brushed his teeth, Alex slipped on her ankle boots. She jammed two pairs of leggings, her jean jacket, and the comfy cable-knit cardigan she reserved for cool autumn days onto a hanger, grabbed her purse and makeup bag, and then stood at the door, tapping her foot.

Chad had been married long enough to take the hint.

Within minutes, they were in his truck, the built-in GPS guiding them to their destination. Alex sipped the coffee that she'd hurriedly poured on their way out of the hotel lobby.

"Chad, I must've been out of my mind when I agreed to do this. Why didn't you try to stop me?"

"Really?"

Alex grinned. He was right. Rarely did he object to any of her crazy ideas. Plus, Alex had been so convincing in parroting Jaclyn's arguments for being on the show that his only real concern had been the amount of time it would take in Alex's already too-full schedule. Hiring Landry had been a huge relief in that arena.

"Okay, I get it. What I don't get is why I would ever agree to doing something like this. At the time, it seemed like a great way to share how my faith journey has impacted my life. Right now, all I feel is sheer terror at being in front of a camera."

"You'll do great, babe." Chad patted her knee without taking his eyes off the unfamiliar road.

"Thanks. I know you're always my biggest cheerleader."

"Um ... Could I be called your support system? Or maybe the man behind the success? Cheerleader ... eh. Not really me."

Alex guffawed, relaxing for the first time since waking up. She'd call him anything he wanted, as long as she could count on his calming, supportive presence.

§§§

"Hm. Still needs something." Brittany tapped one pointy fingernail against her frown. She looked around the dressing room while Alex inspected her image in the mirror over the vanity.

"Britt, you're still a style genius," Alex told her friend. "This dress looked like a potato sack a few minutes ago. Now I look like I stepped out of a magazine."

She marveled at the transformation of her comfortable-yet-shapeless, rust-colored dress. Brittany had rifled through everything Alex had brought, selecting the chocolate-brown leggings and faded jean jacket. With her ankle boots and Britt's turquoise earrings, Alex looked super chic.

But Brittany walked around her friend, shaking her head and clicking her tongue against her teeth.

"It's missing something," she said.

"What? I think I look fine." Alex turned to get a better view in the mirror.

"I'm not going for 'fine' here. I'm shooting for 'spectacular.'"

Alex rolled her eyes at her friend. She understood perfectionism, but having a child had also taught Alex the concept of "good enough."

As Alex was going to make a final protest, a knock sounded at the door, and the women looked at each other, eyes wide.

"Come in," Brittany said, finding her voice before Alex.

Chad stepped into the dressing room, his eyes locking on to his wife. He let out a low whistle. "Wow, babe. You look hot."

His comment sent both ladies into a fit of giggles.

Realizing he'd spoken so openly with Brittany standing there, Chad's cheeks flushed red, and he rubbed his neck. Alex wrapped her arms around his waist and rested her cheek against his chest, drawing strength from him.

Brittany snapped her fingers before asking, "Hey, Chad, do you need your belt?"

"What?" Alex and Chad asked at the same time.

"I've got an idea. Can I borrow it? I'll give it back after the show."

Chad looked at Alex, who shrugged and tilted her head. She had no idea where Britt was going with this crazy request, but having known her as long as she had, Alex guessed Brittany had a brilliant idea brewing.

Chad removed his belt and quickly disappeared out the door to wait for the show to begin recording.

"What in the world, Britt? Why do you need Chad's belt?"

"This is the final piece to your outfit," Brittany answered as she wrapped the belt around Alex's waist.

"It's way too bi—"

"Shh ... I know it's too big. That's the point. If I loop it like this ... and pull this end through here ..." She worked like a seasoned sailor on a boat, and Alex's shapeless dress was soon cinched at the waist. The end of the belt hung off-center, adding another layer of interest.

"One last swipe of lipstick, and you're good to go," Brittany announced.

Alex swiped as instructed, feeling tears of gratitude stinging her eyes. If she cried and ruined her makeup before going on camera, her best friend would surely kill her. She blinked a few times to steady her emotions before turning around.

"You look … well, hot!" Britt said.

Laughing, they left the dressing room, arm in arm.

§§§

"Alex, that was a great segment. You're a natural in front of the camera." Jaclyn shook Alex's hand when they wrapped up shooting a few hours later.

The recording space wasn't huge, but none of Alex's pieces appeared crowded. And Jaclyn took pride in her set design, providing her artist guests with comfy chairs for the interviews. Her cheery logo hung on the homey shiplap background. And the lighting, Alex wondered if the local football stadium might be missing a few bulbs. Overall, Alex felt the professionalism in everything about Jaclyn's production, which put her at ease.

"Thank you for this opportunity, Jaclyn. I gotta tell you, you made it much easier than I expected it to be."

Looking at her watch, Alex couldn't believe how late it was. Although she'd been well-prepared for Jaclyn's questions, they'd done several takes with some of the pieces to make sure the camera angle and lighting were just right. So much went into making the show that Alex had never even thought about.

"So, what's next?" Alex asked, looking around for her husband. She'd seen him about half an hour earlier, but he'd disappeared when the final scene was being filmed.

"I'll edit everything, drop in the opening sequence, add the credits—you know, all the techy stuff—and then I'll send you a file to preview. Your website address will be available to the viewers, so you may want to make sure you're set up to take questions about orders."

"Um ... That sounds like a job for Landry. Let me put that in my notes before I forget what you said."

As she was typing Jaclyn's suggestion on her tablet notes application—another genius invention that Landry had introduced her to—Alex's stomach rumbled loudly enough for Jaclyn and Britt to hear. They smiled, but not at her. They were looking over her shoulder.

"Hey, Miss YouTube Personality, I'll trade you a burger and fries for that belt you've got on." Chad held up several bags from a nearby burger chain.

"You heard the man—hand over that belt. I'm starving!" Brittany said, relieving Chad of a bag as Jaclyn cleared a table on the other side of the camera.

They chattered and shared their favorite parts of the shoot as they passed out food and settled into their chairs. Within seconds of sitting, silence reigned, their full attention directed at the juicy burgers in front of them.

Intrusion

Terry ended his video call with Alex, smiling at how excited Lydia had been to tell her mommy everything they'd been doing. The shoot had gone great, and Alex and Chad were on their way back to the hotel. Tomorrow, they'd head out early for the mountain house.

"Bubba, how many more sleeps before Mommy and Chaddie get home?" Lydia gripped her doll, Baby, in her tiny hand.

"Well, let's see." Terry pulled up the calendar on his phone. "We had one sleep last night, so now we've got …" He waited for her to join him in counting as he pointed to the days.

"One, two, three, four," they said together.

"Four more days. You good with that?" Terry worried his little sister would start missing Alex and go into meltdown mode. He'd heard the horror stories about her wailing the day that he and Alex had left to go to Woodvale last year.

However, Lydia, looking around the room that he'd set up as hers in his office-turned-home, looked more pensive than anguished. "Will we have time to do all the fun things we have planned, Bubba?"

Terry smiled as he scooped her up in his arms, spinning around until she giggled. "We will if we get started right now. Why don't we head downtown to the ice cream shop and get us some cones? We can pick up a pint of Aunt Tilley's favorite flavor and take it by her house on our way home to fix dinner. Sound good?"

Lydia bolted to the front door as she screamed, "Yay! Ice cream! Miss 'Tilda!"

Having never raised a child, Terry wasn't sure if it was too late for ice cream before dinner, but he didn't worry about it. He was the surrogate grandparent, the fun uncle. Whatever label outsiders wanted to put on it, he was the person who got to spoil the little girl, and he took his role as the captain of fun seriously.

§§§

Dottie could hardly believe her luck. Terry Lovell and the little girl, who nobody believed was his daughter, were sitting together at one of the wrought iron tables on the patio in front of the ice cream parlor. Dottie parked about a block away, wanting to have an up-close encounter, not just a drive-by.

The pair were laughing, and Dottie could tell she'd made it up the block just in time. Terry was done with his cone and was helping the little girl unwrap the paper from hers.

I don't have much time.

"Well, look who it is," she called as she walked up to them, out of breath from walking the short distance. She thought she saw Terry tense at the sound of her voice, but maybe she'd just startled him.

"Hello, Mrs. Comstock. How are you today?"

"Please, Terry, how many times do I have to tell you to call me Dottie? Your aunt and I go way back." She patted his arm as she plopped uninvited into a vacant seat at their table.

"Aren't you just the cutest little thing?" she said, reaching for Lydia's cheek.

Lydia shrank back but was unable to escape the vise-like clamp Dottie put on the child's face. Dottie pretended not to notice the little girl rubbing the red mark.

"What brings y'all down here on this beautiful afternoon?" she asked Terry.

"We just came for some ice cream. We're going to take a pint of butter pecan by for Aunt Tilley on our way home."

As Terry answered, Lydia scrambled into his lap and buried her head against his chest. She'd abandoned her unfinished cone on the table as soon as Dottie had arrived.

"I don't see any butter pecan. Why don't you let me sit here with Laura—"

"Lydia," Terry corrected.

"Of course. I'll sit out here while you run in and get Matilda's ice cream. Go on now."

"Will you be okay out here for just a few minutes, Lyddie Bug?" he whispered.

Lydia wrapped her arms around Terry's neck and whispered something in his ear that Dottie couldn't hear. He kissed her brown hair, the sun glinting off the soft locks, and then gently sat her back in her chair.

"I'll be right back."

"Don't worry about us," Dottie cried out, waving as Terry walked in the door to the ice cream shop. "So, Lydia—that's your name, isn't it?—why are you staying with Terry?"

"Bubba's keeping me while Mommy and Chaddie are in the mountains."

"I see. And how often do your mommy and Chaddie leave you with your Bubba?" The little girl was smart. Maybe Dottie could use that to her advantage.

"This is the first time." Lydia narrowed her gaze in suspicion, so Dottie tried another tactic. She knew she needed to work fast.

"You said your mommy was with Chaddie. What about your daddy. Where is he?"

"I don't have a daddy. I have a Chaddie." Lydia stuck her chin out in a stubborn gesture that looked remarkably like Terry.

"Oh, sweetie, everyone has a daddy. Maybe your mommy just doesn't want you to know who your daddy is." Dottie delivered the agonizing words with a sickeningly sweet smile.

Seconds later, Terry walked out the shop door. When he arrived back at the table, tears pooled in Lydia's big brown eyes and her bottom lip quivered.

"Lydia, what's wrong, sweetie?"

"Everyone has a daddy," the little girl wailed.

Terry blanched before turning to Dottie, his face twisted in barely controlled rage.

"I have no idea what you said to her, but I'm telling you right now; don't you ever come around her, or Alex, or Chad again. Is that clear, Mrs. Comstock? I'll be contacting our attorney in a few moments. Do not cross me on this matter." Terry whisked the now-wailing girl into his arms and strode down the street, leaving onlookers to wonder what had happened.

And leaving Dot Comstock smiling at the knowledge that she'd touched a sensitive nerve.

Mission accomplished.

§§§

Terry paced across Aunt Tilley's kitchen, waiting for the kettle to whistle. In three long, deliberate steps, he covered the length of the compact space before he had to pivot on his heel and start over. A few feet away, Aunt Tilley stretched out in the recliner with Lydia curled up against her, both dozing.

Terry raked his hand through his hair, frustration bubbling up in him as sure as if it were the water in the kettle. Before the whistle could wake the sleeping girls, he turned off the heat and poured the steaming water into three waiting mugs. The smell of peppermint tea wafted up, tickling his nose and calming his nerves somewhat as he recalled the innumerable cups of peppermint tea Aunt Tilley had fixed him while he'd been growing up. Did anyone solve any major life issue without a cup? He didn't see how.

As he returned the kettle to the stovetop, a light rap at the cottage door was followed by Meredith quietly turning the knob and slipping inside. She looked radiant in her expensive, tailored suit, stiletto heels, and shining auburn hair gathered in an elegant, low chignon.

Terry smiled despite the trauma that he'd just allowed his little sister to endure.

She slipped off her heels and padded the few steps to greet him, standing on her tiptoes to plant a quick kiss on his cheek.

Terry handed her a mug then motioned for them to step back outside. They sank into the chairs at the patio table, and Terry let his head hang down, staring into his mug as he tried to draw strength from the familiar aroma.

"Do you want to talk about it?" Meredith placed a soft, manicured hand over his.

It was enough to breach the dam that had held back his feelings for the past hour. He poured out details of their day, how much fun they'd been having together.

When the Whites had first asked Terry to watch Lydia, he'd shared with Meredith how excited he'd been about being entrusted with the little girl's care. And they'd been having a great time.

Then Dottie had come along.

"How can one woman be so hurtful, Mere? And, why? You should've seen how Lydia shrank away from her. I'm so stupid. Even a little girl could discern what an evil person that woman is, and yet I let my little sister sit alone with her?"

"Well, you were in a public place …" Meredith began, but Terry's look quelled any further attempt at absolution.

"Don't try to make excuses for my lapse in judgment. My stomach starts to turn every time I let myself think about what could have happened."

"Then don't," Meredith said.

Terry jerked his head toward the beautiful woman, questions he couldn't begin to fashion with his words shining in his eyes.

"Sweetie, you're not an irresponsible person. Alex and Chad know that, or else they wouldn't have left Lydia with you. And, I know I'm new to this, but isn't this the kind of situation where we have to trust that God is in control?"

Terry felt as if he'd been punched in the gut. He'd grown up with a pastor for a dad, lived in a Christian home for girls, and had been instrumental in witnessing to his biological father. But, here he sat today, receiving a reminder of God's complete control from a brand-new believer. The irony brought a smile to his tense face.

"How'd you get so spiritually mature so fast?" he asked, leaning over to kiss her.

She smiled as he pulled away, lowering her lashes and raising the mug to her lips.

They sat there until the crickets began their evening song, talking and holding hands in silence when the tea was gone. Despite the tumultuous events of the day, Terry couldn't remember when he'd ever felt so at peace with his life.

Anniversary Gifts

They'd eaten their burgers late in the afternoon, so Alex and Chad decided to forgo checking out another of Asheville's fine dining establishments, opting instead to call it an early night before the trek to the mountain house in the morning.

Brittany couldn't hide her sadness. Alex, however, promised to bring Lydia back to the area around Christmastime to let the little girl take in the grandeur of Biltmore Estate in all of its holiday splendor.

"It's a date," Brittany declared, embracing her dearest friend as if she never wanted to let go.

"I'll be back in a couple of months, Britt," Alex said, though she also felt sad at having to leave her friend so soon.

Back in their hotel room, Alex tossed her boots toward the closet and peeled her leggings off before searching for her ragged sweats. Chad chuckled at the speed of her transformation from camera-ready to comfy.

"You want to rent a movie tonight? I can run down to the hotel snack shop and get some microwave popcorn. Or we could get into that delicious cake Blakely made us," Chad suggested as Alex plopped down beside him on the sofa, taking his hand in hers.

"Cake sounds good, but I thought first we could do anniversary gifts," she whispered in his ear, giving his lobe a gentle nibble before leaning back to gauge his reaction.

"Alex White," he said, pulling her close, "why do I have the distinct impression that you're up to something?" He cupped her face in his hands and kissed her leisurely.

Hating to break the spell, but knowing she couldn't keep her secret much longer, Alex pulled away, placing a finger on his puckered lips to let him know they'd pick up where they'd left off.

"Hold that thought, mister. I'll be right back." She ran to her suitcase before he had a chance to protest.

When Alex walked back to where Chad sat, confusion was written all over his face. She perched on the edge of the sofa and set the little white gift bag with a bright red bow on the coffee table in front of them.

Chad's brows drew together, and Alex knew his tolerance for the surprise would wear thin soon.

"This is kind of a two-part gift," Alex said, handing him the bag.

Chad reached in and pulled out the little envelope that sat atop the fluffy tissue paper. "Is this part one?"

Alex nodded, barely able to contain her excitement. She clasped her hands in front of her and bounced on the couch.

Chad tried to suppress a grin.

"Maybe we should just wait and do this tomorrow," he said, slipping the envelope back into the bag.

Alex swiftly swatted him on the arm. "Chad, come on. Please."

"I'm just kidding, babe. Let's see what we've got here."

He slipped his finger under the seal and pulled out the thick linen card, scanning the contents. Alex knew when he got to the good part. His eyes bulged, and he covered his mouth with his free hand. The hand holding the card began to tremble, and tears threatened to spill down his face.

"Really? How did …? When …? I don't understand!"

"Meredith helped. Well, actually, Meredith did almost everything. She's been in touch with some of her contacts in the family law practice in Burton. It should all be official very soon. Lydia will be a White by spring." Alex's voice cracked on the last sentence, but Chad didn't notice.

He jumped up from the couch and scooped her up, twirling her around the room as he whooped his joy.

"Aren't you forgetting something?" Alex asked when she could catch her breath.

"What?" Chad stopped short, gently setting her back on her feet.

She giggled at his genuine bewilderment. "It's a two-part present, remember? Don't you even want to see what else is in there?" Alex pulled him back toward the spot where the note detailing Lydia's adoption details still lay on the coffee table.

He plopped down, saying, "Babe, you need to learn how to pull off a surprise. You don't lead with the best part first. Always save the best for last." As he coached her through the finer points of presenting a surprise, he reached into the bag and pulled out a tightly wrapped ball of tissue paper.

"I'll try to remember that in the future, dear," she said, hoping he didn't catch the eye roll she gave him.

Chad ripped the tissue paper away and unrolled the T-shirt before holding it up facing away from himself.

"That's nice. A new T-shirt." He tried to hide his disappointment, but Alex laughed out loud.

"Turn it around, silly," she said, jumping up and turning it around so he could see the front. "Now read it out loud."

"'*Whites. Party of four,*'" he said. "That's sweet, honey. It'll soon be you, me, Lydia, and Midnight. That's cute."

"Nope, that's not what it means." Alex fixed her eyes on her husband, willing him to understand the true meaning of the words. She could almost see the wheels turning in his head as he put the puzzle pieces together, and she could almost hear the exact moment it all clicked.

"You mean …? You're …? Are you sure? Are you okay?" More incoherent babbling followed, which, when coupled with Alex's elation and relief at finally not having to keep the secret any longer, sent her into a fit of giggles.

She launched herself into his arms, holding on tightly as he twirled her around in a joyous dance again. Finally, he set her down, his face sobering and his mouth clenching into a serious line.

"Well, this does complicate things," he groaned as he rubbed the back of his neck.

"Why?"

"Because you got me not one but two precious children for our anniversary. All I got you were diamond earrings."

They looked at each other for a split-second, and then Alex giggled again. Before they knew it, they were both laughing until they cried. It was with tears of joy still in their eyes that they descended on the delectable little cake that Blakely had made for them, polishing it off as they shared dreams for the years ahead of them.

§§§

The next morning, Chad slipped out of the bed, showered, and then went to the hotel's restaurant for breakfast. They had about two hours in the car before they reached the mountain house, and he wanted to be sure they were well-fueled.

Balancing a tray laden with all manner of breakfast fare, he slipped into their room and watched his wife sleep. Knowing his child grew within her, a feeling unlike any he'd ever felt overwhelmed him.

"Thank you, Lord." The whispered prayer was all he could manage, but he felt certain God knew the depth of gratitude those three simple words held.

The heavenly scent of fresh-brewed coffee and bacon filled the room, waking Alex. Squinting against the bright sunlight, she looked around to find the source of the delightful aroma. Sitting up, however, seemed to change her tummy's feelings about how delicious the food smelled.

Clutching her abdomen, she bolted past Chad, who stood at the foot of the bed, still holding a tray of breakfast delights, and barely made it to the toilet. He set the tray down and rushed after her.

"Aw ... Honey, I'm so sorry. I didn't even think about morning sickness. I wanted to surprise you." He held her hair with one hand and a cool, damp washcloth with the other, placing it gently on her neck. "Should I take it away?"

Alex shook her head. "No. I think, if I could just have a little ginger ale, I'll feel better."

Within minutes, Chad had sprinted to the vending machine and was back with a cup of ice and a can of ginger ale. Alex had used his brief absence to clean up a bit and brush her hair.

Sipping the soda slowly, she smiled at her husband as he polished off the eggs and hash browns.

"You feel like eating anything yet?" he asked when his mouth was briefly empty.

"The pancakes smell great."

Alex nibbled at the fluffy, syrup-soaked pancakes and some fruit before declaring herself full.

Chad drew his brows together in concern.

"It's fine," she said, rubbing his arm to reassure him. "Within a few weeks, you'll have to wrestle me for every scrap. It won't be pretty, let me assure you. And let me also assure you"—she tapped his nose—"I will win those fights." She gave him a quick kiss on the forehead, stood, and then sauntered toward the shower.

Confessions

"What are you going to do?" The concern in Meredith's voice echoed from the depths of her blue eyes.

"I haven't decided." Terry paced back and forth across his small kitchen while Meredith stirred the spaghetti sauce. It smelled delicious, but it was far from the most important thing on his mind.

Lydia sat at his enormous desk in the next room, playing a video game on his computer, her hot pink headphones ensuring she couldn't hear the adult conversation.

Ever since his run-in with the odious Dorothy Comstock, he'd done nothing but fret over the whole exchange.

"I had one job, Mere." Terry raked his hand through his hair, relieved on some level that there was still plenty up there to rake through, albeit much whiter than it had been two years ago. "Take care of Lydia. That was my job. How could I botch it so badly?" He splayed his hands palms up in front of himself, as if surrendering to his own ineptitude.

Meredith turned the flame down and put a lid on the pot before closing the gap between them. She took his hands in hers and gave them a little shake, trying to loosen regret's grip on him.

"It wasn't your fault, Terry. And besides, Lydia seems fine now ..."

Meredith began, glancing toward the office where Lydia's attention remained riveted on the computer screen, but she didn't get to finish her thought.

"You should have seen her." Terry locked eyes with Meredith, hoping he could make her understand how thoroughly he'd messed up. "She was cowering, holding on to me tighter than she ever has. And that ... that ... that *woman*," he spat the word out as if it tasted bad, "she just sat there with her sickening, simpering grin, watching the whole debacle unfold as if she were enjoying a show."

Remembering the incident, he felt the rage return. His whole body shook from the force of it, again. His anger at Mrs. Comstock and his remorse at not having handled the situation better had fought for emotional supremacy for two days now.

"Sweetie"—Meredith put a hand on each side of his face, forcing his eyes to meet hers—"give it over to God—completely. I totally understand your feelings and, yes, they're justified, but will all of this stewing over it solve anything? Hm?" Even as he dipped his head in shame, she bent down to hold his gaze.

"I know, Mere. You're exactly right. It's just ... how could anyone be so mean to a child? What kind of sick person is she?" He broke free from her grasp as he spoke and continued his circuit back and forth across the kitchen. "If Aunt Tilley knew what she'd done ..."

"Wait, Terry. You haven't told your aunt about the incident?" Meredith crossed her arms and raised one eyebrow, assuming her most intimidating lawyer pose. It worked.

Terry turned away and pretended to chop the cucumbers for the salad, fumbling through the reasons for his decision to protect Aunt Tilley from the drama. He grabbed at every attempted explanation that he'd invented to justify his decision.

Her fragile health.

Her dislike for Dorothy Comstock.

Her deep love for the whole White family.

"Those are all excellent excuses, dear." Meredith took the other knife and stood beside him, slicing carrots before raking them into the salad bowl.

Terry couldn't see her face, so he couldn't read the intent behind the words. Words that stung because of their pinpoint accuracy. Still, he vowed to go down defending his decision.

"What are you talking about? Those aren't excuses. I'm genuinely concerned about upsetting Aunt Tilley." The high pitch of his voice sounded forced to his own ears. He knew Meredith could hear it, too, and that she'd pounce on any weakness he presented.

"Really?" Meredith asked, her composure that of a marble statue as she set the knife down and wiped her hands on her apron. She turned toward Terry in time to see him nod as he cut his eyes to watch her. "Let's do a little exercise, hm? We'll play it out both ways. What happens if you don't tell her, and what happens if you do?"

"Well," Terry said, turning to face her, confident in his path forward. "If I don't tell her, she doesn't have to go get all upset at the woman who claims to be her long-lost friend. That way, it takes any potential stress off of her from a mistake of my doing."

"Okay, fair points. But what about the people who were sitting on the patio with you? And what about Lydia? Do you really believe the news will never get back to Miss Matilda? And when it does, how hurt will she be to learn you didn't share it with her?"

Meredith's rational assessment of the situation knocked the wind out of his self-confident sails. He swiped one hand down his face in an attempt to buy time.

"Well, crud. I've done it now, huh? How can I make this right, Mere?"

He could feel the anger drain away as the fear of disappointing Aunt Tilley took hold of his heart.

"Well, we live in the South, Terry. All news, good or bad, is easier to deliver when you bring food with it." Her eyes sparkled as she poured perfectly-cooked angel hair pasta in a colander, the rising steam making her flawless complexion glow.

"You're right. I'll call her right now and let her know we'll be over in a few minutes with dinner." He punched at his phone as he spoke but stopped before making the call. "What would I ever do without you?" he asked, pulling her close with his free hand and planting a kiss on her forehead.

"I hope you don't try to figure it out again." She smiled slyly at her reference to their brief breakup.

"Never."

§§§

Matilda suggested they take full advantage of the clear, late-summer evening and enjoy their dinner on the patio. Meredith's spaghetti sauce was a real crowd-pleaser, and Matilda even surprised her guests with a plate of freshly-baked cookies.

Lydia asked to be excused to play with Midnight. Within minutes, the little girl's attention was completely focused on trailing a string behind her and laughing as the cat pounced.

Terry took the opportunity to tell his aunt the details of their encounter with Dottie.

Matilda set her half-finished cookie on her plate. Her mouth had formed a thin, angry line, and her brows were drawn into a tight knot.

"What are we going to do about her, Terry?"

"Well, Aunt Tilley, I don't see there's much we can do. It was an isolated incident, so ..."

Matilda lowered her head at Terry's words, avoiding eye contact. She hoped he wouldn't notice, but such a hope was futile.

"Aunt Tilley, is there something you're not telling me?" Terry's voice held a note of concern and foreboding.

"I didn't think it was anything at the time. I thought I could handle it." Tears pooled in her gray eyes when she looked back up at him.

Meredith grabbed Terry's hand and squeezed it. When he looked at her, she simply shook her head.

"You probably should have shared with me, and Chad and Alex, whenever you first had problems with her. But I can't lecture you about it. I hesitated to even share this latest incident with you."

Matilda's eyes flashed annoyance before she recognized she was annoyed at Terry for threatening to do exactly what she'd done. Then a smile softened her features as she looked at the man before her and reached over to pat his hand with her own gnarled, wrinkled one.

"Why don't we share notes while we clean up from this delicious dinner Meredith made us?" she suggested, scooting forward in her chair and preparing to rise.

"Hey, what makes you think I didn't make this?" Terry asked, indignation coloring the question.

"Because I can eat it." Matilda winked at Meredith, and the two women tried to suppress grins at Terry's wounded expression.

He grabbed another cookie off the platter and took a big bite, munching thoughtfully. "Fair statement. Now, where should we begin?"

Back to Reality

Chad lugged their bags to the truck, smiling as he let his mind wander back over the days they'd just spent celebrating their first anniversary—long morning talks stretching into leisurely brunches, followed by relaxing bike rides or road trips to junk shops. And the evenings ... cooking dinner together, talking, concentrating on each other the way they had when they had first fallen in love. Chad thanked God for the past week.

Of course, the perfect location played a huge role in their magical time together and, as expected, the mountain house had been extravagantly comfortable. Their day trips to surrounding towns to check out the local second-hand stores had threatened to turn the week into a working vacation, but Alex had limited her purchases to a few small pieces that she intended to transform into Christmas gifts. If Chad knew his wife, though, she'd find an excuse to come back to her favorite, newly-discovered, little hole-in-the-wall places that called her with their sirens' songs.

Smiling, he walked through the massive front door and allowed his gaze to wander around the inviting spaciousness of the place. The wall of glass doors leading onto the deck gave the illusion that the whole Smoky Mountain range was a seamless extension of the vacation home. The view displayed the brilliance of the rolling hills in all their seasonal beauty; a kaleidoscope of blooms in the spring; shades of green ranging from the bright yellowy hues of new growth to the deep blue-green tones of evergreens in the summer; fiery reds and oranges in the fall; and stark, bare branches, sometimes blanketed with the peaceful white of snow in the winter.

Inside, smooth river rock surrounded the fireplace and soared up to the entire twenty-foot height of the vaulted ceiling. A large, overstuffed leather sectional shared the space with a couple of deep, comfortable wing chairs, drawing the vacationer in and beckoning them to settle down and enjoy all the place had to offer.

Chad knew how hard Alex had worked over the past year, making sure the cabin met all expectations for a luxury rental. At her direction, contractors had been hired to upgrade appliances, freshen the paint, and install enormous paintings from local artists. She'd thought of every amenity that the most discerning vacationer could ever want. A hot tub now sat on the covered deck, a pair of bicycles invited couples to explore the nearby trails, and a picnic basket in the closet made it easy for families to spend the afternoon at the beautiful clearing beside a nearby stream.

When they'd arrived earlier this week—their first visit since their honeymoon—Chad had been overwhelmed at the changes that she'd been able to effect from Burton. She'd laughed it off, crediting Zeke, the property management company, and her ability to multi-task via the internet. Nevertheless, Chad recognized her style in every detail and knew not a single decision had been made that wasn't deliberate and intentional. The final effect was understated luxury. Comfortable opulence. Not a single creature comfort had been overlooked.

"Earth to Chad." Alex waved her hand in front of his face, pulling him out of his reverie. "Are you feeling okay?" She placed her hand on his forehead, a thoroughly mom-gesture that she'd done a thousand times with Lydia.

"I'm fine," he said, smiling and pulling her close.

While he missed Lydia and the familiarity of their own home in Burton, he hated for their one-on-one time with each other to come to an end. It could be the last time they'd be able to focus solely on each other for a long time, especially once the new baby came.

The thought of the new baby pulled his grin even wider. *Will I look like a goofy clown all the time, walking around with this silly look and a dorky permanent smile?* He totally didn't care. God had brought them through a dark and difficult time. It felt good to revel in the blessings He now poured out.

"Do you know how blessed we are?" he asked, placing a light kiss on her lips.

She smiled up at him, love shining in her liquid-pooled brown eyes. "I do." Alex stood on tiptoe and kissed him back. "I've known for a long time."

Taking her face in his hands, Chad kissed her forehead, her nose, each cheek, and then he wrapped his arms around her, pulling her into a kiss that conveyed all the love he felt, the joy she brought to his life. When he finally pulled away, her eyes remained closed and her breath came in deep gulps. He drank in the sight of her.

"You know," she whispered, looking up at him through the thick veil of her lowered lashes while she toyed with a button on his shirt, "I know the owners of this place. I bet they wouldn't mind if we stayed just a little while longer."

Needing no further invitation, Chad scooped her up in his arms, continuing the kiss as he strode toward their room.

§§§

Driving across the North Carolina state line and back into South Carolina, Alex spoke to Terry, letting him know she and Chad would arrive a bit later than they'd discussed yesterday.

"Yeah, just a couple of hours later than expected. Chad drove past this amazing little second-hand store, and I made him turn around." Alex tried not to make eye contact with Chad, who glanced away from the road with eyebrows raised in question. "Tell Lydia I love her. Thanks, Terry. Bye."

Alex ended the call and looked at her husband, daring him to call her out.

Never one to shrink away from a dare, he took the bait.

"Wow, Mrs. White. I never knew the depths of your subterfuge." His sly grin and teasing voice belied the harsh words.

"What was I supposed to tell him? The truth?"

"Good point." Chad had no desire to broadcast the details of their private lives with anyone.

"Besides," Alex said, "Terry asked if Lydia could stay one more night. They've got a few things they haven't been able to do."

"That's cool. I miss Lyddie, but I know she's having a great time. Wanna go out to dinner?"

"If you don't mind, I'd love to just put on my sweats, order a pizza, and watch a movie. I've tried not to think about it all week, but I'm going to be really busy after Jaclyn's podcast airs tonight. Landry's been sending me emails that I've ignored for days, but reality sets in tomorrow."

Thinking of the work ahead of her made her head spin and her body long to climb into bed and pull the covers over her head. Alex didn't dread the work of creating new things. She loved that part. It was the hard stuff that really scared her, like finalizing her website design, picking out new shipping labels, approving a slick new inventory system that Landry had found, fielding requests for guest appearances—something she'd never considered before agreeing to do Jaclyn's podcast—and asking Landry if he'd be interested in a full-time position.

In truth, he worked enough hours that he should probably already be considered full-time, but she'd never looked into the need for making it official. She would talk to Meredith tomorrow to get recommendations for a corporate lawyer who could help her set up a framework that would allow her to grow a staff.

"What're you thinking about?" Chad asked.

"Staff."

"What?"

"Chad, I think—I can't believe I'm saying this—I'm going to have to hire a few employees. I can't get to everything I need to do, and I don't want to go about growing my business the wrong way. On one hand, I'm just a person who makes cool stuff out of junk. Do I really need a staff? But, on the other hand, if I don't, am I being a poor steward of the resources God's entrusted me with? Ugh!" The utter absurdity of it hit her, making her second-guess her own decisions of a few seconds ago.

"Look, babe, I haven't wanted to say anything, but I'm so glad you're thinking in that direction. Landry's been great for you, but I do think it might be a good idea to consider letting him take on a bigger role … and maybe even taking on some more help. Dad went through the same thing when he was trying to decide whether to hire more mechanics for the garage. And, of course, I had a lot to think about when some girl swooped in and totally changed everything about my business." He grinned, and she knew he was remembering the deal she'd cut with him to trade repairs to her car for a makeover of his shop.

"Stop," she said, swatting his arm playfully. "I'm being serious."

"Me, too. Those changes you made were the best things to happen to the garage since Dad opened it years ago. But don't you remember how hesitant I was to take the leap? Don't wait so long to move your business in the right direction, babe." He reached out and patted her knee, and she took his hand and held it with both of hers, letting her thoughts wander.

Yes, it would be nice to have one more night of peace and quiet before the life of a wife, mom, and business owner consumed her once again.

§§§

"I'm a little bit hurt that Miss M. didn't want to join us," Chad said, taking a big bite of his loaded pizza.

Alex nodded, unable to answer through her mouthful of a veggie-loaded bite. They were cuddled up, enjoying their dinner on the sofa, a luxury they rarely allowed themselves with a toddler who was prone to spills and accidents. Chad proffered his slice to his wife, but she shook her head.

"I'm avoiding cured meats. Actually, the list of what I am avoiding is longer than the list of what I can have." She rolled her eyes, shoving another big bite into her mouth.

Chad marveled at how fickle the nausea seemed to be. It definitely wasn't confined to the morning hours, but it also didn't seem to be associated with any particular food group.

Munching on his meaty mouthful, he carefully considered his question before asking.

"So, babe, when do you want to tell folks our news?"

"You mean that I'm going to be hiring some more help? Well, I thought I'd leave that to Landry. He'll probably post something on social media and ..." She tried to finish without laughing, but the stricken look on Chad's face must have been too much for her. Placing a hand gently on his cheek, she spoke softly. "Whenever you want, dear. Do you think we should tell Lydia first?"

"Yeah," Chad said, nodding. "That should take care of the rest of the town."

They looked at each other for a split-second, remembering how Lydia had announced their engagement at church.

"Maybe we need to make a plan," Alex suggested.

"Great idea," Chad agreed. "How 'bout you send out a text invite, and I'll buy some steaks and burgers? Next weekend, the world will know.

But, for now, it's our secret."

"Agreed. Our secret."

Chad kissed his wife, unsure how he'd ever keep this joyous news a secret for almost a week.

LeighAnne Clifton

The Harvest Tea Preparations

"Alex, will the pieces for St. Augustine be ready to ship by next week?" Landry asked, never missing a beat as he tapped away on the computer at his desk.

On the Monday after she and Chad had returned from their trip, she'd extended the offer for full-time employment, along with the promise of benefits and a proper office space. Landry had accepted before she'd even had a chance to present her well-rehearsed diatribe extolling his valuable skills and unequaled work ethic.

By the time he'd shown up on Tuesday morning, she'd fashioned a desk out of a couple of end tables that she'd picked up off the side of the road weeks ago and an old piece of laminate countertop that she'd cut to fit perfectly. For now, Landry was crammed in the corner of her garage-turned-workshop.

They agreed they'd have to figure out a more suitable office setup on a permanent basis. He couldn't be expected to work with Alex sawing, drilling, and hammering.

Now, looking at Landry, his hands poised over his keyboard, ready to answer the shop owner in Florida, Alex knew she needed to figure out something soon. A thin layer of sawdust had already settled on his hair, papers, shoes, and computer. And it was only noon of his first day in the workshop!

"Yes, they'll be ready. Now, are you ready to break for lunch?" she asked, dropping her brushes in the bucket of cleaner and rapping at Miss Matilda's door.

When her friend finally moved into her new house at Together for Good, Alex would miss her terribly. The Dixons still called almost daily, although their calls had lately been more to keep Miss Matilda apprised rather than ask her advice. She knew the older lady was itching to get back to the home and all it represented, but Alex selfishly wanted to extend her stay as long as possible.

The transition time between summer and fall had provided Burton with a brief spell of tolerable temperatures, and Alex took advantage by carrying the lunch tray to the patio table. Landry had already escorted Miss Matilda out, and they were both settled in their seats, chatting like the old friends they were. Everyone helped themselves to heaping helpings of chicken salad and fresh fruit.

They were talking about their options for a permanent and proper office space for Landry when their attention was diverted to the crunch of wheels rolling into the driveway.

Alex's face lit up at the sight of Chad's truck. Then her heart clenched.

Oh no. Something's wrong. Lydia? Terry?

Why did her mind automatically go to the most horrific and frightening conclusion?

Excusing herself, Alex tried to relax as she rushed to meet her husband, who rarely came home for lunch and always called when he did.

"What's wrong? Is Lydia okay?" She clutched his greasy shirt, both wanting to know and being terrified to hear.

"Take it easy, hon," Chad said, hugging her quickly and rubbing her back. "Everything's fine. Can't a man have lunch with his wife?"

Alex eyed him with suspicion. Chad was up to something, but she couldn't put her finger on it. She'd play along ... for now.

Taking his hand, she led him to the patio table. Once he'd greeted Landry and Miss Matilda, he eased himself into the other seat. Alex had brought an extra fork, so he shared her food.

"Chad, either you're trying to figure out what herbs I used in the chicken salad, or you've got something to tell us. Something that couldn't wait until tonight." Alex couldn't stand not knowing what was behind the contemplative look on her husband's face.

She crossed her arms and leaned back in her chair, willing to wait him out. She was, after all, the mom of a toddler and had matched wills with one more cunning, and stubborn, than he.

"You know what?" Landry asked as he rose. "Why don't Miss Matilda and I just—"

"No, y'all stay," Chad interrupted him with a raised hand. "I just wanted to give Alex a heads-up about a ladies' event coming up at church."

"Why would I need to know about that?" Alex asked before taking a big gulp of her tea, washing down the bile in her throat that had been rising since Chad's arrival.

"Because they're going to ask you to be the speaker."

Alex spluttered and choked. "Me? Why me?"

"Isn't it obvious, dear?" Miss Matilda laid her hand on Alex's shoulder, speaking in the tone she often used to calm a scared girl at the home. Alex had been on the receiving end of that same tone more than once. "You're a beautiful example of what faith can do in a life. Think about where you've come from, what you've done, the lives you've touched. Did you do all of that on your own?"

Alex shook her head, unable to answer. Too many questions competed in her head for their turn to go first. "How do you know about this, Chad?" Why would the ladies ask him before they even mentioned it to her?

"Well, today's Tuesday, so ..."

It started to click in Alex's brain. Chad's outreach to the widows and single moms at church brought in many of Miss Matilda's friends. The same women who planned most of the women's ministry activities.

Alex had a barrage of questions ready to fire at her husband, but a cell phone calendar reminder pinged, interrupting her tirade. Thinking it was hers, she looked down at the phone laying on the table between her and Miss Matilda. A reminder had certainly popped up, but not for Alex.

"Miss Matilda, why do you have a scheduled event called 'Help Chad convince Alex'?" Alex swiveled her head, leveling an accusatory stare on first one culprit and then the other.

She'd been ambushed.

"Uh-oh. He got here a bit earlier than we'd discussed." Miss Matilda's voice was adequately contrite, but her face indicated she was quite proud they'd pulled off their scheme. Too late, Miss Matilda swiped the phone off the table and tucked it in her pocket, attempting to let remorse consume her features.

"Babe." Chad got up from his chair and pulled her to stand with him. Holding her face in his hands, he came clean, confessing the whole plan. "Miss Evelyn came in this morning and asked if I thought you'd be willing to speak at the ladies' Harvest Tea in October. I promised I'd ask you. But, really, it's like Miss M. said. Who has a better story of the power of faith in our lives than you? And besides, remember Miss Evelyn is the lady who thinks I'm the cute, young mechanic. I had to say yes to her."

As hard as she wanted to stay mad at him and Miss Matilda for plotting behind her back, she knew they both loved her and had only her best interests at heart.

She remembered the day the church had found out about their engagement when Lydia had spilled the beans. Miss Evelyn had immediately besieged Miss Matilda's phone with offers to help. In the process, she'd endeared herself to Chad by heaping compliments on him.

She'd have him eating out of her hand for a long time.

Glancing at Landry, who'd watched the whole exchange, back and forth, as if it were some strange sport, an idea hit Alex.

"While you're here," she said, squeezing her husband around the waist in a big hug, "let's talk about our options for a more suitable place for Landry's office. I can't have the man going on calls for me with sawdust in his hair."

Landry swatted at his hair, his expression horrified as he watched the fine powder catch the sunlight as it floated off in the gentle breeze.

"I agree." Chad chuckled. "What are our options?"

He took his seat, and the four of them were soon brainstorming the pros and cons of various office space configurations and locations, all thoughts of the Harvest Tea long forgotten.

§§§

The ladies stirred coffee in their foam cups as they found their seats in the fellowship hall. Dorothy Comstock took a seat on the last row, giving her a view of all the participants while not calling attention to her note-taking. The Ladies' Harvest Tea Committee meeting was underway, and although she wasn't officially on the committee, she'd managed to find an older lady who needed a ride.

It's really a win-win. Jo Ellen gets to come to her meeting, and I get to hear everything that's going on. Totally worth a few hours out of my day.

Dot focused her attention on the podium as Evelyn cleared her throat and called for the ladies to settle down. She then said a quick prayer before launching into the business at hand.

"Ladies, I believe the decorating group has things well in hand. Is that correct, Mrs. Drummond?" Evelyn asked.

She sought confirmation from the pastor's wife, who'd decorated for the tea every year since they had come to the church. This would be her twentieth tea, and she had the process perfected. The ladies on the committee saw no need to mess with a good thing.

"Yes, Evelyn." Mrs. Drummond stood and faced the group. "Everyone is welcome to come and help the day before. We'll have plenty to keep everyone busy." Smoothing her skirt beneath her, she sat back down.

"Thank you. I'm sure it will be as lovely as always." Evelyn smiled at the kind, sophisticated woman, knowing most of the ladies in the room were thankful to have such an involved and caring pastor's wife.

A smattering of polite applause confirmed Evelyn's sentiments.

"As you know, as chair of the committee this year, it's my responsibility to secure an engaging and entertaining speaker. I'm pleased to announce that Alex White has agreed to share her testimony with us."

Another round of applause, this one more vigorous than before, broke out with Evelyn's announcement.

Mention of the girl's name put Dot's senses on high alert. She'd been sowing tiny seeds of half-truths from the information that she'd gleaned during her many reconnaissance missions, but she couldn't believe her luck today. She'd spent the whole summer sneaking around, gathering data, and disseminating only the ugly parts about Alex and those closest to her. Although Matilda Gault was the true object of Dot's character assassination attempt, she felt sure that a solid blow to Alex's life would have the same intended effect.

Dot realized she'd let her mind wander and chided herself for possibly missing important details. Not a problem; she'd just grill Jo Ellen on the way home, stopping to buy her ice cream if she had to, and get all the juicy details she needed to proceed.

A plan began to formulate in her brain.

"Does everyone know their assignment for the event?" Evelyn asked, obviously ready to dispense with the meeting formalities and move on to the pastries that Riker and Blakely had sent over. "Good. We'll see everyone here the day before the tea. Be sure to call your group leader if you run into any problems."

Evelyn barely had the words off her tongue before the women descended on the trays loaded with all sorts of delicious offerings from the girls' bakery.

Riker and Blakely would also be catering the tea. Their bakery had become not only a favorite destination for yummy treats, but also the go-to for small to medium events. Dorothy knew the girls' stories paralleled Alex's, so she decided to make her time at the meeting really count.

She barreled up to the table, making sure to squeeze in the line behind Evelyn, much to the chagrin of the ladies who'd been waiting patiently. Dot grabbed a napkin but didn't bother using the tongs to pick up her selections. She missed the daggers being shot her way by the angry women who would never cause a scene in the church. She wouldn't have cared even if she had noticed.

"These are delicious," she said with her mouth full of raspberry Danish.

Evelyn cringed, but manners dictated that she remain cordial.

"Yes, they really are. Those girls are so talented. God truly blessed them." Evelyn tried to extricate herself from the conversation, but Dot grabbed her upper arm, halting her escape.

"I guess He did, huh? First, those poor girls find themselves ... well, you know, in a difficult situation. Then sweet Matilda helps them out. What a blessing." Dorothy assumed the compassionate expression she'd practiced in front of the mirror, the one she believed exuded concern for others.

"Um ..." Evelyn began. "Yes. Matilda was a blessing to them. And to all the girls who've come through Together for Good."

"Hmm. Isn't it interesting that Alex and these talented bakers all started businesses right here in Burton? What a coincidence?" Dot continued to probe for information, all the time feigning an air of concerned curiosity.

"Well, I don't know about coincidences," Evelyn said, wriggling her arm out of Dot's grip. "The Lord provided for all of them, putting them in the place He wanted them and opening doors of opportunity."

"Of course," Dot agreed. She could tell she wasn't going to get anything else out of Evelyn. "Well, I'd better find Jo Ellen and get her home." Dot turned back toward the food table, reached between two ladies for another napkin, then cut in front of two other women to load the napkin up with goodies. *Might as well have a little something for my trouble*, she justified to herself.

Ignoring the stares leveled at her, she went to find Jo Ellen's walker and hurry her out of the fellowship hall.

Dorothy Comstock had plans to make.

Announcements

Chad said a silent prayer for his wife while he formed a few hamburgers and set them on a plate. They'd been back from their anniversary trip for almost a week, and in that time, Alex's pregnancy-related nausea seemed to get worse each day. He'd spent the last several days bringing her ginger ale, crackers, dry toast, and sports drinks, hoping something appealed to her. And if it did, that it stayed down.

"Hey, Lyddie, why don't you take Midnight to visit Miss M.? I'll text her and let her know you're coming," Chad called into the living room as he covered the plate of burgers and set it in the refrigerator next to the steaks.

"Yay! Let's go, Midnight!" Lydia scooped up the fluffy, snow-white ball of fur and carried her to the kitchen door. The cat's front paws stuck out in front of her and bounced with each step the girl took.

Chad never ceased to be amazed at how patient their feline family member was with Lydia, enduring stroller rides, tea parties, and endless costume changes.

Chuckling, Chad washed his hands, shot a quick text to Miss M., and then took the stairs two at a time to check on Alex. He walked into their room just in time to hear the sounds of her heaving coming from the adjoining bathroom. A quick rap on the bathroom door elicited nothing more than a strangled grunt from his wife, which he took as a signal to enter. The sight before him broke his heart.

Alex knelt beside the toilet, elbows resting on the rim, head pressed against her hands. She'd kept Chad at arm's length during the early days of her pregnancy with Lydia, but he had a front-row seat this time around.

"Babe," he said, taking the folded washcloth that she'd set on the counter and soaking it with cool water. As he squeezed the excess water out, he asked, "Is there anything I can do? Anything I can get you?" He placed the cloth on her neck and rubbed her back.

She shook her head. Then she looked at him as if she'd had an idea. "Maybe some crushed ice?"

"I'm on it," he called, already out the door before he finished speaking.

Although he was back with the ice and a spoon in little more than a minute, he found her on the bed, eyes closed, feet propped on a pillow, and the washcloth spread across her forehead. The minty smell of toothpaste hung in the air.

Knowing better than to try to sit on the bed and jostle her, Chad pulled up a stool and gently touched her arm. "Here, sweetie. Try this," he whispered. Holding a spoonful of ice in front of her, he hoped to entice her to get some form of hydration in her body.

She opened her eyes, looked at the spoon in front of her, and giggled.

Chad saw in those gorgeous brown eyes the mischievous light that had been absent for the past few days.

"I'm not a two-year-old, Chad." Alex took the cup and spoon from him, placing a few chips of ice on her tongue to see how it would settle.

"Good?"

She nodded and scooped up a bit more.

"Maybe we should postpone the cookout tonight. You're not up to having guests."

The hurt in those eyes, that just seconds ago had been alight with playfulness, gouged at Chad's emotions. He knew how much she looked forward to making their big announcement tonight. But, at the same time, he didn't want her overdoing it, taxing her energy and stressing her body. He told her of his concerns, for her and for their child.

Alex reached out as she told him, "I get it, honey. I'm a little bit worried, too. After the miscarriage, every little twinge or symptom gets me all nervous. But we can't live like that. I want to enjoy this pregnancy as much as possible."

"Aw, babe. I know we've gotta have faith that God's going to take care of you and the baby. You're right. We just need to trust Him and live each day." He took her hand in his and kissed it softly.

"Would it make you feel better if I let you and Char handle all the prep?"

"Yeah," he said, letting go of the breath that he hadn't realized he'd been holding. "I've got almost everything taken care of, so there shouldn't be that much for her to do."

"Cool. Lydia's T-shirt is all wrapped and ready to give to her. It's on the top shelf in our closet." Alex squeezed Chad's hand before grabbing the spoon for another mouthful of ice. "I love you."

"I love you, too." He knew the words could never convey all he truly felt—how amazed he was at her strength and perseverance, how proud he was of her ambition and success, and how thankful he was that she'd become his wife. He hoped that, somehow, for now, the words would suffice.

§§§

Alex sat on the patio in the comfy Adirondack chair, sipping her ginger ale and watching all those she held dear bustle about. Charmain had stepped in and picked up the slack without questioning Alex's flimsy excuse for sitting this one out.

"How's that ankle, sis?" Charmain asked as she carried another food-laden tray from the kitchen and set it on the picnic table.

A twinge of guilt stabbed Alex's conscience, but she tamped it down with the promise that all the secrecy would soon be over.

"Um ... Still a bit sore," she fibbed. "Thanks for helping Chad."

"No problem. I'm pretty used to bailing out my dorky big brother." Charmain waved Alex's gratitude off. Then she gave her sister-in-law a quick side hug before scooting off to see what else needed to be done.

"Hi, Alex. Sorry to hear about the ankle." Yvonne plopped down in the chair next to Alex, concern evident on her face.

Alex made a mental note to check with Chad about changing their plans. She couldn't go through this whole cookout under the ruse that she was nursing a sprained ankle. All the guests thought they'd been invited over to celebrate the end of summer. Alex knew she and Chad needed to make their announcement, and soon.

"Thanks, Yvonne," Alex answered, eager to change the subject. "I haven't talked to you or Marquis since your anniversary getaway. Did y'all have a nice time?"

Since the two couples had gotten married on the same day, at the same place, it wasn't difficult for them to remember one another's anniversary. Miss Matilda had told Alex that the Dixons had celebrated their first anniversary with an overnight trip to a nearby little bed and breakfast. Charmain had stayed at Together for Good. Although, according to Miss Matilda's intel, none of the current residents were due for a couple of months.

"We had a wonderful time," Yvonne answered, her face lighting up with excitement as she talked. She told Alex all about the beautiful place they stayed, their fancy meal in the inn's restaurant, and the lovely early fall weather they enjoyed as they strolled around the town. "It really was perfect. What about y'all? How was the mountain house?"

"We had a great time, too. So relaxing, especially after all the craziness that's gone on for the past few months."

Besides Chad, only Miss Matilda, Terry, and Meredith knew about the miscarriage. Yet, Yvonne had had a front row seat for the long list of upheavals their circle of friends had been involved in—Miss Matilda's stroke, Terry and Meredith's relationship, Alex's foray into the worlds of podcast guesting and employee hiring ... to name a few. And, of course, Yvonne knew firsthand about the challenges and rewards of taking over the operation of Together for Good.

"I hear you, girl," Yvonne said, chuckling as she stood. "I'll leave you to rest. I've got to find Marquis and make sure he isn't sampling that yummy-looking cookie tray Riker brought."

"If you catch Chad doing that, tell him I've got eyes everywhere."

"Sure thing."

Alex scanned the backyard from her patio post. Terry pushed Lydia on the swing while Meredith stood in front of the little girl, tickling her toes at the apex of each ascent and making Lydia cackle with joy. Miss Matilda and Landry strolled arm in arm up and down the driveway, their heads tilted toward each other, deep in conversation. Miss Matilda had traded in her cane for Landry's strong arm and seemed content with the upgrade.

At the burgeoning picnic table, Yvonne and Marquis filled cups with ice and poured tea in some and water in others. Every now and then, Char emerged from the kitchen with a platter, or a bowl, or a casserole dish. It became increasingly difficult for her to find space to squeeze in each successive offering. Away from the action, Chad manned the grill, engulfed in the hickory-scented cloud of charring meat that was making everyone's mouth water.

He must have felt her watching him through the smoke, because he turned and smiled at her, waving and blowing her a kiss. Alex's heart flip-flopped in her chest.

She beckoned him over, eager to discuss her proposed change of plans for the evening. He glanced at the grill before signaling to her that it would be a few minutes before he could get away. She nodded then resumed her examination of their guests.

How could she have come to love these people so dearly in such a short time?

Overcome with gratitude, Alex closed her eyes to say a quick but deeply sincere prayer of thanks for God's provision for her friends and family, for her home in Burton, for the baby growing inside her.

"Hey, you awake?" Chad touched Alex on the shoulder, startling her out of her prayerful calm. "I'm sorry, I didn't mean to scare you."

"No, it's fine. I was just thanking the Lord for all He's blessed us with." She smiled at her husband, knowing he understood.

He knelt beside her and stroked her cheek. "How are you feeling?"

"Pretty good. That's what I wanted to talk to you about. I think we need to make the announcement before we start eating. I can't keep up this charade of being hurt. I'm starting to feel really guilty about lying to everyone."

"Fine with me. I'll go get Lyddie's gift. We'll let her open it, and then we'll start eating. Be right back." He rose, kissed the top of her head, and then bolted off.

Within seconds, he was back at her side, the brightly wrapped package in his hand. Chad whistled a quick, ear-splitting blast to get everyone's attention. Then he motioned for Lydia to join him and her mother.

The sight of the gift wrapping and the fluffy bow piqued the little girl's curiosity, and she hurried over to see what surprise Chad had for her.

"Chad," Charmain said, stepping up and touching his elbow. "Could I say something before you give Lydia her surprise?"

"Um, Char, now's not really—"

"It's fine," Alex said. "What's up, Charmain?"

Charmain's uncannily poor timing in all situations was legendary, so Alex assumed her beautiful sister-in-law would be dropping some terrible news about another job gone wrong. At least Alex and Chad could offset her announcement with their own happy news.

"Here goes." Charmain drew in a deep breath. "I'm going back to school, to become a sonographer. For the first time in my life, I really feel this is what God's calling me to do. I hope to work at Together for Good someday soon."

After a brief stunned silence, the group erupted in cheers. Everyone circled around Charmain, congratulating her on her new career choice.

Alex and Chad exchanged an incredulous glance. They'd prayed for clear direction for Charmain's career path.

Yvonne and Marquis cried, overcome with joy as they embraced Charmain. With Miss Matilda absent and injured, they had no one to perform ultrasounds, which Alex knew from firsthand experience was a huge outreach tool. When a young mother was able to see her baby's heartbeat and its tiny limbs moving about inside her, the child's humanity became real, tangible, irrefutable. Having that capability on the premises again would be invaluable, and the Dixons knew it.

When the melee began to die down, Chad cleared his throat.

Terry clapped his hand on Chad's shoulder. "Mind if I say something right quick?"

Chad looked to Alex, who shrugged. They'd waited this long. Might as well see what was so important that Terry needed to speak now.

Terry looped his arm around Meredith, who dipped her head as she ran her fingers through her fiery hair. Alex could swear she saw a pink tint creep up the lovely lawyer's neck and into her cheeks. *What's going on?*

"Y'all know the wonderful news of Meredith's salvation, right?"

Applause erupted again.

Terry smiled at Meredith and continued speaking when it was quiet again. "So, now that this beautiful woman is our sister in the Lord, I've asked her to be my wife … and she's accepted!"

A collective gasp echoed through the twilight, immediately followed by whoops and cheers. Everyone hugged Meredith and shook Terry's hand.

Alex kept her seat, eager to congratulate her dear friends but not daring to divulge their secret yet. This had truly turned out to be a night of celebration.

"Chaddie," Lydia said, tugging on his shirt, "who's the present for? Is it mine?"

Everyone laughed. The little girl had been patient, but her capacity for waiting had reached its end.

Alex patted her lap, inviting her daughter to join her. Lydia climbed into her mommy's lap and watched Chad expectantly.

"Okay, Lyddie Bug, here's your present. We got it for you while we were on our trip last week. We hope you like it." Chad handed the gift to the little girl, who tore into the exquisite wrapping with abandon.

Alex helped her open the lid and unfold the tissue paper. Together, they lifted the shirt so that just the two of them could see the front.

"Mommy, I can't read it."

Laughter rippled through the crowd.

Alex whispered in her daughter's ear, and Lydia's eyes grew wide. Her mouth formed a tiny *O*.

"Really, Mommy? Chaddie?" She whipped her head from Alex to Chad.

They both nodded, neither trusting their voices in the moment.

"What's your shirt say, sweetie?" Terry asked.

"Bubba, you won't believe it!" Lydia turned the tiny pink T-shirt around for the guests to see. Printed across the front were the words, *"Mommy and Daddy say I'm going to be a big sister."*

Holding her daughter in that moment, Alex remembered when she'd first learned of her existence. It hadn't been accompanied by joy and celebration. Quite the opposite. The discovery of her first pregnancy had brought fear and uncertainty. But now, as Alex watched the people assembled before her through the happy tears swimming in her eyes, she knew God had truly brought about a miracle. Not just the baby who would be born soon, or the child sitting in her lap, or the woman who'd survived a life-threatening health scare, or the friends who were willing to leave everything they knew to help women in need.

No. God had worked all these things, and so much more, for His purposes.

These people surrounding her, cheering for her and Chad, hugging and high-fiving … these people were doing amazing things for God's kingdom, each in their own way. And she, Alex White, had the privilege of serving alongside them, serving with each of them in different ways.

"Do you think she caught the part about *Daddy*?" Meredith whispered in Alex's ear, breaking into her thoughts.

Alex shook her head and smiled. "I don't think so. We'll get to that part." Alex finally rose from the chair, no longer needing to pretend her ankle was injured, and hugged the lawyer who already felt like part of the family. "Thank you for all you've done."

"It's been my pleasure, truly."

Alex found her husband chatting with Miss Matilda, who embraced the girl who she'd literally found along the side of the road.

"Well, dear, I guess good things really do come in threes," Miss Matilda said, still basking in all the good news that had been announced tonight.

"I've got one more piece of good news for y'all," Chad said, raising his voice so all present could hear. "Dinner's ready. Let's pray, and then we can dig in."

Everyone joined hands and bowed their heads, aware of how much they had to be thankful for.

Plan in Motion

Dorothy Comstock knew she couldn't implement her plan alone. Despite the elaborate groundwork she'd laid, she still needed an unsuspecting newcomer to all the local goings-on. She sniffed out her prey all over— at the church's new member meetings, the rec center's quarterly informational session, and other local gatherings where new residents would be likely to frequent. Her prime opportunity presented itself at the Chamber of Commerce's monthly meet and greet, right under the noses of her intended targets.

The gods must be smiling on me.

Arriving at the municipal building twenty minutes late, she figured everyone who counted must already be there. She hoped she'd missed all the boring introductory speeches that the mayor and council always gave.

Although Dot had never owned a business, she had enough friends in the municipal offices that she kept her finger on the pulse of the city's social calendar. Slipping into a few functions a year, especially if she did so on the arm of an unsuspecting man arriving alone, had never been difficult.

Tonight, she'd dressed to impress. Smoothing her silver spandex pants over her ample hips, she admitted to herself that she probably should have opted for the control top panty hose. No matter. Her hot pink and neon orange print tunic with bell sleeves and shoulder cutouts would demand attention, which was exactly what Dot wanted.

She waited patiently in her car, checking to see if there were other late-comers.

A fancy red BMW whipped into the parking lot and snagged the first spot it came to. That was Dot's cue. Someone was frantic over their tardiness, and Dottie intended to put their mind at ease. *It's just the neighborly thing to do*, she thought with a smug grin.

Dot continued smiling as she watched a middle-aged woman scramble out of the expensive car and grab her purse, a bag, an insulated mug, her keys, obviously rushing and panicked over her late arrival.

Dot calmly exited her car and approached the woman. She'd never seen her before, and Dot felt sure she knew everyone in Burton.

"Excuse me," Dot said, approaching the woman who was now juggling her belongings.

The sound of Dot's voice startled her, and she jumped, dropping her purse.

"Oh, I'm so sorry, dear. Let me get that for you." Dot bent over carefully, trying hard not to rip the skin-tight spandex pants, and retrieved the purse. She slipped the handle onto the woman's shoulder. "There you go. I'm Dorothy Comstock, but my friends call me Dot. And you are …?"

Dot ran a quick, appraising gaze up and down the woman. Dark hair, with a bit of gray at the temples. Lovely skin, and just a few smile lines around the eyes. Shapely, but fit and toned. Within a few seconds, Dot surmised she could work with this woman.

"Thank you for your help, Dot. I'm Teresa Bell. I just moved here from Florida a few weeks ago. I bought the bridal boutique from Gretchen. I got caught up with a customer tonight, but I really must get inside." As she spoke, Teresa Bell moved toward the entrance, and Dot matched her step for step.

"Oh, I understand." Dot's voice soothed Teresa Bell's frazzled nerves. "We must cater to the customers, right? I was just heading in myself.

Here, let me get the door for you."

And, just like that, Dorothy Comstock gained entrance into Burton's Chamber of Commerce's September meet and greet.

§§§

Chad and Terry carried the ladies' drinks to them at the high-top table that they'd been able to snag. These Chamber meetings tended to be a rehash of the previous month—Mayor's comments, news of the latest pothole repairs, and other such pressing issues—but every now and then, something happened to liven things up.

Chad sipped his diet Coke, looking around the room at the usual attendees.

"I don't remember ever seeing you at these functions, Alex." Terry handed Meredith a club soda with lime, putting his hand on her back and standing close.

"That's because I've never been," Alex replied, taking her ginger ale from Chad. "Now that I actually have an employee, with the possibility of adding a few more, I figured I should finally take the plunge and join the Chamber. I suppose I've graduated from a one-woman operation to what you'd call a 'cottage industry.'"

"What about you, Meredith? Just tagging along for the ride?" Chad asked.

"Actually"—Meredith cut her blue eyes toward Terry—"in all the commotion last weekend, we didn't get to tell you the rest of our news. I've resigned from the law firm." She beamed, obviously thrilled at her decision.

"That's big news, Mere! What's next for you?" Alex asked, trying to keep her inquiry vague, not intrusive.

"I've found a condo about a block off Main Street, and I've already started moving some of my stuff in. Once we're married, Terry will move in until we find a house."

Terry squirmed at the comment before taking his fiancée's hand and leading her to a group that included the mayor.

Chad knew Terry had been working on his own house plans for a couple of years now, but something always came up. Maybe now, with Meredith by his side, he could focus his energies on his life, his home, and his wife. Chad knew how important those things were. God had shown him so clearly over the last year.

Alex took a sip of ginger ale but choked on it as a neon-clad monster walked in.

"You okay, hon?" Chad asked, patting her back gently.

Alex nodded then inclined her head toward the door where Dot and some woman who they'd never seen stood surveying the crowd.

"Who let her in here? She's not a Chamber member." Chad's hackles went up every time the wicked Dorothy Comstock made an appearance. It seemed bad things tended to follow her.

"Relax, sweetie. Maybe she's showing that lady around," Alex said, trying to calm her husband.

Still, Chad put his hand on the small of Alex's back and steered her away from view of the entrance. He refused to take any chances that their paths might cross. He spotted Terry and Meredith chatting in a corner and directed Alex toward them. Looking back one last time, he saw her—how could anyone miss her in that ridiculous get-up—pointing and talking incessantly to the poor woman who seemed trapped in Dottie's gossip web. *Better her than me.*

"I see Mrs. Comstock has a new victim, um … I mean … friend," Terry said, watching the only woman, besides his ex-wife, who he'd ever confessed to having an urge to punch.

Chad grinned at the thought of the refined and cultured man ever taking such a violent step, but he had to admit it'd be kind of entertaining to see it.

"Oh no." Meredith seemed distraught at the sight of Dot's prey. "I believe that's Teresa Bell. Remember, Terry, I told you about the new owner of the bridal boutique? How did Dot get her claws—excuse me, how did Mrs. Comstock meet her so soon?"

As a lawyer and a Southern lady, Meredith prided herself on her manners and decorum. Chad had seen another side of her, though. He knew she could get feisty when she needed to. He liked that side of her. Everyone needed a little salty to balance the sweet.

Realizing his wife had been silent since they had joined their friends, Chad looked at her. Her face had gone ashen, and the hand holding her ginger ale trembled.

"Babe, are you feeling well? Let's get you home," Chad said, taking the cup out of her hand.

She shook her head. "No. I'm fine. That woman is … she's evil, Chad."

"I know. I agree."

"It's a pretty big gathering tonight," Terry said. "Let's try to steer clear of her. It shouldn't be too hard, seeing how she's wearing that neon beacon."

Terry's attempt at humor made them chuckle, and they all attempted to relax. They never lost sight, however, of the bright pink and orange figure as it floated around the room, talking to the mayor, the council members, and most of the business owners.

A select few chose to avoid her advances.

§§§

Dot could have told those holier-than-thou minions of Matilda Gault that the only thing to be gained from avoiding her was trouble. She'd spent months gleaning information. She'd sat back and listened to folks prattle on incessantly, feigning interest when the boredom consumed her. She'd asked leading questions and expertly guided the answers in the direction that she wanted them to go. She'd formulated a plan, and Burton, South Carolina would never be the same once she set it in motion.

Standing against the wall, watching the unsuspecting pawns in her game mill around, Dot felt a modicum of pity for them. They went to church and prayed to their God for wisdom, and strength, and forgiveness.

They called it faith.

These stupid, weak-minded people. When will they learn that wisdom is what we find out for ourselves? Strength lies in what we can attain. And faith? Well, that's just a myth.

Sunday mornings had to be the longest, most difficult of her information-gathering expeditions. But, in the rural Southeast, Dot understood the importance of faith to the people of the town, and she played along ...

Until she was ready to change the rules of the game to suit her purposes.

And that time would be here soon. Really soon.

Fissures

Matilda let Landry guide her into R&B's Café, an outing they both looked forward to each Tuesday and Thursday morning. Now that she was stable and walking well with a cane, Matilda looked forward to getting out and taking in the sights of downtown. Finishing the excursion with a cup of tea and a yummy treat made by two of her former girls was the proverbial icing on the cake. She smiled at her own pun.

She was so proud of all that Riker and Blakely had accomplished. When they'd decided to go with the simple combination of their initials as the establishment's name, Charmain had suggested they really play it up. The rhythm and blues music-themed décor bordered on kitschy, but when combined with the accompanying homey touches—sunny yellow gingham café curtains, black-and-white checkerboard tile floors, and a comfy reading nook by the window—the place lured in locals and tourists alike, encouraging them to linger for a while. Of course, Riker and Blakely had relied on Alex's skills and connections to source all the furnishings, and she'd come through for them as only she could.

"You want the usual today, Miss Matilda?" Landry asked, pulling Matilda out of her musings and back to the present.

She smiled at her handsome escort. "Yes, dear. That would be lovely.

I'll get a table." Matilda concentrated on her posture as she walked to the little table for two in the corner. She and Landry liked it because it afforded them an unobstructed view of the door and the counter.

Hanging her cane on the back of her chair, she heard the bell above the door ding as she was lowering herself into the seat. A nice-looking woman who Matilda didn't recognize took her place in line behind Landry.

Blakely had Landry's drink order ready within seconds—it was their regular day and time, after all—and he carefully carried the mugs to their table with the proprietor on his heels. She carried a plate with a huge cinnamon roll and two forks, the pair's standard order.

"Here you go, Miss Matilda," Blakely said, giving the older lady a hug before hurrying back to the counter.

Landry and Matilda dug into their pastry, closing their eyes as they savored the yeasty, spicy delight. After a few bites, Matilda guessed the tea had cooled enough to wash down a bit of the sweetness, so she picked up her mug and watched the counter.

Riker emerged from the kitchen, wiping her hands on a pristine white cloth and shaking hands with the lady who had been in line behind Landry.

"Miss Matilda, I've got a couple of super important emails I need to answer. Do you mind? It'll just take a minute." Landry looked distressed at his breach of etiquette, but Matilda was more than amenable to having his attention otherwise occupied for a little while. Her curiosity about the newcomer had been piqued.

"By all means, dear. Don't let me keep you from your work. I don't want Alex accusing me of monopolizing her best employee."

"Thanks." And with that, he focused his full attention on the tablet he'd pulled out of the backpack that he carried everywhere.

Matilda believed a bomb could have exploded and Landry would have never known it, so absorbed was he in his work.

Meanwhile, Riker had led the fashionably dressed woman to a

table nearby. Matilda continued to sip her tea and nibble her pastry, pretending to watch folks stroll down the street, but she couldn't help hearing snippets of the conversation beside her.

"I'm Teresa Bell, the new owner of the bridal boutique," the woman introduced herself.

"Nice to meet you, Miss Bell, and welcome to Burton. I heard Gretchen sold the place. What can I do for you?"

Matilda smiled. She knew Riker was getting ready for the lunch crowd, so idle chitchat wasn't in her schedule this morning. She needed to get right to the purpose of this visit.

"I believe we could help each other. I understand you cater weddings. Is that right?"

"Yes, ma'am. Nothing too big, but we've had several happy clients since we started."

"That's what I hear. Your first gig was beautiful, from what everybody says."

Matilda smiled again, remembering how hard the girls had worked to pull off Alex and Chad's wedding. And it had been beyond beautiful. Stunning. Breathtaking. Those words more appropriately described it. Then again, it had to be. The girls' future careers had depended on the success of the event. And what a success it had been.

"Well," Riker hedged, trying to remain humble, "we worked very hard. Plus, we were both expecting at the time, so that was an extra challenge." She chuckled.

"Oh my. Both of you? That must've been quite demanding. Where was the wedding?"

"At Together for Good, the pregnancy care home right on the edge of the town limits. The grounds are beautiful," Riker said with confidence, speaking fondly of her former home.

Matilda's senses went on alert with the direction the conversation was taking, but what could she say? She wasn't supposed to be listening.

If she were smart, she'd extricate herself from this awkward situation before she heard any more, interrupt Landry's emails, and talk about the weather or some equally mundane subject. She didn't have time, however, to engage her better judgment before the discussion beside her resumed.

"You know, I hear that there were two weddings that day? How exciting that must've been."

The question was harmless, and Teresa Bell's voice held no rancor, but Matilda felt a chill creep up her spine.

"Yes, ma'am. Funny thing, too. The second couple who married that day are actually running the home for a while."

Enough, Riker. A complete stranger doesn't need so much information.

"Hm ... I guess that makes sense."

Out of the corner of her eye, Matilda saw the woman nodding her head slowly while Riker scowled, confused.

"What do you mean? They stepped in to help out in an emergency. Of course, it makes perfect sense." Riker's voice held an edge of suspicion now.

Riker hadn't acknowledged Matilda as the one whose place the Dixons had taken over, but she glanced uncomfortably toward the table where the beloved older lady sat. Matilda pretended to concentrate on the crumbs on the plate, but every girl who'd lived at the home knew of her exceptional hearing.

"That's not what I've heard," Teresa Bell continued, oblivious to Riker's discomfort. "I heard that they've told folks they're all settled in, ready to make this their job for the long haul. They said the family and friends of the old lady who used to run the place don't have any confidence she'll ever be capable of doing so again."

Matilda thought she'd choke on her tea. Landry, oblivious to her eavesdropping, looked up to see her pale face and the tears poised to spill at any second.

Riker looked over and mouthed, *"I'm sorry,"* before rushing the woman out of the café, mumbling something about needing to get prepped for lunch.

"Miss Matilda, are you feeling okay?" Landry asked, putting his hand on her gnarled, wrinkled one.

"Could we leave now, dear?"

"Sure thing," he said, jumping up and shoving his things into his backpack.

Before they'd made it to the door, Riker had packed up the remains of their pastry, thrown in a few cookies, and put their tea in to-go cups.

"Miss Matilda, she's a newbie. Don't listen to her," Riker whispered in Matilda's ear as she embraced her goodbye.

Matilda nodded and walked out the door that Landry held open for her. Gone was her exemplary posture. Now she hung her head in utter shame.

Shame at listening in on a private conversation.

Shame at daring to believe she was getting her former strength back.

And shame at being naïve enough to believe anyone else could do her job.

§§§

Terry lined up take-out cartons from the Chinese restaurant on Meredith's kitchen counter. The few belongings she'd moved to Burton were still in boxes, so he wanted to surprise her with dinner when she got home.

She'd only been in her new position with the local child advocacy group for a couple of weeks, but Terry could already tell she invested a great deal of her emotional energy in the cases. The least he could do was have dinner waiting on her, allowing her to do nothing but kick off those high heels and relax.

He heard the key turn in the lock and hurried to set out the plates that he'd found in the meticulously marked box and chopsticks from the restaurant before she walked in. In a few long strides, he was at the front door, ready to kiss her hello after—from what he'd learned talking to her earlier—a trying day.

"Hello, sweetheart. Welcome home. I've got dinner!" Terry leaned down to kiss her, but he pulled back when she turned her icy blue stare at him, her eyes squinting as they did when she was miffed with someone.

She may have a fiery temper to match that gorgeous red hair, but those eyes will positively freeze you in your tracks.

For about the hundredth time, he thanked the Lord that he'd never had to go up against Meredith in a legal situation. Although he knew her to be kind, compassionate, and fair, he'd also seen the competent, experienced, and sometimes ruthless attorney who'd made a name for herself in family law.

"Bad day?" Terry asked, attempting to relieve her of her briefcase and purse, but she jerked away from him, her nostrils flaring as she took a step back.

He held his hands up, not exactly sure what he was surrendering to, but wanting to make it perfectly clear he was doing so.

"A bad day, Terry? You wanna know if I've had a bad day?"

He had noticed her cultured, practiced courtroom diction slipped away when she was angry, leaving behind the deep Southern drawl from her youth. It was alluring, but he didn't dare smile, no matter how appealing it was.

"Um, do you want to talk about what happened?" he asked, watching her slam her belongings down on the rented sofa. Her enormous custom-made sectional wouldn't make it from North Carolina to Burton for several weeks.

Meredith was obviously madder than a wet hornet, leaving Terry clueless as to how he figured into the situation. From her combative posture—her hands jammed onto her slim hips and her chin jutted toward him—he inferred he was most definitely a part of the problem.

The thing that remained was to figure out exactly what he'd done.

"I'm not some opportunistic gold-digger, you know." She kicked off her heels and began pacing, arms crossed and gaze never leaving Terry's. He'd seen "the walk" in the court scenes on TV shows, but he had to concede one point—it looked much better on Meredith than it did on those actors trying to play a part.

"I'm well aware of that," he said, trying to concentrate on the situation at hand. "I never said you were."

"So, why would people think that the only reason I'm marrying you is for your money? I've got my own money, you know!" She flailed her arms wildly, and her voice had edged up until she was almost squeaking by the time she'd finished her sentence.

Still having no clue regarding the source of such ridiculous allegations, Terry wanted nothing more than to hold the woman he loved and kiss away her doubts. He wanted to make all the ugly insinuations disappear and to make her understand that he loved her because of how wonderful she was, exactly the way God had made her.

He had to tread lightly, though. She stood poised before him like a cat ready to bolt, or pounce, at the slightest provocation.

Against everything within him, Terry stood his ground, motionless but definitely not emotionless. "May I ask what precipitated this charge?"

"It's all over town. My goodness, Terry, we just announced our engagement, and already there are busybodies talking about us." Meredith had moved past rage now. Her voice shook with the hurt and confusion of being the target of nasty rumors.

Seeing his opening, Terry went to her and wrapped her in his arms. She stood stiffly and unyielding for several seconds, but Terry had no intention of letting go. Running his hand slowly up and down her back, he could feel her tense muscles gradually begin to relax. Soon, she wrapped her arms around him and rested her cheek against his broad chest.

"Wanna talk about it?" he asked.

"Oh, Terry," she said, leaning back so she could see his face. "I felt like such a fool. I know I'm relatively new to town, but I thought that would give me at least some degree of protection against petty rumors. People don't even know me."

"Why don't we fix our dinner, and you can tell me the whole story?" Terry suggested.

"Okay," she sighed out. "It does smell delicious."

They scooped chow mein and moo goo gai pan on their plates while Meredith told of her visit to the city's licensing office to inquire about what she needed to do to set up her practice in town. While there, she had overheard two women in an adjoining cubicle talking, and loudly.

"I hate eavesdropping, Terry. But, for heaven's sake, if someone doesn't want to be overheard, the least they could do is lower their voices. It was as if they wanted everyone around to know their business."

"So, what exactly did they say that upset you so?" Terry asked, scooping up his food with chopsticks.

"The first lady asked if the other had heard you and I were getting married. She obviously didn't know I was only a few feet away, or maybe she did and just didn't care. Anyway, the second lady then said, yes, she'd heard. She said I'd snagged a real cash cow, what with the inheritance and all. They both agreed that was the real reason I was marrying you."

Now it was Terry's turn to be angry. What right did people have discussing his love life? Or his finances? Or their perceived intersection of the two? Or—and this was the one that infuriated him the most—his beautiful, kind, generous fiancée?

"Did you recognize either of the voices?" he asked.

Meredith shook her head. "I don't know everyone in town like the rest of y'all do." She took a bite and chewed slowly, a pensive look crossing her features. "You know what?" She swallowed, and Terry could swear he saw a lightbulb turn on over her head. "Come to think of it, I walked out of the office with that lady who came to the Chamber meeting with Dorothy Comstock. Could that be a coincidence?"

The mention of the woman's name still set Terry's blood to boiling. If he found out she was responsible for such hateful lies after all the other trouble she'd caused, he'd have a really hard time conducting himself as a gentleman.

Deep down, he truly believed she was responsible for spreading this untruth. And if she was willing to gossip and tell falsehoods once, how many more times would she do it? How many times had she done it already? What did she have to gain? How far was she willing to go to hurt others?

§§§

Dottie couldn't believe her luck. She'd invited Teresa Bell to lunch on Wednesday, hoping to pump her for information about her first few weeks in Burton. Little did Dot know she'd strike oil when the pumping started.

The ladies walked into a cozy roadside diner on the outskirts of town and found a table near the back. Dot didn't need the prying eyes of people she knew witnessing their little lunch date. The irony of her strategy was completely lost on the town gossip.

"So, tell me," Dottie said, opening her napkin and smoothing it into her lap, "have you made any new friends in Burton?"

"I've met some very nice people," Teresa Bell said, perusing the menu.

"Really?" Dottie leaned forward, inviting Teresa Bell to share without having to ask outright.

"Oh, yes. I went to the café, like you suggested. The girls there are very sweet. We chatted about their business, but I didn't really get an opportunity to propose a mutually beneficial business deal, even though our clientele would dovetail so nicely."

"Why not?" Dottie asked, trying to act interested in Teresa Bell's prattle when she really just wanted to hear what she'd learned. She didn't give a fly's eye about Teresa's business or how she planned to manage it.

Patience, Dorothy, she chided herself.

The waitress took their orders, and then Teresa Bell continued her tale.

"So, anyway, we were talking about their first catering gig, just like you suggested. When I asked her about the second couple who got married that day being intent on taking over the girls' home, things kind of got crazy real fast."

"Crazy ... how?" The woman sitting across from Dottie now commanded her full attention.

Easy, Dottie, old girl. Be cool.

"Well, it was strange. The girl I was talking to—she has a strange name. It's not Riley, but it's something like that. Anyway, when I started talking about the home, the old lady at the next table had some kind of ... like a spell or something. She and the young man she was with got up and left abruptly. It seemed to upset Riley—or whatever her name is." Teresa Bell had a faraway look in her eyes as she recounted the events from earlier in the week, as if she were reliving the scene.

"Um ... So, what did the old lady look like?" Dottie asked, tamping down her excitement as she stirred a packet of artificial sweetener into her tea.

She and Matilda were the same age, so she tried not to take offense at the "old lady" comment. She had no problem overlooking an age-related jab if it meant gathering some crucial information.

"Well, she was short, gray hair. You know, old-lady-looking. Oh, I almost forgot. She walked with a cane." Teresa Bell took a sip of water when she finished.

Dottie couldn't believe her luck. Could she really have sown a seed of doubt, bitterness, or anger in the life of the unflappable Matilda Gault?

Tucking away the thought to relish more fully later, she continued to ask Teresa Bell about her week. The woman had proven to be a useful pawn in Dot's plan, so the least she could do was listen to her prattle on for a bit.

"Everything else I've been doing is just the legwork for getting the business set up. It's nice to be in a small town where you can get almost everything done in one place. I got most everything taken care of at the municipal building. In fact, the lady in the licensing office and I really hit it off. She's got two grown kids and goes to the same church you do." Teresa sipped her water again. "She thinks that beautiful red-headed attorney is marrying the architect for his money. Something about a will."

Dottie's heart soared. Had it really been this easy? Find some unsuspecting and trusting stranger and set her loose. Of course, Dottie gave herself credit for laying much of the rumor mill groundwork, without which none of the hurtful allegations Teresa Bell had disclosed would have surfaced.

Their food arrived, and they shared companionable banter as they enjoyed their salads. Dottie was in such a good mood that she ordered them each a slice of pecan pie to go. She didn't argue, though, when Teresa Bell offered to pick up the check.

Yes, indeed. A really good day.

All Wrong

Mrs. Drummond's sleek Cadillac was already in the church parking lot when Alex dropped Lydia off at kindergarten before heading to the fellowship hall to decorate for the Harvest Tea. It still didn't seem right that her little girl was a kindergartener, but Lydia thrived on the routine and the lessons, coming home every day with a new fact or skill.

Alex grabbed her bag from the seat beside her then walked into the church, checking her email as she went. She didn't notice the two cars pulling into the parking lot as the fellowship hall doors closed behind her.

"Good morning, Mrs. Drummond!" Alex called across the space that was already filled with dozens of round tables awaiting the artistic touch of the pastor's wife.

"Well, hello, Alex," Mrs. Drummond said, circulating among the tables and placing a folded tablecloth on each one. "Are you here to help decorate, or to scope out where you'll be standing when you speak tomorrow?"

"Um, the first. Just point me in the direction where I can be most useful." Although she'd prepared, rehearsed, and refined her remarks for the tea, Alex still felt a lump in the pit of her stomach at the thought of facing so many people at once. *Who am I to tell these godly women anything they don't already know? Why did I agree to this?*

Mrs. Drummond handed the stack of tablecloths to Alex. "If you would, finish putting one of these at each table. Once some of the more, um ... basic decorating helpers get here, they can get them laid out on the tables. I've got other things for you to do once I get all of the decorations out of storage."

The older lady disappeared into the storage closet while Alex continued the task she'd been assigned, only to be interrupted by the harsh sound of arguing as people approached the space from outside.

Alex stopped and listened to the raised voices, tilting her head in disbelief that they could belong to the people she suspected. When those same people burst through the door, Alex stared at them in shock.

"What kind of brother are you, Chad?" Charmain yelled. "I can't believe you'd say such things. And after all I've done for you, and Alex, and Lydia!"

"Get over yourself, Charmain. You know I didn't say those things. And besides, we've done a lot for you, too, you know!" His deep voice reverberated off the soaring ceiling.

The sister and brother stood toe to toe, locked in a sibling battle of the wills that had played out most of their lives. Their clenched fists, flared nostrils, and flushed cheeks told Alex they'd been at this one for a while. And they'd reached an impasse.

"Hey, y'all," she said quietly, tiptoeing toward them. She felt as if she were approaching a pair of animals locked in mortal combat. The slightest disturbance could cause them to direct their anger at her, a situation she had no intention of causing. "What's wrong?"

Alex instantly knew she'd asked the wrong question.

The White siblings turned from each other and faced Alex, both wearing a smug, self-satisfied expression that told Alex each believed the other to be the offending party. Chad crossed his arms, Charmain planted her hands on her hips, and they both began to speak at once. They might have a bitter wedge of disagreement between them, but they still had a couple of crucial things in common—they were both loud and livid.

Alex held her hands up and closed her eyes, indicating her unwillingness to endure such a melee.

"Why don't you tell me everything ... one at a time?" Alex suggested. "Ladies first," she added quickly when she saw both parties draw a breath to start yelling again.

"Thank you," Charmain said, tucking her hair behind her ears and taking a deep breath. "My friend, Joyce, said her boyfriend heard one of Chad's mechanics say that Chad had told him he didn't think I'd follow through with my schoolwork, that I'd just quit again ... like I always do." Her eyes flashed at her brother, raw hurt evident despite her anger. Or maybe because of it. Alex wasn't sure.

It was a convoluted accusation, but Alex thought she got the gist of it.

"Charmain, I'm sure Chad didn't--"

"Alex," Charmain interrupted her, "you can't be the mediator if you're going to take sides. How are you sure he didn't say it?" Charmain turned her ire on her best friend, which made Alex squirm.

The truth was that Alex and Chad had both had their doubts about Charmain's latest career choice. As far as Alex knew, though, they'd only spoken of such things in private.

"Well, Char, why don't we just ask Chad?" Alex started again, using her best diplomatic voice in an attempt to bring the temperature down on the argument, knowing she needed to support her husband at the same time.

"Babe, you know I'd never say such things, especially at the garage." Chad's green-eyed stare made Alex doubt her ability to maintain any semblance of neutrality in this argument.

She nodded at her husband.

"Well, what a welcome surprise!" Mrs. Drummond called, coming out of the storage closet. "A strong man to do some of the heavy lifting." Her face was alight with joy, even as she struggled to heave a huge plastic bin onto the nearest table.

Chad rushed to her aid.

"Oh, sure. Now he's the picture of a Southern gentleman," Charmain spat at him. "He goes around talking about his only sister like I'm some lazy, good-for-nothing—"

"Char, just stop it." The harshness in Alex's voice cut Charmain's rant short.

"If you'll excuse me, I'm just going to get some more bins," Mrs. Drummond said, making a hasty retreat.

"Chad's coming with you," Alex said, giving her husband a nudge in the ribs with her elbow.

He took the hint, stepping quickly to catch up with the pastor's wife.

Alex turned back to her sister-in-law. "Where's this coming from, Char? You're one of the most self-assured people I know. When have you ever worried about what people thought about what you did?"

Charmain bowed her head and stared at her new red ballet flats.

Alex waited, giving her time. She knew that sometimes a person could endure the onslaught for only so long. Then they ran the risk of snapping under the pressure. And whether Charmain's pressure was applied by others or it was self-imposed, maybe today was the day she had simply broken under the weight of it. Alex wanted to be there to help her pick up the pieces. Just like Charmain had done for Alex more than once.

§§§

Charmain felt the sting of tears, and she blinked rapidly to stop them from spilling down her cheeks. She didn't want anyone to see how deeply the allegations had hurt her. But, when Alex came alongside her and touched her arm, Charmain's composure crumbled.

"Why am I such a failure, Alex? Why can't I be confident and successful

… like you or Meredith?" She dabbed her eyes and blew her nose with the tissue that Alex dug out of her mammoth bag. "All I've ever wanted to do was make Chad proud of me."

Alex watched her friend in mute disbelief.

"Char, you've always come across as the picture of confidence. I've admired you since the day I met you. I mean, look at you! Gorgeous, outgoing, fearless. To be honest, I've found myself jealous of you more than once."

Charmain put her face in her hands, causing her words to come out muffled but intelligible. "None of that's real, Alex. I'm just a scared woman trying to figure out what I want to be when I grow up. The problem is … I'm grown, and I still haven't figured it out." Her body shook with the sobs of pent-up anguish.

Alex wrapped Charmain in a hug and rubbed her back soothingly.

Charmain felt like a fool. In the space of a few minutes, she'd flung nasty accusations at her brother and fallen apart in front of her sister-in-law, the two people she admired most. They had it all together. They'd both taken the hardships life had dealt them and forged on, creating successful careers, a loving, satisfying relationship, and a beautiful, growing family. *Why can't I find all that?*

"Alex, I really do want Chad proud of me. After Mom died, Dad just shut down, checked out. If it hadn't been for my brother, I don't know where I'd be. He's my rock. I want to show him all his efforts weren't wasted." She lifted her red-rimmed eyes, searching Alex's face for the understanding she desperately needed.

"Char, I'm going to be completely honest with you, okay? Several months back—in fact, it was on the day Chad and I first found out about the inheritance—I voiced my desire to help you find a career path that really excited you. Something you'd want to stick with for the long haul. We were dreaming about all we could do, all the people we could help.

The thing is, though, nobody else was around. We agreed to pray about it and see where the Lord took you."

The logical side of Charmain's brain told her this was a more plausible explanation of the ugly rumor she'd heard. But, if there was a nugget of truth in it, how did it start making its rounds if neither Alex nor Chad blabbed their thoughts to the wrong person? It just didn't add up.

"I don't understand. If it was just the two of you, how did a rumor so close to the truth start making its way around town?" Charmain felt her anger at her brother begin to cool. Still, someone was trying to discredit her in her brother's, and the town's, eyes. Who would do such a cruel thing?

Both women puzzled over the question, wrapped up in their thoughts, when the door to the hall opened again.

Terry and Meredith walked on each side of Miss Matilda, matching her slow but deliberate pace. The scowl on the old lady's face was completely out of character, sweeping Charmain's problems from her thoughts.

"Miss Matilda, what's wrong?" Charmain asked.

Chad brought two big bins of decorations out of the storage closet just in time to hear Charmain's concerned question.

"I think all of you know exactly what's wrong," Miss Matilda said, her voice shaking with emotion. "And it's time we got to the bottom of it right now." She plopped down into the nearest chair.

Chad, Alex, Charmain, Terry, and Meredith stood in front of her, looking at each other with questions in their eyes, but no one dared to be the first to speak. Charmain wasn't sure about the others, but she hated being on the receiving end of Miss Matilda's displeasure.

How much worse could this day get?

§§§

Since her disastrous trip on Tuesday to R&B Café, Matilda had cried and prayed, sulked and prayed, thought and prayed. Now it was Friday—she'd told Landry she wasn't feeling up to their standing Thursday date this week—and she was no closer to understanding why the people she loved so much had seemingly betrayed her, discarded her, lost confidence in her ability.

Kicked her to the curb.

She'd sat in silence the whole ride to the church with Terry and Meredith, only accepting their offer for a ride because she didn't have her car at the Whites' house. She'd seen the glances her nephew and his fiancée had given each other, especially when they'd try to engage her in conversation and she'd supplied monosyllabic responses.

"My!" Peggy Drummond said from behind an armful of burlap and grapevine wreaths. "Looks like the decorating committee will be getting lots of extra help this year!"

Matilda saw the puzzled look in Peggy's expression, but the woman had been a pastor's wife far too long to give away her emotions.

"I wish I were here to help, Peggy, but, apparently, there are people here"—Matilda shot a scathing look at the young people—"who think I'm no longer capable of such things."

"Aunt Tilley, what are you talking about?" Terry asked, holding his hands out, palms up, as if in surrender.

"Just because I'm still getting my strength back doesn't mean I ever lost my hearing. I've heard what my friends and family are saying about me." Matilda stopped, scared if she tried to say more that the floodgates would burst.

The five people before her shared confused looks.

What if I got this all wrong?

Oh, Matilda, you fool. What have you done?

"Miss M., we honestly have no idea what you're talking about," Chad said, rubbing his neck with one roughened hand as he wrapped his other arm protectively around his precious wife.

"Matilda," Peggy said softly, moving to stand behind her now that she'd set down her armload of decorations, "may I try to help y'all get to the bottom of this?"

Matilda nodded, staring at the tissue she was shredding in her lap.

"Thank you. Let's start with you, Matilda." Peggy put her arm around the sweet, quivering lady and squeezed gently. "What have you heard that's upset you so?"

Matilda took a deep breath before repeating the heart-piercing information. "I heard a woman tell Riker that my friends and family have no confidence that I'd ever move back to Together for Good again, much less ever be able to help in any way." Even to her own ears, her voice sounded pitiful and whiny. Matilda then looked at the floor, unable to bear the pity she anticipated seeing in their eyes.

Peggy turned her attention to the young people. "Is this true?"

"No!" they chorused in unison.

"Aunt Tilley"—Terry moved toward her—"we're scheduled to break ground on your new house in a couple of weeks. Why would I move ahead with the house if I had any doubts about your ability and competence?" He knelt in front of her, taking her hands in his. "We're so proud of how hard you've worked to reclaim your health. You suffered a stroke! We could have lost you. Do you know how thankful we are that you're still with us?"

Matilda finally raised her head just enough to see her nephew's handsome face. Meredith's love had made the stress and pain of the past few years melt away, and it looked good on him.

She reached out and placed her hand on his cheek. "So, who was the woman saying such things? And where would she have heard this?" Matilda questioned, wanting with everything within her to believe Terry had spoken the truth but still wondering about the allegations.

The intensity of the moment was shattered by laughing and chattering voices approaching the fellowship hall.

"I believe the rest of the decorating committee is here." Peggy said, checking her watch. "Maybe y'all can work through this some more in the parlor," she suggested.

The group moved across the fellowship hall and toward the smaller room used by the prayer team, grief counselors, and one of the smaller Sunday school classes. They hadn't made it out of the fellowship hall, though, when they heard a voice. A voice that lit a fire of dislike and disgust in the belly of every one of them.

"Well, what do we have here?" Dorothy Comstock called as she walked in, her face split in a mirthless grin and sheer malevolence shining in her eyes. "I thought none of you would be speaking to each other by now."

In the Open

Peggy Drummond stepped forward before the others had a chance to say something they would regret. "Dorothy, are you here to decorate or cause trouble? Because if it's the second, I recommend you turn right around and leave the way you came in."

Alex's jaw hung open. She'd never heard Mrs. Drummond speak such firm words, or in such a harsh tone.

She watched the two women stand off in the middle of the half-decorated fellowship hall, a study in contrasts. Mrs. Drummond epitomized Southern elegance in her bubblegum pink cashmere sweater set, flowing black knit slacks, and buttery soft black flats. Not a hair was out of place, and she held herself with the posture of one who knew not only who she was but Whose she was.

As Alex examined Dorothy Comstock more closely, she saw the woman for who she was, and a wave of pity assailed Alex's heart. This old acquaintance of Miss Matilda's—Alex had trouble believing they'd actually been friends—looked disheveled and unkempt. Her wrinkled blouse could have been pulled from the bottom of a hamper full of clothes. If so, the skirt she'd selected to go with it most definitely didn't "go with it." Alex thought about how mortified Brittany would be at the sight and had to stifle a giggle. *Not an appropriate reaction in this situation, Alex. Get it together.*

Somewhere in her peripheral vision, Alex saw Terry pull up a chair for his aunt.

Still, the pastor's wife and the town gossip stared at one another in silence. A silence that grew more uncomfortable by the second for the others present.

The ladies who had entered a few seconds ago with Dorothy huddled by the door, obviously scared to venture inside, yet not one dared to leave and miss a single second of what was about to happen.

Finally, Peggy Drummond took control. She crossed her arms and tilted her chin up, striking an imposing figure. "Mrs. Comstock, I hate to have to do this, but I must ask you to leave. I feel certain I will have the support of my husband and the Harvest Tea committee."

Alex glanced around to see her friends staring at Mrs. Drummond with the same look of shock that had been on her own face just seconds before.

"I beg your pardon?" Dot said, advancing on Peggy as if she intended to do her bodily harm.

The movement was enough to rouse Chad and Terry out of their shocked stupor. They rushed to Mrs. Drummond's side, prepared to defend her.

"Thank you, gentlemen," Mrs. Drummond said, casting a grateful glance at each of them. "That won't be necessary, though. Will it, Dorothy?" She focused her gaze on the woman in front of her.

"I knew it," Dorothy whispered so quietly the women standing beside Miss Matilda could barely hear her. "I knew that God of yours wasn't all you said He was." She gained steam as she spoke and crescendoed in a top-of-her-lungs shriek, "He *doesn't* love everyone! He *doesn't* forgive everything! I was *right*! You've proven my point ... and I've *won*!" She turned a blotchy beet red, her hands clenched at the ends of her stiff arms, and her body shook in impotent rage. Her breath came in short, shallow pants, and her eyes bulged. Then she turned on the scuffed and worn heel of her shoe and began marching off.

"Why did you do it?"

The question stopped Dorothy Comstock dead in her tracks.

§§§

"Why did you come back, Dot?" Matilda spoke evenly and calmly, standing up and walking toward the woman who she'd known so many years before. "Was it the familiarity of Burton? Because you grew up here? Or was there something else that drew you back?"

"Oh, dear, idealistic Matilda, still as stupid and tenderhearted as ever, I see. Honestly, I can't believe someone hasn't scammed you out of a fortune by now. It would be so easy." Dorothy's face contorted into a wicked grin, as if she took joy in offending Matilda. "If you must know, Matilda, I came back to get my revenge against you."

Silence so thick that Matilda thought she could reach out and touch it hung in the air for several seconds.

"Dorothy," Matilda spoke in the soothing tone she used with her girls, "I have no idea what I've ever done to you, but—"

"Don't you pull that apology crap on me, you sanctimonious—"

"That's quite enough, Mrs. Comstock," Mrs. Drummond interrupted her before any vulgar language flew. "This may be the fellowship hall, but it is still the house of the Lord, and it will be revered as such."

Dorothy barked out a toneless laugh, crossed her arms, and began pacing in front of the group. "The Lord. What has the Lord done for me?" She jabbed at her chest. "I'll tell you. He's taken everything away from me, that's what! And it's *all ... her ... fault!*" She pointed at Matilda.

"I can assure you of one thing, Dot Comstock," Matilda continued using her regulated voice, even in the face of such vehement accusations. "Whatever you've lost, the Lord has taken away for a reason."

"What do you know about pain and heartbreak? When have you ever experienced loss?" Dorothy was shrieking again. Her face had turned a disturbing purple. "What do any of those people standing behind you know about losing anything that's dear to them?"

Terry, Meredith, Chad, Alex, and Charmain swiveled their heads to look at one another. Then, as if on cue, they all started laughing.

§§§

Their outburst wasn't ideal. Or even appropriate. Alex recognized that point. But the absurdity of Dorothy Comstock's statement was so shockingly incredulous that they could think of no other reaction.

Looking around at these people who had become her family, not by birth but by love, Alex understood how each of their losses, and their responses to the pain, had been used by God to shape them into the empowered people they were today.

How different might life be had they allowed those deep, aching losses to make them bitter? What if they hadn't relied on their faith in the Lord to strengthen and comfort them through the difficult days when each one first faced their trials? What if they'd abandoned His abiding comfort during those times over the years when, out of the blue, they were reminded of what they'd been asked to walk through? And of how far they'd come?

For Meredith, it was when she had seen a young person who would be about the age her child would be now. Finally, that wound had begun to heal with the help of her faith in Jesus.

For Terry, it was last year when he had faced his biological father and helped lead him to faith in Jesus Christ. It had taken him a long time to come to terms with the fact that he had been adopted, but the privilege of participating in his father's salvation had been a balm to his wounded spirit.

For Chad and Charmain, it was in ministering to others who lost loved ones to the unfathomable pain of suicide. Losing their mother that way was a pain no child should have to suffer.

The Lord walked Alex through her own pain—assault, miscarriage, an emotionally absent mother—and He used all of these dear friends to come alongside her and help her through each day.

But all of these heartaches and sorrows dimmed in the light of the promises of the Lord's eternal love. Alex hadn't known about such wondrous love when she'd arrived in Burton a few years ago, when Miss Matilda had introduced her to the joy of knowing Jesus.

So, what went so wrong with Mrs. Comstock?

Alex took her husband's hand and mouthed the word, *"Pray."*

He nodded and bowed his head.

"Mrs. Comstock," Alex said, stepping forward to stand beside her dear friend and mentor, "just so you know, every single one of us has experienced life-changing, heart-breaking losses. But, what exactly did Miss Matilda do that upset you so? We're all curious." Alex held her breath, praying the woman wouldn't come at her with claws bared.

"*Do*? I'll tell you what she did." Dorothy took a couple of breaths in an apparent attempt to calm herself then seethed, "She took my husband away!"

Alex thought the collective gasp behind them would suck the air out of the room.

"Dorothy Comstock, I did no such thing!" Matilda protested, indignant at the accusation.

"Well, you might as well have," Dorothy returned, attempting to salvage her argument.

"You'd better explain yourself, and fast, lady." Matilda narrowed her eyes. "Because I'm quickly losing patience with you."

Alex had seen Miss Matilda truly upset only a few times, and there were only a few things that could set her off. When someone messed with her family, her faith, or her girls … the grace Matilda Gault extended ran out pretty fast.

"You don't even remember, do you?" Like a deflated balloon, Dorothy's countenance collapsed. Her anger dissolved into anguish.

"No, Dot, I have no idea what I've done."

Mrs. Drummond stepped between Alex and Matilda and whispered, "Why don't y'all move to the parlor?"

Alex nodded, not wanting word of this exchange making its way around the church by the time the tea started tomorrow afternoon.

"That's an excellent idea. Let's go, Dot." Miss Matilda turned, expecting the other woman to follow.

Dorothy stood without moving. "I think your friends should join us, Matilda." She sniffed. "What I've go to tell you affects them, too." She pulled a hanky out of her sleeve, blew her nose loudly, and then strode toward the parlor, leaving the others to look at each other with questions in their eyes.

§§§

The parlor was quintessential Southern charm—overstuffed, tufted sofas in muted brocades with lots of throw pillows; coordinating wing-back chairs; cherry side tables, polished to a glossy finish, perfect for holding a cup of coffee or a glass of sweet tea; and a matching coffee table, free of clutter and ready for occupants to place their Bibles. Windows on three sides bathed the taupe walls in morning light.

Before the group even had time to claim their seats, Dot stepped behind the podium at one end of the room and began speaking. "Just to be perfectly clear," she said, in a voice too loud for the small space, "I'm the reason the rumors about all of you have been going around town." She paused, hoping to cause an uproar among the people gathered before her. When they looked at her in silence, she continued with her explanation. "I came back to Burton in May. I'd been planning to come back here to get my revenge on Matilda for several months. When I got here and found out she was in the hospital, I worried I was too late. So, I put my plan into high gear."

A knock at the door drew everyone's attention away from Dorothy. Terry was closest, so he opened it a few inches. After speaking in hushed tones for a few seconds, he threw the door open wide and ushered in Yvonne and Marquis, who looked around at their friends.

"Mrs. Drummond said we should come back here," Yvonne said, sounding unsure of herself.

Dorothy saw Matilda stiffen when the couple entered, and she took a measure of satisfaction in knowing her plan had worked.

Meanwhile, Alex scooted closer to Chad and patted the sofa beside her. The Dixons settled in quietly.

"Dorothy," Matilda said, ignoring the entrance of the couple who had taken over her job, "what did I do to you that made you want to hurt me so badly?"

"I'm so glad you asked," Dorothy sneered. Her eyes seemed to focus on something far away as she recounted the story of her youth. Her countenance changed, softened somehow, as she recalled her younger days.

She and Matilda had graduated from high school together, although they hadn't been close friends. Dorothy had married Bob, her high school sweetheart, days after graduation. They'd been blissfully happy ... mostly.

They dreamed of raising a big family, but after a few years, when no babies came, they began to worry. They saw doctors and visited adoption agencies, but the stress of it all put a strain on their relationship.

"All of this was happening about the time Matilda was working with her sister and brother-in-law at Together for Good during her college breaks," Dorothy said, venom in her voice directed at the woman everyone else present loved dearly.

"Oh, my word! I do remember you and your husband coming to the home," Matilda gasped, her voice almost a whisper. "It was so long ago, and we never saw you again. What happened?"

"I'll tell you what happened!" Dorothy screeched then closed her eyes, trying to regain her tenuous grasp on her self-control before continuing her narrative.

"We met those girls. I couldn't even look at them. They had everything I didn't—those beautiful, swollen bellies, that gorgeous glow. And yet, they hated themselves. They wanted to give away their babies. It was just so unfair. Why could they be given the very thing I wanted more than anything in the whole wide world?" Tears poured down Dorothy's face as she dredged up the memories, leaving tracks in her makeup and on her heart.

The group assembled before her sat silently, barely breathing, not daring to interrupt her account.

"We heard Matilda tell the girls about God's love, how Jesus died to save them from their sins—all that stuff. Bob hung on every word." Dorothy rolled her eyes. "I told him if God cared about us, He'd give *us* the babies, not those girls who had no way of providing for them." Dorothy hung her head in her hands and sobbed, her body shaking with the force of her past as it came rushing back to haunt her.

Alex took the box of tissues off one of the side tables to her.

Once the woman had again composed herself, she continued.

"I'm going to cut to the important part. Bob decided all that God stuff was real. He told me that, if I was going to continue to be bitter and blame God, we'd have to either seek help or part ways. A year later, we were divorced. A year after that, he was married to one of the girls he met at Together for Good. They've got five kids now and live in Texas."

Matilda and all the young people stared at Dorothy, waiting for more. When all that followed was her own blank stare, Matilda took the lead.

"So, I'm still not sure I understand why you came back, Dorothy. And why you'd want to seek revenge against me. What did I do?"

"Matilda, do I have to spell out everything for you?" Dorothy bellowed. "That stroke must have affected more than you realize! *You* were the one who introduced Bob to God! *That* is the reason he left me! *That* is the reason I haven't been able to find happiness in a marriage since then! It's *all ... your ... fault!*" Dorothy closed her eyes and swallowed hard. "Don't you see?" she hissed. "I had to come back here; how else could I hurt you and everyone close to you, just like you hurt me?"

Around the Hall

The sight of the fellowship hall took Alex's breath away when she stepped inside. After yesterday's revelations, they'd all slipped out the back door of the parlor and gone home to rest, pray, and consider how the Lord would have them proceed, with Him, with each other, with Dorothy Comstock.

The woman had dropped a big load on them, and they all needed to consider how her actions had impacted them individually and collectively. But they'd do so without Dorothy around to continue to sow her brand of discontent and strife.

This morning, Mrs. Drummond had called Alex to notify her that Mrs. Comstock had packed her bags and left town late last night. She gave no forwarding address, or apology. Alex prayed the woman would one day find the peace her soul so desperately needed. Then she turned her attention to the loveliness all around her.

Sunlight poured in the high transom windows, bathing everything with a warm glow. Alex wandered around, letting her fingers glide across the pristine white cloths. Juxtaposed against each immaculate cloth was a wide strip of rustic burlap. In the center of each burlap strip sat an artful mound of assorted autumn produce—corn, nuts, and a variety of squash. The tables were set with gleaming China and silverware. Little pitchers of cream and bowls of sugar had already been placed at each table. All of the service pieces were artfully mismatched, and the effect was eclectic and inviting.

Several of the men in the church had volunteered to serve the ladies today. Alex wondered if they were doing so out of a spirit of graciousness or simply to figure out what the ladies did at one of these things. Probably a bit of both, truth be told. Whatever the case, the gentlemen looked dashing in their matching outfits of black slacks, crisp white shirts, and black bow ties.

She spotted Chad filling crystal glasses with ice at the long table that served as the main drink station, situated right outside the church's industrial-sized kitchen. Other men were carrying the glasses to the tables, and still others were coming behind and filling them with water once they reached their destination.

Alex had heard the now-infamous story of how Reverend Drummond, when he'd first come to the church, had spilled a tray of ice water glasses, complete with ice and water, on the church's oldest member. The next year, a new protocol for beverage distribution had been instituted, and Reverend Drummond never darkened the doors of the Harvest Tea again.

"You look like a cross between James Bond and a maître d' at a fancy restaurant," Alex told Chad, placing her hand on his freshly-shaven face.

He chuckled as he slung a napkin over one arm and blew on a pointed finger.

"Well, you look stunning. I can see why they asked you to be the star of the show," he said.

As always, Alex was uncomfortable in the spotlight and had stressed over the selection of her outfit. And, as always, Brittany had been just a Facetime call away.

Alex approved of her friend's choice of a teal sweater dress and boots, with a flowy cardigan in jewel tones that picked up the exact colors of the lovely vegetables on the tables. Her bump had begun to pop out a bit sooner this second time around, but she intended to enjoy every second, and this dress played up her burgeoning figure.

She swatted her husband's arm, dismissing his compliment, and then kissed his cheek before turning to join Mrs. Drummond, who waved at Alex from the front of the room.

§§§

Chad knew Alex wasn't completely comfortable in these situations. Mrs. Drummond had been gracious enough to allow Alex to pick who would sit at the head table with them. The choice had been simple for her. Miss Matilda already occupied the seat to Alex's right.

Chad saw Mrs. Drummond check her watch.

The Harvest Tea had been a big deal at church for as long as he could remember. He was so proud of Alex for being selected to speak. The women's committee usually found someone from out of town, but someone must have convinced them that Alex had an important story to tell. His heart swelled with pride.

Chad suspected Charmain would arrive just as the festivities got underway. He'd heard Mrs. Drummond pull Yvonne aside yesterday and ask her to get the girl moving a bit faster than usual. Marquis was already here, so there was a good chance Yvonne was tapping her foot in Charmain's house, rushing the girl to get out the door.

Chad smiled sympathetically at the thought. He'd been on Char duty more times than he could count.

Chad felt better about his relationship with his sister than he had in years. They'd gotten a lot out in the open yesterday after Mrs. Comstock had dropped her bombshell. He truly believed Charmain was finally on the path God intended for her to be, and he couldn't be prouder. At Alex's insistence, he'd been sure to let her know just that.

Across the room at the table where filled water pitchers awaited the men, Chad watched Meredith interrupt Terry long enough to whisper in his ear and place a tiny kiss on his cheek. The lovely attorney smiled as she slipped into her seat next to Miss Matilda. She didn't look back, so she didn't see Terry place his fingertips on his cheeks in the exact spot where her lips had been moments before.

Even from this distance, Chad could see Terry swipe at his eyes before grabbing one of the nearby water glasses and taking a long swig. Chad thanked God for bringing Meredith to Burton.

§§§

Meredith found her seat next to Terry's aunt Tilley. She placed a hand on the older lady's shoulder as she slipped into her place.

"Hello, dear," Matilda said, her face radiant.

"Matilda, before things get too crazy, and while we've got a few moments alone, I want to thank you."

"*Me*? Why? Whatever have I done, dear?" Her gray eyes shown bright, making Meredith wonder if she'd make it through the words of thanks that she'd rehearsed.

"You didn't give up on me. None of you did," she said, squeezing her arm. "This place is beautiful, but it's also so meaningful that it's here among these women who have helped me learn what it means to become a woman of God."

Meredith watched her face, waiting for a reply.

Matilda drew a frilly lace hanky from her pocket and dabbed her eyes. Her nodded affirmation was all Meredith needed.

§§§

Matilda felt a bit silly being the first person seated at the head table, so she was glad when she saw Meredith coming her way to join her. Chad had been gracious enough to drive her here and escort her in.

My, girl, she mused, *you do have some very handsome young men accompanying you around. Aren't you the blessed one?*

There had only been one man whom she'd ever really cared about in a romantic way. Their paths had crossed at the worst possible time, and she'd had to walk away from her chance at love. She never regretted it, though. Matilda loved the life she'd chosen, convinced it was the way God had intended for her to go. He'd given her a purpose and a mission field. He'd given her strength and wisdom. And He'd blessed her with some of the dearest people ever created. No, a lifetime of romantic love could have never compared to the fullness she'd experienced.

Could it?

Matilda looked around the beautifully decorated hall until she found Alex and Chad. Tears stung the backs of her eyes as she remembered everything they'd endured to get to where they were. Across the hall, Meredith placed a tender kiss on Terry's cheek, and he looked at her with nothing short of sheer adoration in his eyes. God had done wonderful work in the lives of these young folks, for sure.

And now, did she, Matilda Gault, have the faith in her own heart, the faith she preached to every girl who ever came through Together for Good, to believe she'd soon be healed and back to work?

She bowed her head, determined to take her questions to the Author and Perfecter of her faith right there.

§§§

As Terry watched Meredith take her seat, he saw his aunt Tilley bow her head to pray. He hoped all was well, but he didn't dare interrupt her. Besides, his emotions were still a bit raw after his sweet encounter with Meredith. *How did I ever think Gail was the woman God intended for me?*

He thought back to all of the wasted years that he'd spent trying to make her happy. He understood now that nothing in the world would ever make her happy, short of a legion of minions designed to do her bidding night and day. He smiled at the thought of Gail ordering around a legion of minions.

It had taken a painful realization, an even more painful divorce, and the wisdom of a young girl to make Terry open his eyes to the sham his life had become. He'd tried to thank Alex a thousand times in a thousand ways, but she always brushed off her contribution to his life change by telling him that she was just where God had wanted her to be.

Maybe.

But, as Terry looked back on the man he'd been and the man he was now, he was overwhelmed at the difference. He thought he'd been a man of faith, grounded in his belief in God, but when everything he had believed to be true about his life crumbled, from who his parents were to what his wife was truly like, he had felt his foundations crumbling beneath him.

Not a feeling anyone, especially an architect, wants to feel.

That was when he'd gone deeper, grown in his faith, learned what it was to be a brother, biologically and spiritually, and eventually grown to forgive the woman who'd given everything she was and had to raise him. Now, as he stood ready to marry the woman who truly complemented him, spiritually, intellectually, emotionally … in every way imaginable, Terry clearly saw God's hand.

§§§

"Ha!" Charmain said in triumph as she and Yvonne stepped through the door. "Twelve minutes to spare. Told you we'd make it." She side-hugged Yvonne before rushing off to find their seats.

Yvonne grinned at her friend, who most folks had mistaken for her sister when they had first met. She'd known Charmain for a long time and knew her proclivity for bad timing and her aversion to punctuality. Sometimes she was just good, old-fashioned late. Sometimes she showed up at exactly the wrong time.

Today, however, Charmain had put forth an incredible amount of effort to make it to the Harvest Tea on time. Yvonne guessed it had a lot to do with Char's deep affection for Alex. But she thought it also went deeper than that.

Ever since Charmain had announced that she intended to become a licensed sonographer and work at Together for Good, Yvonne and Marquis had noticed the girl dropped by more often. She'd bring the residents thoughtful little gifts, like journals or fuzzy socks. She pitched in at mealtime and in the garden.

Yvonne knew this took no small amount of work on Charmain's part, considering how hurtful Yvonne had been during her stay at the home many years ago.

Whatever Char's motivation, Yvonne continued to be thankful for her new friend and prayed she'd find the job that made her happy. Yvonne also prayed that job would be with them.

§§§

Marquis stood at the end of the serving station designated for tea service preparation, setting out the metal baskets and lining them with frilly napkins.

He heard Charmain's exclamation when she and Yvonne walked in and turned to see them. His lovely wife, who hadn't yet found him in the growing crowd, made her way to the front table. He knew how touched she'd been for Alex to ask her to join them in the place of honor.

Marquis ran his hand over his face, gathering the emotions that threatened to well up within him. What had he done to deserve the life he had?

Nothing, man; that's what.

It was true. He'd made so many mistakes. So many. And yet, Jesus had called him back, forgiven him, washed him clean of all unrighteousness. Not only that, but the only woman he'd ever loved had come back to him, he'd found a job where he could truly make a difference in the lives of women and their unborn children, and he had some of the most loyal friends a man could ever ask for.

If there was anything in his heart that he could ever count as lacking, it was their son.

Yvonne had put him up for adoption when Marquis had walked away from her. What else could he have expected her to do? His heart broke every time he thought that their child was out there somewhere, being raised by someone else.

Were they teaching him about God? Was he smart? Was he athletic?

Today, though, Marquis would push thoughts of the boy aside and concentrate on being a faithful servant to these ladies who had welcomed him and his wife with open arms.

He began stacking teabags in each lined basket. It would soon be time to place them on the tables.

§§§

Alex took her seat and looked around as ladies filed in and the place filled up, her heart threatening to burst within her. Each lady here today had impacted Alex in some way over the past few years. Some had taught Bible studies, some had kept the nursery or led children's church, others had sung in the choir, and others had thrown a beautiful bridal shower when she and Chad had gotten married. Many of these ladies had helped move the Dixons into Together for Good. And, of course, there were the girls who'd made sure her wedding, and that of the Dixons', had been nothing short of perfection. Riker and Blakely worked tirelessly to serve the people of Burton.

Alex reached out and took Miss Matilda's hand. She was rewarded with one of the older lady's beaming smiles.

"Is anything wrong, dear?"

"No, ma'am. Just the opposite. Everything is very right."

Miss Matilda patted Alex's hand and nodded. Silently, they sat and watched their dearest friends come together.

Tea Talk

The men now wandered around the room, carrying the fare of the day, lovingly prepared by Riker and Blakely. Some presented trays laden with finger sandwiches to the women, others carried scones and clotted cream or delicate petit fours, and others circulated with tea pots, always at the ready to keep the ladies' cups filled.

Mrs. Drummond and Alex had gone over the order of the program several times, so Alex knew exactly when she would take the podium to speak. Consequently, her appetite waned. Although she no longer suffered from morning sickness on most days, the stress of speaking in front of a large crowd, no matter how friendly, clenched her stomach into a knot.

"We'll wrap you up a plate to take home," Miss Matilda whispered. "And one for Lydia, too."

Alex smiled. Of course, the lady who had been taking care of her for five years would still be doing so, even during her own recuperation from a stroke.

Alex nodded and hugged the woman who was so many things—a friend, mentor, confidante, sounding-board, truth-speaker.

Mrs. Drummond patted her back, indicating it was time to begin the program.

Alex took a fortifying sip of her peppermint tea while Mrs. Drummond introduced her. Then, as the ladies politely applauded, she scooped up her note cards, said a quick prayer that the Lord would supply her with His words, and stepped behind the microphone.

"Mrs. Drummond and the Harvest Tea committee, I want to thank you for the opportunity to share a few words today," she spoke directly to their official host.

Mrs. Drummond, a Southern lady to the core, nodded her elegantly-coiffed head in response.

"And, I most especially want to thank each of you here today.

"As I look around this room, with its beautiful decorations, delicious food, and wonderful fellowship, I see people who have had a huge impact on my faith journey. Not only mine, though, but on the journeys of many girls who have been residents at Together for Good. You've shown us what faith looks like, what it feels like and, yes, even what it tastes like. Because, let's be honest, we're a bunch of Southern church ladies. We'd just as soon bake a casserole as look at you."

The ladies chuckled in agreement, acknowledging their belief that most life-altering events called for a chicken casserole or a chocolate cake. Major events required both.

"Growing up, I had everything I wanted. Looking back, I was what you'd call a spoiled brat. What I didn't have, and didn't know I even needed, was faith in Jesus. I didn't have that until I came to Burton, through circumstances I'd have never chosen, but I'm so thankful for now. Not because I'm glad I went through difficult times, but because I now have the wisdom to see Who brought me through them."

She'd considered how many details of her assault she should share. In the end, she and Chad had agreed that keeping everything in general terms was best. The day would someday come that she would owe Lydia an explanation of her true parentage. Alex didn't want half-true stories of her situation circulating around town, potentially reaching her little ears before Alex was ready.

Alex continued talking about the challenges and triumphs of being a single mother, college student, and business owner. Each a daunting task on its own, but in conjunction with the other two ... well, life had become a delicate juggling act at times.

"Over the past year, since I married my very handsome husband"—all eyes turned to Chad at the drink station, and Alex could see pink creep into his cheeks—"I've become especially cognizant of the need for the support of family. Not necessarily those related by blood. I'm talking instead about those family bonds cultivated through a common faith, shared experiences, and a true respect for each other. I'm so blessed to have such a family."

She paused as she allowed her eyes to roam from Chad, to Terry, to Marquis as they circulated the room, serving the ladies. She saw Riker and Blakely, young women also striving to grow their own business and raise their children to know the Lord. Finally, she looked to her left and right at her core support group, mouthing, *"Thank you,"* in each direction.

"I pray that the Lord has provided all of you with a similar support system."

Alex said another quick prayer before she launched into the part of her remarks that she'd revised last night as she was processing the havoc that Dorothy Comstock had wreaked on their circle of friends.

"Ladies, we have the privilege and comfort of being able to rely on our faith in difficult circumstances. My friends and I have all had to face some hard stuff over the past few months, but our faith in the Lord has carried us. I'm sad to say, however, that sometimes our faith in each other has been found wanting, especially when we've been undermined by untrue and ugly rumors.

"I want to issue you a challenge today. Don't believe the words that come after 'someone told me ...' Don't repeat those words. Gossip and rumors are the enemy's work, and he delights in using them to destroy the relationships that are dearest to us. Stand in the gap and stop the gossip."

Looking around the room, she saw some of the women shift uncomfortably in their chairs. Others looked at her with confused expressions.

"I'll close with this reminder, sisters. The words *gospel* and *gossip* only differ by three letters. Think about it; you can spread either one to people around you. So, if the first three letters of both words stand for Giving Out Some—for the G, O, and S—then let's consider what those last three letters can stand for.

"I think we should think of the word *gospel* as standing for Giving Out Some Peace, Encouragement, and Love. Aren't those the very things Jesus came to Earth to teach us about?

"On the other hand, when we gossip, we are actually Giving Out Some Strife, Innuendo, and Prevarication."

She paused to let it sink in, smiling when she noticed that some of the younger ladies were typing notes on their phones.

"So, think about what it is that you want to spread—gospel or gossip. Love on your family, however it is God has given them to you, and grow in your faith, encouraging each other on the journey. Thank you."

Alex gathered her cards, stepped back, and then looked up, searching the room for Chad's loving eyes.

The ladies' applause as they rose to their feet overwhelmed her, and she felt the familiar sting behind her eyelids.

She hoped someone had had the forethought to record it. Because, for the life of her, Alex couldn't remember a single second of the past ten minutes, and Landry had given her strict instructions to be prepared to critique and polish her presentation for upcoming appearances.

Finally, she found Chad's familiar green eyes, his handsome smile. He was whooping, clapping, and whistling like he was at a rodeo, and it made her forget the tears.

§§§

Chad had never been so proud in his entire life. He'd been over-the-moon happy on his wedding day and deeply grateful on the day he had found out they were having a baby and he would get to adopt Lydia. But watching his wife, who he knew more than anyone was a force to be reckoned with, his heart swelled with an inexplicable pride. She'd overcome adversity and emerged stronger for the struggles. She'd touched so many people with her kindness and love. And, despite her youth, she had so much to teach women twice her age about life, and love, and faith.

Epilogue

Chad watched Alex doze, tendrils of hair clinging to her skin, still damp from the exhausting work she'd recently completed. Their son, born just an hour ago, had been whisked away after he and Alex had gotten to hold him. The nurses promised they'd bring him right back once they'd done everything they needed to do. In the meantime, they recommended the new mom and dad rest.

A knock at the door made Chad's heart quicken, as he thought he'd be alone with the tiny infant. Instead of the nurses, however, it was Charmain with Lydia.

"Can we come in?" Charmain whispered.

Chad nodded.

Despite everyone's efforts to be quiet, Alex's eyes fluttered open, and she smiled when she saw Lydia. "Hey, there! Guess what you've got?" she said, scooting over to make room for the little girl on the hospital bed.

"Be careful," Chad whispered in the little girl's ear as he lifted her to sit next to her mommy.

She nodded, taking her new role seriously.

"I will, Cha—I mean, Daddy."

They grinned at each other, as they had since the adoption had been finalized a little over a week ago.

Lydia had almost gotten accustomed to using his new moniker, but when she slipped up, they shared a look as if they had a secret only they knew.

"Mrs. White?" a voice called softly from the door.

Without waiting for an invitation, the nurse entered, holding a tiny bundle in her arms. She walked to the bed, but Alex directed her to let Chad hold him.

Standing beside the bed, staring into the impossibly blue eyes of their son, a lump formed in Chad's throat that he'd been fighting since they'd arrived at the hospital a few hours ago.

"Can I get a family picture?" Charmain asked, pulling her phone out of her purse.

"That would be great, Char." Alex said, snuggling Lydia under her arm while Chad leaned in close with the baby.

"So, what's the little monkey's name?" Charmain asked. She remained standing, and Chad was glad she didn't seem to intend to stay.

"Paul," Chad announced.

They'd decided months ago it was the perfect choice. The apostle Paul had penned the book of Romans, the source of the name of the pregnancy care home. It was also the Biblical book that had introduced Alex to Lydia's namesake, the strong woman of faith.

"And his middle name?" Charmain wanted all the details.

"Chadwick. Alex insisted." Chad blushed. He then shared his weight, length, and time of birth with his sister. He knew Charmain would be on the hook for all the pertinent information once she got back home to the second cottage behind Together for Good.

She and Miss Matilda had moved in just a few days ago, and it seemed to be the perfect situation. They'd been roommates for several months and got along beautifully, each woman's strengths complementing the other's weaknesses. Once Char received her certification, she'd be on the premises to help out and do the sonograms. She'd even talked about starting a mobile sonogram to serve the more rural population.

"I'm going to run and get a cup of coffee and see which doctors are here. I want to run the mobile sonogram idea past a few of them. I'll be back in a few minutes to take Lyddie home." She was gone before anyone could thank her or say goodbye.

Although the Whites had been sad to see the ladies leave their guest house, it wasn't going to remain vacant for long. Landry would move in next week and turn the second bedroom into his office. It was shaping up to be another busy summer.

Chad smiled. He couldn't remember a summer that wasn't. And he wouldn't have it any other way. Today, though, they'd take time to settle into the newness of their growing family. Today, all Chad desired was to be surrounded by his wife and children, privileges he never thought he'd be blessed with.

He shifted Paul to one arm and wrapped the other around his girls. "Could we pray?"

"I think that's a wonderful idea," Alex said.

Chad's heart was full almost to bursting as he led his family in prayer, modeling the faith he hoped to pass on to the two precious children in their arms.

What We Don't See

Reader Questions

Thank you for continuing this journey with Alex and her friends. Below, you'll find a few questions to help you delve deeper into the main themes of the book and to encourage discussion with others. Each question set is divided into information you gleaned from the book and truths you've experienced in your own life.

I hope you enjoy diving a little deeper.

B = Questions related to the book.
P = Questions related to your personal experience.

What We Don't See explores the faith journeys of several characters. Both the book's theme and its title were taken from the two verses at the beginning of the book (Hebrews 11:1 and Romans 8:25).

B. What are some ways the characters in *What We Don't See* struggled to deepen their faith? How did they share their faith with others?

P. What are some of your favorite verses about faith? Why? How do these verses speak to you in difficult times? In happy times? When you question God?

Several characters had to deal with faith-testing situations (Matilda, Alex and Chad, Terry and Meredith, Yvonne and Marquis).

B. Each character processed their faith struggle differently, as we all do in life. Describe a few characters' different approaches to the struggles they faced.

P. Which characters' struggles were most relatable for you? How did you handle your own difficult situation? How did it grow your faith in God?

It wouldn't be a **Together for Good** *book if there weren't a few secrets revealed. Both Meredith and Dorothy have secrets they've been keeping for a long time, but they deal with them in very different ways.*

B. How was Meredith encouraged and put on the path to healing when she revealed the truth about her abortion? How did Meredith and Dorothy pursuit of the closure of their pain differ?

P. Who is someone you know who processes pain differently than you? How do you deal with it? How do you comfort them? Witness to them? Walk alongside them?

Alex and Terry inherit a fortune, but money isn't a major part of the story. They both desire to use their wealth to provide for their families and do good things for others.

B. Do you think the other characters (Miss Matilda, Chad, Charmain, Meredith) were envious of Alex and Terry's inheritance? Were they supportive of the choices made to wisely use the money?

P. If you inherited a large amount of money, what would you do with it? Would you bless others? Take a vacation? Take friends and family on a vacation? Stash it away for a "rainy day?" Get creative! You can afford to be generous in this question!

Although faith is the "unseen" topic of What We Don't See, there's a more sinister unseen force at work. Dorothy's gossip-mongering threatens to tear the friends apart.

B. Why do you think Dorothy is often gathering her intel without the characters' knowing? Why does she seek to hurt, discredit, and divide Miss Matilda's circle of friends?

P. Sometimes gossip can be sneaky or even irresistible. How do you guard against spreading rumors, hear-say, or falsehoods about others? Do you have a plan for removing yourself from a situation when you recognize gossip being shared? How do you shut down a gossip?

Alex shares an acronym for identifying the basic differences between the Gospel and gossip.

G – Giving	G – Giving
O – Out	O – Out
S – Some	S – Some
P – Peace	S - Strife
E – Encouragement	I – Innuendo
L – Love	P - Prevarication

B. Her friends obviously understood the source of her advice. What about the other women at the Harvest Tea, many of whom had been the targets of Dorothy's information-gathering missions? What do you think they did after hearing Alex's wise advice?

P. How will thinking about the differences in these two words change the way you interact with others? Do you think of the Gospel as Peace, Encouragement, and Love? Do you see gossip as sowing strife, perpetuating innuendo, and potentially spreading lies?

LeighAnne Clifton and her husband, Bill, call South Carolina home. After meeting while both earning their degrees in chemical engineering at the University of South Carolina, they married and settled in Aiken. Both recently retired and are pursuing some of the things they've been putting off for some time, like yardwork, home improvement projects, and travel. They have two grown children, a son-in-law, and a pair of spoiled cats. They currently serve in their church on Sunday mornings, teaching third graders.

What We Don't See is the third in the *Together for Good* series, and it follows the characters that readers grew to love in *All Your Heart* and *Ready to Forgive*.

LeighAnne loves to upcycle old junk into beautiful, one-of-a-kind pieces. She shares her thoughts on Christian living, DIY projects, and the latest book news on her blog:

https://alive-leighjourney.com